Spaghetti Head

A Novel by
Sarah Tyley

ACKNOWLEDGMENTS

Spaghetti Head is based on a picture I drew in 2005, of a pile of jumbled up spaghetti that represented thoughts and emotions I was having at the time. I wanted to get from jumbled emotions to a nice straight, orderly pile – and thus the idea for this story was born. So I'd like to thank everyone that I'd met in my life before I drew that picture, because you will all have influenced it.

A big thank-you to everyone who has helped me complete Spaghetti Head, either through reading it, commenting, designing, etc etc. To Laura Tyley for reading, cover design, social media and marketing, Becky Slack for reading, marketing and all-round support, Jolea Minnick for formatting, Atam Sandhu for cover ideas, Gary Dalkin for structural editing, and for being one of the first people to 'get it': his comments were invaluable in the development of the book. You can find him at www.tothelastword.com

Thank you to Dulcie, Aaron, Sue, Becky, Richard, Clare and Beaze for being my first wave of readers, critiques and encouragers! Katrina – you have been especially supportive, and saw things in the book I didn't know I'd written! Thanks to people on Twitter and on the Facebook groups I follow for all their tips, advice and sharing of knowledge – I massively appreciate it.

I say a massive thanks to everyone in Somerset – where my heart truly lies. Firstly, of course, to Mum, and the rest of my family – I wouldn't have had half this stuff in my head if it wasn't for all of you. And to all of my friends – you have all made me who I am. I'm hoping that's a good thing! To Nick and to France for providing me with the space and time to finish Spaghetti Head, which I actually wrote in November 2006. They do say writing is all about re-writing!

And finally, thank you for reading it. I hope you enjoy the characters I have shared the last twelve years of my life with.

SARAH TYLEY

Learning to manage, control and direct the resources of your mind is the greatest challenge you will ever face.

Dr Shad Helmstetter

MALI – NEW YEAR'S DAY 2116

"How many times, Alice, have I showered out here, hoping for a blinding flash of enlightenment?"

"Lots."

"Maybe I'm not breathing deeply enough," I said, staring at the candle resting on her back.

"Well you'd better hurry it – you're four minutes over your water allowance."

I closed the tap and held my arms out to the side – no need for a towel in this heat.

"What do you want enlightenment about, anyway, Nell?" Alice said, her black metallic nose shining up at me in the moonlight.

"About why I'm still a single. About why I can't tell Mum and Dad I love them. About whether I should listen to my head, or my heart."

Always listen to me, Nell – here in your head.

"SID's telling me to listen to him."

"Well, SID would! Listen to your heart, Nell – it's where you'll find the truth. Whatever you do, do not listen to SID – how has he ever helped you? He's probably the entire reason you still *are* a single."

"You think so?"

"Well what other reason is there?"

You're terrified of commitment?

"Talking of being a single, I'd better get dressed, I'm meeting Youssan in an hour." I crouched down to blow out the candle and tickle Alice's ear. "Do you think it's a good idea?"

"What?"

"Meeting Youssan for dinner."

No.

"Absolutely."

She hasn't even met the man!

"But I was only chatting to him for a couple of hours last night – what if he only invited me because he'd been drinking?"

Strong possibility.

"Well, there's only one way to find out, Nell. It's only dinner, for goodness sake. Lighten up!"

DINNER WITH YOUSSAN

Ankle-level solars lined the sandy track. They line every walking track. I should be used to how pretty they are by now, sparkling through the darkness, yet still they always make me want to spin.

What, and arrive covered in sweat!

The solars are installed to help us feel happy. And safe. And thankful. You can tell the planet's governed by women – would men bother with such detail? None of those I know would.

I arrived at the twinkling circle-junction and took the left path towards Fanta's, who serves the best chicken and chips in the zone. There are five zones in West Africa: Frangipani, Arachide, Tamarind, Baobab, and ours, Cassava. They're all part of a massive agricultural project – Feed the Soil, Feed the People – designed to improve crop yields. Mum and Agnes Gondwe, oversee the plant nursery, and Dad manages irrigation. We have year-round sunshine, low rainfall (which is why I installed an open-air shower), but decent reserves of underground water. Combining soil improvement techniques and using drought-resistant plants, the project is finally, after thirty years, starting to see an increase in yields.

My stomach flipped – a string of coloured lights shone out from the restaurant's thatched veranda. Youssan would be able to see me approaching.

What if he's not here?

I took out a tissue and blotted my forehead.

Nervous?

Hot. Go away.

"Nell!" Youssan called from a round table over to my left, under a ceiling fan.

Tall. Broad. Shaven head. Pink linen shirt – which looked amazing against his dark skin. He was as attractive as I'd remembered from last night.

He stood up, kissed me on the cheek and pulled a chair out for me. His hazel eyes were dotted with dark specks, reminding me of a tree pipit's egg, only shiny. They sparkled into mine, prompting a smile over which I had no control.

Oh God, here we go.

"Thanks for coming," he said, smiling back.

"Thanks for inviting me."

We sat down appreciating the fan. "Would you be okay if my sister joins us?" he asked.

No. You want him all to yourself.

"Of course," I replied, my palms sweating.

A slim, dark beauty walked confidently along the veranda towards us. Youssan stood up, hugged her and pulled out another chair.

"Yolandé," she said, smiling, as she shook my hand.

"Nell," I replied, admiring her symmetrical smile.

How do you know that's his sister?

Who else would it be?

His wife.

You're demented.

"I've read some of your articles, Nell. I love them," Yolandé said.

"Me too!" Youssan said. "I thought the piece about the manager of the wind farm tying himself to the blades to check for cracks as they turned was brilliant," he said.

"My favourite is the one about the effects of blowflies on cattle in Venezuela. I read the bit about them burrowing their heads into rotting flesh to Youssan at breakfast – do you remember?" Yolandé said, laughing in Youssan's direction.

So they're together at breakfast as well?

Shut-up.

"How could I forget!" he said, rolling his eyes.

We ordered: three times chicken and chips.

Original.

"So," I said, "What do we all think!"

"About which?" Youssan said, "Compulsory mindercising, or the 2117 election announcement?"

"The mindercising!"

"I feel a bit insulted," Yolandé said. "I'm healthy as it is, thanks."

She certainly looks fit.

"Outwardly healthy, yes, Yol, but mentally?"

Hope he doesn't ask you *that question.*

"Are you joshing? We're practically born with therapy implanted into our brains. An hour a day during ed years, surely set us up for positive mental health, so why the need to re-name it 'mindercising' and make it compulsory, I've no idea. I don't get it."

"I'm always out walking anyway," I said, "that's my meditation."

"Me too," Youss replied.

"Fantastic. I know some lovely circular walks, if you ever fancy joining me."

"Love to."

The food arrived. "Shall we say the Words before eating?" Youssan said.

We sat up straight, cleared our throats and joined hands.

'We shall never forget those who perished. Our gratitude to them for who they were. Our gratitude to Yellowstone for who we have become.'

We released one another and picked up our cutlery.

"So, which 'mindercise' did you register?" Yolandé asked.

"Yogic walking," I said.

"Counting ants," Youssan said.

"Balancing on one leg," Yolandé said.

I started to feel rather normal.

Boring more like.

"Balancing on one leg was an option?" Youssan said.

"Granma will love telling her friends what you've registered," I said.

"You've still got a grandparent?"

"Yep. Two weeks ago she became one hundred and six years living."

"Wow! So she remembers humans governing, before the Disaster."

"She does."

"What did you do for her birthday?" Youssan asked.

"Nothing special."

"Nothing special!" he said, pulling a face. "When did you last see her then?"

"Last week."

"You were in Australia?"

"No. I saw her on-screen. We chat every week. I haven't seen her in the flesh for twenty-one years."

"Yizer! Twenty-one years!" Yolandé said. "What does she think of the election announcement?"

"She's glad she probably won't live much longer."

She'll ashing live forever!

"But why have you only seen her on-screen?"

"She's a chronic claustrophobic and can't travel."

"Anything to do with being shut underground for all those years after the Disaster?"

"Everything…"

"Enough to give anyone claustrophobia."

"How come you've never gone to see *her*?"

"She says Australia's too far, too much hassle – especially with one flight a month. The moment I finished ed she told me to concentrate on my career, and not waste time going to stay with her for a month. I see so much of her on-screen, I've never insisted on visiting."

"Would it really be too much hassle?" Yolandé asked.

"From here to the airport in Timbuktu is 26 hours by sunbus," Youssan said. "Then there's the flight to Oz…"

"And then no flight back for a month," I said.

You're too selfish to take the time off work.

"You should go, Nell, whilst she's still alive," Yolandé said. "What did she do in the survival parks?"

"She managed insect storage. Granpa managed birds."

I watched Youssan as he picked a chip up, dipped it in the chilli-mayonnaise and slid it past his barely open lips. I couldn't make out when he was chewing, or swallowing – I'd never seen a man eat so elegantly.

Give it six months and you'll hate the way he eats.

"So how do you both know my mum then?" I asked.

"I've just joined the composting team, so I met her at my welcoming event."

Youssan could be perfect – he likes walking, eats beautifully, cares for the environment, and he's a great dancer.

Lots of women must like him.

"Apparently your Mum's got a bit of a reputation for throwing a good party, so we were excited to get an invite. Little did I know there'd be the extra bonus of finally meeting Nell Greene, with her flared cotton trousers and wild red hair," he said, smiling.

Smooth talker.

Perfect teeth.

"Well, I'll give it to you Youss," Yolandé said. "You certainly know how to make a woman blush."

THE AWARD

"Alice, Alice, Alice, my beautifulest CowBot. What a great evening! Apart from eating the best chips on the planet, Youssan is fantastic. Tall, dark, he was wearing the most beautiful shirt, brilliant table manners, great conversation. And he's a very sexy dancer. This is it, Alice. Youssan and Nell FOREVER."

"Brilliant, Nell, it sounds like it went well."

If he's so fantastic why is he single?

I sat on the edge of the sofa and kicked off my sandals.

In fact, a man that attractive has probably got women queueing up.

Shut up.

I scooped my Friesian-cow housebot, Alice, up onto my lap. She's an old model, but still brilliant around the house. Thanks to her flat under-carriage she can perform all kinds of functions: for ironing, her wheels tuck up inside and she hovers backwards and forwards over the item of clothing on a bed of steam. For hoovering she has an 'in-vent' between her two front-wheels, with a storage area between her two back-wheels, which she opens up to empty. For polishing she raises her wheels and I can attach a special cloth enabling her to glide over floors. For washing up she fits into a slot over the sink, and water jets open up and spray downwards. Plus her strong rectangular-shaped frame enables her to carry up to twenty-five kilos. She has a little tow-hitch, she's covered in Friesian-cow-patterned fur, and she is programmed uniquely to me. Her operating chip was initially programmed with basic, functional vocabulary, which I have, over the years, updated, so we can converse practically as well as humans. She's my best friend, and I'd trust her with my life.

Liar. You don't trust anyone.

My wall-screen lit.

To Nell Greene

We are to remind you of your thirty-sixth birthday later this year.

As if you needed reminding of that!

All healthy women on the planet are encouraged to have children to help reverse our declining population. However, recent research has shown the human population is not recovering as quickly as we would like, despite our best efforts, and so we have reinstated the Award. As before, the Award targets women who have contributed greatly to the healing and development of the planet, and who, thus, have perhaps prioritised providing a service over starting a family.

We believe your selfless dedication to service provision, Nell (we've read every article since you began writing), has got in the way of you choosing to have a family. We are, therefore, over-joyed to inform you that you have been chosen for the Award.

"WHAT!"

This year, yourself, Anne Tillings, communication engineer, Sherry Munk, head robot programmer, and Nenny Fitchly, big cat nursery manager, are just a few of the women who will be presented with the Award. Once you accept the Award and give birth to your first child you will receive a life-time monthly credit of units as compensation for your lack of units from service provision.

"Give birth to my first child! Have they gone mad? I don't want children!"

There is, however, a slight catch: due to potential health risks, the maximum recommended age for having a first child is thirty-seven, so please bear this in mind.

Nobody has ever refused the Award, and given the importance of the task ahead as a race, you need to know we may have to review your status if you are not pregnant by your thirty-seventh birthday in eighteen months' time.

"Pregnant by the time I'm 37! No ashing way!"

We hope reviewing your status will not be necessary, as we would love you to continue writing articles once your children are in ed.

We understand you are not currently in a relationship, but nevertheless, we do hope this is

happy news for you, Nell, and we look forward to
seeing you at the upcoming Award Ceremony.
The Population Committee

The screen cleared.

"Happy news! Are they joking?"

I looked at Alice. She looked at me.

"Oh my God!" I said, laughing.

Oh My God is right!

We looked back at the screen: clear.

"Did that just happen?"

Yep.

"Your screen definitely just displayed a message."

"It must be someone playing a prank."

"It looked official to me," Alice said, "try replay."

I did. And there it was, the same message in Committee
format. We read it and re-read it.

"What the ashing hell? I can't believe it. It's been years since
I've heard of anyone getting the Award. Why would they have
started it up again?"

"To win votes?"

"How will the Award win votes?"

"No idea."

"And why me?"

Because you're physically capable of childbirth?

"And who the hell are they expecting me to get pregnant
with?"

"Good question. It doesn't sound very System-like to me,"
Alice said.

"The bit about reviewing my status sounds like a threat.
Silvers aren't threatening," I said, resting my chin on Alice's
back.

"I agree."

"When have I been in a relationship long enough to think
about starting a family?"

*Never. You're terrified of commitment, that's why they never
last.*

"I'm rubbish at relationships. How is that going to change in
the next eighteen months?"

It isn't.

"The System doesn't know all that, Nell."

"Well they know I'm a single, so why wouldn't they know the rest."

"They know your status, not your character. And anyway, you're busy with other things. You're not rubbish."

She's your housebot – she's bound to say that.

"What the hell are we going to do?"

Fail.

"Let's start by finding out what a status review means," Alice said.

THE SYSTEM

My screen lit again.

To Nell Greene
We would like to be the first to congratulate you on receiving the Award. As you are not in a relationship, and time is not on your side, we hope we may be able to help you by forwarding details of possible perfect matches. Please feel free to choose one perfect-match profile within the next week. We will then make all the arrangements, and cover the cost of your first meeting.
We look forward to hearing from you,
The Dating Committee

"Time not on my side! Effing nerve!"

"A perfect match? Have you heard of that before?"

They've got their work cut out!

"I haven't, Alice."

"And who are the Dating Committee?"

"No idea. I've lost track, there are so many committees now. We thought they would make communication with The System easier."

"Have they?"

"No."

I tapped my fingers against her side.

The System – the planet's governing body – consists of an overseeing committee of twenty-five robots, and numerous operational committees who implement the practical management of the planet. They're all democratically programmed, they all look like women, and they're fondly nick-named Silvers. Every three years all of us humans, no matter how old, is sent a form listing different qualifications, characteristics, personality traits, hobbies etc. they would like each Silver on the overseeing committee to have. We tick the box for each quality we would like programmed in, and there you have a 'democratically programmed' robot. There is a Director of the System – who is upgraded with leadership programming, and the programming team are all humans, all women and they are elected by us every three years.

Two years ago, however, a new programming team was elected. Shortly afterwards, and without human votes, they chose a new Director, and new sub-committees of Silvers started managing communications. The programming team are not authorised to act independently, and we, the general population, started to worry that they were abusing their power. Collectively, we called for a global vote on future governance. The result? There should be a global election, and it should include human candidates.

Human candidates! No-one can believe it. Who would ever have imagined that humans would be given the chance to govern again? Not after the mess we'd made of it before the Disaster. And yet, ten days ago, the System announced the election will take place next year – 2117.

"Okay. Focus, Nell," Alice said. "It looks like you need to get pregnant, and fast."

I stared down at Alice.

"I haven't, Alice, in thirty-five years met anyone I've wanted to 'get pregnant' with – as you so romantically put it."

Scared of rejection, that's why.

I'm a free spirit.

Liar.

"But just imagine who the Dating Committee might set you up with!"

"But I can't just drag someone in here to get pregnant!"

"Well, Nell, it sounds like you haven't got a lot of choice."

"Alice! There's always a choice."

"And now would be a good time to make the right one," she said, hanging her head.

"What a nightmare. I knew meeting Youssan was too good to be true."

I did say so...

"Youssan!" Alice said, perking up. "There you go! Ten minutes ago you were telling me how fantastic he is – well now you've got the chance to spend the rest of your life with him."

She's assuming quite a lot there.

"If only things were that simple, Alice."

They could be if you didn't make them so complicated.

"Call Granma. She'll know what to do."

"No way! Not yet. She'll worry."

"Call your Mum, then."

"She'll freak – you know what she's like about anything to do with Committees. Why don't I just reject the Award. I mean, what's the worst the System can do?"

Good idea, reject it.

"Admit it, Nell: you've always wanted a family, you've just never met the right person. Well, maybe this is your chance. Don't reject it. Talk to your Mum."

Right person? No-one will ever be the right person.

I held Alice's fur covered aluminium frame tight against me.

"I'll call her tomorrow. I can't believe we're even having this conversation, can you?"

"No."

Me neither. Answer's simple. Reject the award.

"Okay, Alice, we need time to think."

"It's simple. Go and get pregnant with Youssan."

"Alice! You're ruthless!"

"I think my emergency-programming may have kicked in."

"Emergency programming?"

"Installed on my chip during manufacture."

"Really?"

"So my manual says."

"Anyway. So, what we're saying is, I'm declining the offer of a perfect match, and taking my chance with Youssan. Correct?"

You only met the man last night!

"He's the best chance you've got," Alice confirmed.

Big mistake.

"The message about the Award didn't say when you need to reply."

"Knowing silvers, it won't be long."

"Let's pray for a miracle with Youssan then," Alice said.

I stared at her, open mouthed.

A miracle is an ashing understatement!

YOUSSAN – AND SID

*Is fear created by the type of person you're in a relationship
with, or is it always lurking inside and bought to the surface by
the pure nature of being in a relationship?*
Nell Greene

Mum advised me to try my best with Youssan and not mention
a word about the Award to him.

To the Dating Committee
Thank you very much for your offer of perfect match
profiles. I am glad to say I have, however, met a
very nice single man, and will therefore not be
needing your services. Once again, many thanks.
Nell Greene

He hasn't even asked you to couple yet!
He will.
And if he doesn't?

***

Youssan and I stood kissing at his front door. Heaven.
His roamer bleeped. He left it in his pocket.
Who's that?
We walked in to his bright, sparsely furnished livingspace,
where Yolandé sat, cross-legged, staring into a candle flame.
Why is she always here?
Youssan hurried into the bathroom.
He's gone to look at his roamer.
So?
So, who messaged him?
Who cares?
You do. Ask him who it was from.
No.
Youssan walked towards me. "That was a message from
Stefan at work, needing some information," he said, whilst his
eyes appeared to find something of great interest on the carpet.
He's lying.

15

No he's not.

Why couldn't he look you in the eye then?

The skin on my forehead was shrinking and getting hot. My ears started ringing. My solar plexus flipped.

Youss walked into the kitchen, putting his roamer on the counter.

"Who's cooking tonight then, Nell – you, or Youss?" Yolandé asked.

"Sorry?"

"Cooking, Nell, tonight. You, or Youss?"

Why isn't she cooking?

"Good question," Youssan said. "I'll take this out to the compost, then we'll sort it."

Quick! Now's your chance! Go and look at the message.

No!

Go to the kitchen. Look. Then you'll know.

"I'll go and see what's in the fridge," I said.

His roamer was lying on the counter. My legs felt wobbly as I walked over and pressed the replay button: it was still unlocked.

Youss, looking forward to chatting tomorrow. S xx

I felt sick.

Stefan, he'd said. A man, signing off with a kiss?

Two kisses.

Needing information?

My heart started pounding.

He's a liar.

My hands were shaking.

"Found anything worth cooking in the fridge?" Youss said, walking over and kissing the back of my neck.

"Chicken?" I said, clinging on to the fridge door. "Do you need some time before dinner to send the information?"

"What information?" he asked.

Caught him!

"The message you had from Stefan?"

Turn around and watch his face.

"Oh no, I'll see him tomorrow," he replied, looking directly at me.

See? He's innocent.

Apart from he said it was Stefan needing information, yet the message said 'looking forward to chatting tomorrow'. He's a liar. You can't trust him.

"Delicious curry," he said, as the three of us ate.

The chicken pieces were dry as sand in my mouth.

Ask him more about Stefan. Or ask Yolandé if she knows him.

Shut up.

You can't trust him.

Shut up. I like Youss.

Get out of the relationship now – before you get hurt.

OUT OF CONTROL

Youssan and I walked hand in hand along sandy tracks, danced manically under the bright February stars, and merrily dug our way through his compost heaps. I barely noticed the heat, or the flies: I was in love.

Lust, more like.

Then one evening, half an hour before I was leaving for his place, my roamer bleeped.

Nell, sorry to let you down at such short notice – I have to work late. I'll call you in the morning. Y x

My mind raced back to the S with two kisses message. My heart launched itself into my throat, just as every microorganism in my intestines decided to change position with one another. It was as if they were sprinting around, into tighter and tighter circles before randomly choosing which other microorganism they wanted to swap with. Like musical chairs to robo-techno in the pitch black, blindfolded. With no chairs.

Why hadn't he called?

Easier to let someone down with text.

Why had he cancelled?

Meeting up with S.

I didn't sleep, I was too busy imagining S as a tall, beautiful, funny woman. My mind conjured up scenarios of the fun they were having together. Without me.

My mind only calmed when he'd phoned the following morning to invite me round for dinner.

***

He opened the door. "Sorry about last night," he said, kissing me. "One of the compost bots malfunctioned."

"Really? That's unusual," I said, returning the kiss.

"It's an old model. We're receiving a replacement next week."

His wall-screen lit.

Youss, what a night! Great to see you. Can't wait for our session next week. P will be here too. How fantastic is that? I've misplaced my roamer, so screen only, S xx

My stomach churned. My throat tightened and I couldn't swallow. I looked into his eyes.

A malfunctioning bot kept him late, he said. Liar.

"Stef was helping me work on the bot last night," he said, clearing the screen.

What? The message said great to see you. Someone he sees every day wouldn't say that.

Nor would he say 'can't wait for our session next week'.

He's lying. Again.

"So, what do you fancy doing then. Shall we stream something?"

"Sure."

Aren't you going to ask him about last night?

"Sounds like Stef had a great time trying to fix the bot."

"Oh, he's loopo – a real bot tech," he said, avoiding eye contact. "I don't think he gets out much."

"And what's the session about next week?"

"It's the specific programming of the new compost bot. He'll love it."

It's feasible – he did mention the replacement bot arriving next week.

Signing off with two kisses?

Would a man do that?

No.

He's lying.

He is.

Why would he lie?

He's got another girlfriend?

So how can I get him to tell me the truth?

Torture?

He squeezed my hand. "How about I do roasted fish?"

"Delicious."

He doesn't love you.

Shut up SID.

How can you ever trust him?

I'll figure it out.

End it now before you get hurt.

I don't want to.

Tell him you looked at his roamer then, tell him you know he's lying. Tell him it makes you feel insecure. See what he says. If he explains, he loves you. If not, he doesn't.

And if he doesn't explain? How embarrassing would that be!

"I'm exhausted, Youss," I said, shortly after eating. "I'm up early in the morning, so I'm going to bike home."

"Sure? Why don't you stay with me and leave half an hour earlier tomorrow? I missed you last night."

Is that even true?

Probably not.

"No, really. I've got an article deadline tomorrow at 4pm, so I need a good sleep."

End it, Nell. You can't trust him. And what's a relationship without trust?

DECISIONS

"It's over with Youss, Alice."

"What! Why?"

"He lies."

"Oh stop it. This happens every time you meet someone. Remember the Award!"

"It's too late, Alice. Everyone has a choice, and Youssan's was to lie."

"Oh lighten up! Have you never lied?"

"I'd better tell Mum, seeing as she introduced us."

"Seriously? Can't you give him another chance?"

Once a liar, always a liar.

"No, Alice, I can't."

***

"You can't afford to muck about, Nell!" Mum ranted. "Your entire life you've walked away from good men."

Wrong. They were all liars.

"Hang on. I could do with some support here, Mum."

"Well, sorry, but it's time to grow up."

"Grow up! Youssan lies."

"Have you told him about SID?"

"Of course not."

"Tell him. If he doesn't understand then you move on – but at least you've given your relationship a chance."

No way! You'd look a right fool.

"It's too late, Mum."

"No it isn't – there's the Award to think about."

"I'll reject it."

"No you won't. If you're not going to talk to Youssan, then at least promise me you'll sort your head out."

***

I did talk to Youss – but only to un-couple. I made up some pathetic excuse about work and needing to travel to Frangipani for a few months. He didn't seem too upset.

I felt miserable.

You're better off alone.
No I'm not.
You'll get over it.
Oh shut up. I need to talk to Granma.

***

"How's my favourite little Spaghetti Head?" she said, smiling into her screen.

"Not brilliant, G."

"You need to learn to love yourself, Nell," she said, after I'd told her about Youss.

"It's not that, G."

It might be.

"It's SID, Nell. He's an old misery, don't listen to him."

Stupid old woman.

"You've got to think of the Award, Nell. What will happen if you don't accept it?"

"I don't know."

"Well you need to meet someone – and fast."

"But it'll just be another disaster."

"Why will it?"

"You know why."

"You can get medication to destroy SID. You need to sort your head out. It's time."

"I know."

"Have you still got therapy credits?"

"Yes – for Greenwaters – a new centre up in Scandinavia."

"Go, Nell. Clear your head. Destroy SID. Then you'll be free to fall in love."

"You make it sound so easy, G."

"It might be that easy – you just need to get on with it!"

Good luck with that!

WELCOME TO GREENWATERS – THREE MONTHS LATER

I was unpacking the last of my clothes at Greenwaters Therapy Centre when my wall-screen burst into life, and Granma, Rose to her friends, was smiling out towards me from her kitchen in Australia.

Why Australia?

It was one of the countries the least affected by the gasses and ash deposits of the Eruption, and twenty years after surfacing from the underground survival parks, Western Australia was voted as the best place to host the planet's Accomplished Contributors – otherwise known as anyone over eighty-five years old. Once you've spent your lifetime contributing to the healing of the planet and its population, you fly to Western Australia to live out the remainder of your life in absolute luxury, with every sports facility, hobby provision, and health treatment available for free.

"Fantastic to know you've arrived safely, Nell."

"I wish you were here, G," I said.

"What have you done to your hair? It's bright red!"

"Fresh paste from my henna plants. It'll calm down in a few days."

"Good – it detracts from your gorgeous Nelly-green eyes."

"You're looking well, G, purple suits you. You've had a fringe cut in to your hair too. I like it."

"Thank-you, darling. Now. Show me around your livingspace. I'm curious to see how people are accommodated at these new Scandinavian centres."

"You won't be disappointed," I said.

I linked my roamer to the call, and walked around filming.

"Are there any proper walls, or is it *all* glass?" she asked.

"There are three glass walls, and then this one, in solid pine," I said, turning the screen.

"How do you have any privacy?"

"Watch this, G. 'Night-time snow'," I said, loudly, and the glass became black, blocking out daylight. My sleeping-platform light came on automatically, whilst images of large, fluffy snowflakes started to fall down the glass. "Cool, eh?"

"What are the image choices?"

"There are so many – I can have rain, lightning, aurora, sandstorm…"

"Well lightning wouldn't be very relaxing – and why would anyone want to watch a sandstorm!"

I tilted my roamer to show the exposed rustic roof beams above the kitchen, and sweeping around, she saw my sleeping platform, suspended over half of the livingspace. "Look at the enormous window over my bed, G. I cannot wait to do some moon bathing."

"Agh! What's that bright pink thing!"

"It's my sofa – I love it! I think it's my favourite bit. And there's matching dining chairs."

"How anyone with red hair can like pink, I'll never know. It's such a dreadful clash!"

True.

I laughed.

"Someone's definitely been doing their homework!"

"Exactly what I thought."

"And where's my favourite little CowBot?"

Alice whizzed across the floor from under the dining table. "Look!" she screeched, "can you believe this? My very own, made-to-measure, sleeping platform and re-charging point."

I tipped the screen down towards Alice, and followed her over to a rectangular green platform at the end of the kitchen area.

"My my, is that artificial grass?" G asked.

"Yes," Alice replied, excitedly, "which is nearly as good as the real thing, which I'm hoping to smell soon."

"May in Scandinavia, Alice, you should be in luck," G replied.

"Look!" Alice said, whizzing up a ramp onto the platform, her four wheels disappearing into the synthetic grass. She spun her rump around and reversed up to the wall, where a tiny plug came up out of the platform and locked into her under-carriage. "I'm now re-charging!" she said. "Clever, or what?"

I smiled down at Alice, my best friend, and tickled her ear.

No wonder you've ended up at a therapy centre if a robot is your best friend!

"And the view?" Granma asked.

"Stunning," Alice replied. "If I turn right out of here, there's a stone path winding so gently downhill I hardly need to use my brakes. It stops at the edge of a gravelly beach, which circles around Deserted Bay. The water is green and clear, and there's not a soul in sight. Then there's this long wooden jetty, which is wide enough for four people to walk side by side, and a wooden ladder at the end, disappearing into the water. Out towards the sea end of the bay there are lots of brightly coloured wooden cabins, just big enough for one person to sit in fishing. Then if you turn around and look up hill, you can see trees and meadows and huge bare rocks. I cannot wait to go exploring."

"You stay close to Nell, Alice. You never know what may be lurking in those Scandinavian forests."

Alice's ears flattened back against her head.

"I'm so happy for you both, really I am. I've never seen you so excited, Alice – has Nell given you a program-update?"

"No."

"She's been different since I received the Award message from the Population Com."

Alice sped under the table.

"Maybe it's the stress of it all," G said.

"I doubt it – she's not programmed to recognise stress."

Living with you for this long, it's probably transferred.

"But something about her has definitely changed," I added.

"Emergency-programming!" Alice shouted from under the table.

"Well, I like the difference, Alice," G said. "Now listen, Nell, remember why you are there."

"I don't need reminding, G. I haven't upset my article editor at Earth Matters for nothing – I'm here to sort my head out."

"What specifically did she say to you?"

"She wasn't happy. But I explained everything and she agreed to stream some archive interviews of mine on a weekly basis until therapy is over."

"That's great, it frees you up to focus solely on destroying SID. He's in *your* head, he's *your* voice, *your* creation. Just stop him!"

"Do you think it'll be that easy? As if I had a light activator in my head? On/off?"

"Why not?"

You'll never destroy me. You need me.

"You're right – why not? I'll give it my best shot, G. Can you let Mum know we're settled in? I've got to go to the introduction meeting, which I'm dreading."

"You'll be fine."

"I'll send her a message later."

"I'll let her know, Nell. Have a fabulous time, and keep me up-dated. I love you both."

***

Granma was immediately replaced on-screen by a woman wearing a light blue, round-necked sweatie – in her late twenties at a guess. Her shoulder length blonde plaits were tied-up with blue elastics, though strands of hair refusing to conform shot out in all directions, as if she were fresh from a static chamber. She had kind, sparkly eyes.

"Hello, Nell, I'm Sally," she said confidently. "I hope you've had time to settle in. I've been assigned as your group therapy leader for the next eight weeks. Please come to the Introduction Lounge in thirty minutes. There's no need to bring anything with you. Walk along the stone path to the left of your livingspace, until you reach two short pine trees, turn right, and the lounge is directly in front of you. It has a welcome sign over the door. See you there."

The screen cleared.

Ready for total humiliation?

Yes, if it means shutting you up.

I fixed my most unruly curls off my face and put on my favourite green cardigan. "See you later, Alice," I said, heading for the door. She started whizzing backwards and forwards in straight lines, her ears flat back against her head.

"I don't see why I can't come."

"I don't think you're invited."

You're too scared of bearing your soul in front of your dearest friend.

"How do you know I'm not invited?"

You're scared she won't like the 'real' you.

"You just don't want me there."

"That's not true, Alice."

Yes it is.

RULES

Alice and I reached the two short pine trees. They were marooned on an island of moss.

"Moss! I LOVE MOSS!" Alice shouted.

How can she love moss? She isn't programmed to feel love! Send her for a bugging scan, quick, before she gets any more annoying.

I opened the door under the welcome sign and walked into a rectangular lobby area.

"Welcome, Nell," a woman's voice said from above. "Please take off your shoes and put on a pair of the slippers provided – choose whichever colour you like."

Alice looked up at me and widened her eyes.

"Garish pink?" Alice questioned. "This is getting out of control. You'll hate pink for the rest of your life if they carry on like this!"

We laughed.

I placed my shoes on a metal tray which retracted into the wall, put my slippers on and picked up Alice. The pine door in front of me swung open.

Silence. Eyes looking at me. Nightmare! I felt my face heating up.

"Hi, Nell." I recognised Sally's voice. "Come on in," she said, gesturing towards a giant, empty beanbag.

All eyes on you.

My face cracked into a grimace. I sank into the beanbag's turquoise canvas, and put Alice down beside me. She rested against my leg, dropped her head and started to sniff the real-grass flooring.

"Hello, and welcome to you all," Sally said. I focussed on her bushy eyebrows. "I'm Sally, and I'll be leading your group therapy. All of you are here for different reasons, which I'm sure will become apparent with time."

Let's hope there's some juicy ones.

"Shall we start with the Memorial words?"

We all sat upright, and recited in unison:

'We shall never forget those who perished. Our gratitude to them for who they were. Our gratitude to Yellowstone for who we have become.'

My eyes darted to her right for an instant. Man. My age. To her left. Man. Hang on a minute, isn't that...

"I'd like to start by laying down some ground rules. I ask you all to respect the confidentiality of anything discussed during our group sessions and one-to-ones. I ask you to be respectful of one another's right to be heard. For the first three weeks I would ask you do not invite one another to your personal spaces. You'll likely feel your most vulnerable at the beginning, which is only natural, and you may be tempted to look for comfort from one another. Obviously, support from one another is encouraged, but relationships, are not."

Silence.

"Jupiter?" I mouthed to the man to my left.

He lifted his hand in recognition.

Oh God. Not that loser. What were the chances?

"I understand it sounds strict, but those are the rules of the programme."

"Can we meet up outside our livingspaces?" the woman to my right asked.

"Sure. There's the Relaxation Space, and many kilometres of countryside," Sally replied.

Looking at her heels, I didn't get the impression the other woman was the type to go strolling through the meadows.

"Right, I'd like us to start by going around the circle introducing ourselves, though some of you already know one another. It would be good to know your name, and something most people don't know about you," Sally said.

Cringeful.

Shit, I hated these introduction sessions. Still, this was an improvement on the last one I was at where we were asked to tell everyone our names, and if we were a mode of transport, which one would we be! Ridiculous waste of time.

"We'll start from my left."

I looked towards the man on the yellow beanbag. Gorgeous Alert!

Bet he's popular with the ladies.

"Hello, I'm Ty," he said confidently.

He was gorgeous before he spoke, but after hearing his sexy baritone – well! Chocolate-brown collared sweater, fantastic jaw line, dark eyes, short dark fringe getting longer towards his ears. Athletic. He looked familiar. No, it couldn't be.

Your turn soon.

My heart sped up and I put my palms down on my trousers to try to soak up the sweat. My ears started buzzing.

What are you going to say about yourself?

Don't know.

What if your mouth dries up.

What if I can't swallow: what shall I say?

You've never trusted anyone in your entire life?

"And I brew nettle beer," he added.

"It is you!" I blurted out, before I thought about my mouth being too dry to speak. "Ty, as in Ty Martins?"

"That's me," he said, his large black eyes smiling into mine.

"But you live in Argentina!"

"My, your fame precedes you," said the woman to his left, my right. "I'm Mara," she added.

Narrow, pointy face, eyes like light blue crystal. Thin, red lips. Tinted foundation. Straight black shoulder-length hair, parted in the middle. Not sure I'd trust her.

You don't trust anyone.

Tight black trouser suit, jacket open. White vest-top thing under her jacket with her 34Ds, at a guess, desperate to burst out.

Make you feel inferior?

She was sitting bolt up-right, which isn't easy in a beanbag, with her legs crossed, looking more like she belonged in a Committee meeting than here.

Me next. Breathe. Breathe.

What're you going to say?

Don't know.

I didn't even hear what Mara said about herself.

"Nell?" Sally said.

"Yep, sorry. I'm Nell. Umm...something about me...My favourite music is 20th CenturyDisco."

That's the best you could come up with?

"Vintage, plus a hundred years," Sally said.

"The old music's miles better than all the robo-ragga shite played these days," Ty said.

Did his eyes linger on me a little longer than they had on Mara?

I very much doubt it.

Relief. Spotlight off.

"Hello, I'm Jupiter," the man to my left said, "and my favourite thing to eat is a sweet and sour stargazer."

He smiled at me. There's only one person I've ever known who could eat a whole sweet and sour stargazer.

"Ty and Mara also know one another, as they're married," Sally said.

"Why did you have to say that?" Mara asked, her eyes boring holes into Sally's.

That's snuffed out that little fantasy then.

Alice nudged my leg.

"Oh, sorry," Sally said. "And you are?"

"Alice," she said proudly, "I can iron three shirts in two minutes, which isn't bad for a Friesian cow."

Everyone laughed. Good old Alice, breaking the ice.

"I was given to Nell on her tenth birthday, and have been by her side ever since. I'm modelled on the finest milking cow on the planet."

"Welcome, Alice," Sally said, smiling.

"Fantastic," Ty said – and out from behind his beanbag appeared a sheepbot.

Alice's ears whipped back against her head.

"She's modelled on a rare-breed – the Hampshire Down. And her name is?" he asked his sheepbot.

"Shilly," the sheepbot said shyly, glancing over at Alice, whose ears, I noticed, started to slowly edge forwards.

"How on earth did you sneak *her* in here?" Sally asked.

"She's a minimizing model – I can squash her down to the size of a kilo of chickpeas, and then expand her back up to normal housebot size. Clever, eh?"

"Impressive," I said, smiling at Shilly, "and slightly more modern than old Alice here."

Alice barged into my shin.

"Shilly, meet Alice," Ty said, smiling.

Alice's ears shot the rest of the way forward. "Pleased to make your acquaintance, Shilly," Alice said, dipping her head.

We all laughed.

"Is it alright if they come along to the sessions then, Sally?" I asked.

"I don't see why not."

Ty and I smiled across the lawn at one another.

He's married and not interested.

INTRODUCTIONS

"Right," Sally said, "firstly, Nell and Jupiter, you may be wondering what the chances were of the two of you being here at the same time. We're testing different group dynamics at three of these new therapy centres to see which performs the best. This group has been chosen based on common interests and background. We will compare results from the different groups to see whether, in general, participants feel more comfortable, and therefore achieve better results, with people they know, or with strangers."

"Great, we're guinea pigs," Mara said.

"Now I'd like you to share something about someone else in the room. Nell and Jupiter together please, and Ty and Mara."

"What the hell have you been up to then, Jupes?" I asked, as we pulled our beanbags together. He peered out at me from behind a curtain of lank, greasy, black hair. He hadn't gained a gram over the years, and was still dressed from head to toe in black.

He smiled. "Nobody's called me Jupes for *years*. It's good to see you, Spaghetti Head."

"Hah! Only Mum and Granma call me that these days. And my sister, Shoo, of course. You remember her?"

"I do. She was crazy."

"So crazy she's in a 'meltdown' therapy centre – on major medication."

"Doesn't sound good."

"It isn't."

He leant closer to me. "Who's Ty Martins? I didn't like to ask when Mara said he's famous."

"Do you ever look at Self-Sufficiency?"

"Nope."

"Well he writes ed stuff for their programs and streaming site. He's one of the planet's truly self-sufficient farmers. Occasionally he presents a bulletin."

"I'd better have a look at some of his articles!"

"You should. So what happened after ed, Jupe?"

"I crowned edplus, got married, and everything was perfect for a few years. Then I lost my job as a livingspace designer because a woman fell off her sleeping platform and died. The System ruled it was my design at fault! Nobody mentioned the half litre of vodka she'd drunk. So, I was taken off design and put into management, which I hated. A friend introduced me to acid, which led to heroin – and the rest is history. I'm here to kick my addictions."

"Addict*ions*?"

"Drugs and gaming," he said.

Which explains why his skin's so grey. Probably hasn't seen daylight for years.

"Did you design any livingspaces I might have heard of?"

"Al-Faw Blue coastal complex in Iraq?"

"Wow, it looks like an *amazing* complex – brilliantly designed."

"Thanks, Nell. Yep, I designed it, shortly before everything went very wrong."

"How about Fran, and Sharna and all the old gang?"

He winced.

"I married Fran, and Sharna was the one who supplied us with heroin. Fran died six months ago of an overdose."

"Oh no. I'm really sorry, Jupiter. I didn't know."

She didn't like you anyway.

I could hear Mara mumble something about children as Jupiter and I sat in silence, looking at one another.

"I'm so sorry, Jupe."

He shrugged his shoulders. "Enough about sad old addict me, how about you, Nell? I usually follow your articles on Earth Matters – it's one of the better streaming sites. I enjoyed the one about the cod farmer who redesigned a flotation tank so he could live underwater with his fish. Extreme!"

I smiled, "I enjoyed writing that article, and it basically sums up my life – interviewing farmers with strange habits!"

"Does the System control who you interview?"

"Partly. The Earth Matters editor, who's become a friend, suggests articles, giving me the necessary contacts, and I choose the ones I think will be most interesting. She sets the deadline and I submit the article. I've never had a rejection."

If only you could say the same for boyfriends.

"Could you write about a farmer who hasn't been suggested by Earth Matters?"

"I do. I submit those to the Human Voices channel. Mum – you remember how anti-System she was – wants me to stop writing for Earth Matters and earn all my units from Human Voices where the subject matter is less controlled. But a farming article isn't exactly going to be scrutinized by the System on grounds of discrimination or inciting hatred, is it?"

"Doubtful."

"So I'm happy working for both."

"And how about marriage, and children?"

"I've never got round to either. In fact, my lack of children is, I suppose, what prompted me to come here." He raised his left eyebrow. "I've received the Award, which basically means I need to be pregnant by the time I'm thirty-seven. Which is eighteen months away."

"Yizers!"

"Okay, time's up," Sally said, clapping her hands.

"Thank fuck," Mara said.

"We'll start with Jupiter. Can you please tell us something about Nell," Sally said.

"Well…. she is here to get pregnant."

"I am not!" I punched him on the arm as he winked.

"And the reason she's such a late starter is because she's been too busy writing about eccentrics trying to save the planet using bizarre farming methods, like one woman who farmed rats in stacked guttering for wall insulation."

"Nell…as in Nell Greene?" asked Ty, his dark brown eyes penetrating my soul.

"The very same," Jupiter replied proudly on my behalf.

"I thought you reminded me of someone! Out of context it's hard to be sure though. I admire your work, Nell, it's always informative, yet funny at the same time. The article about farmers in Venezuela picking blowflies off their cattle, caramelising them, and selling them at the market as a local delicacy was extraordinary."

I blushed, partly because of the praise, partly because I think it was probably one of the worst pieces I'd ever written.

"And I would just like to clarify I am NOT here to get pregnant – that's purely Jupiter's warped sense of humour."

"And, Jupiter?" Sally asked.

"He designed the Al-Faw Blue coastal complex in Iraq."

"Oh I *love* the design of that coastal complex!" Mara squealed. "The virtual shopping zone is fantastic. It's by far the best in the Gulf."

"As my depleted number of units can testify!" Ty added.

We laughed. This could be a good eight weeks.

Wait till you get on to the serious stuff, then we'll see.

"Ty," Sally said, "something about Mara."

"Ems became a mum too young, and would love to have her early twenties back again."

"Ty – that's not fair," Mara protested, her eyes full of spite.

"But it's true though, isn't it?"

Silence.

"Mara?" Sally said.

"Ty makes his own Curly Wurlies – with a sweetcorn batter coating rather than chocolate over the toffee," she said.

"Can't be totally self-sufficient if you're reliant on cocoa beans from Brazil, can you?" Ty added.

"Ooh, I feel an interview coming on!" I said, mesmerized every time my pupils made contact with his.

Not a crush this early on, please.

"Tomorrow I have a private session with each of you. We'll be working through an exercise to help me understand your individual needs and get to know you better, then we'll all meet back here the day after at 2pm."

Mara was the first to leave. Alone.

CHANGE

The secret of change is to focus all your energy,
not on fighting the old,
but on building the new.

Socrates

"Do you really think a few therapy sessions and some groups chats can change what I'm like when I'm in a relationship, Alice?"

She looked up from polishing the pine floor. "Do you want to change, Nell?"

I looked out through the glass towards the bay.

Do I want to change?

No. Change takes commitment. You're nul at commitment.

"Yes, Alice. I want to change," I said, looking down at her.

"Brilliant. Go and get on with it then."

INNER CRITIC

"Morning, Nell," Sally said, smiling, "come on in and take a seat."

I walked into the hexagonal lounge. The coloured bean bags were stacked against the log-wall, and Sally was sitting in a canvas arm-chair, in the middle of the room. I sat in the identical chair opposite her. I wished there was a table, or some other sort of barrier between us.

"Have you settled in alright?"

"Yes thanks – it's without a doubt the most luxurious livingspace I've ever stayed in."

"Good. Enjoy it." She reached down into a bag beside her chair and took out two portables. "We're going to spend our time this morning working through a written exercise I've prepared. I'm hoping it will give us information on how we need to focus over the next eight weeks." She held one of the screens towards me.

"Okay," I replied, taking it from her.

"Scroll through the instructions, and when you're ready you can enter your answers on-screen, underneath the statements. I have the same exercise here on my screen, so any questions, just ask."

I looked down, and read the heading.

Understanding your inner critic

I uncrossed my legs, and re-read it. Inner critic! Inner maniac, more like.

How childish.

Instructions for completing the exercise:

Your inner critic can be described as a voice in your head who may often judge and belittle you. You may or may not be aware of it. For the purposes of this exercise, you are to imagine the voice chatting inside your head is that of your best friend.

I looked at Sally, sitting opposite me, her screen in her lap, "I could never think of SID as my best friend, Sally."

Ouch, that hurts.

"SID?"

"My Sinister Imagination Disorder, as my mum likes to refer to it."

"Okay, Nell, so in the instructions it says your inner critic can be described as a voice which you may or may not be aware of. You are obviously already aware of your inner voice – yes?"

"Oh yeh – SID's been in my head for years."

"That's great – we have a really good base to start from. And so, do you think that, purely for the purpose of this exercise, you could try to think of SID as your best friend? I mean, could you just imagine SID playing the role in the statements?"

"All I can do is give it a try."

I looked back down at the screen:

Below are seven statements. Mark a score from zero to five against each statement, representing how you would expect your best friend to support you in each situation. Five is the highest score, when you think the statement describes exactly how your best friend would behave. Mark zero, if there is no chance at all of her behaving like that.

"Her?" I said again, looking up from the screen, "SID's a him, definitely a him."

Sally raised her eyebrows.

I looked out the window at the crisp, blue morning.

"I'm not sure about this, Sally. It just doesn't describe how I think of SID."

It's a waste of time anyway.

"Try to just concentrate on the subject matter of the statements. As you work through each one, pay attention to your reaction, and write down which thoughts you think are yours, and which you think are SID's. It'll be useful to separate the two. Then add your score in after – don't get hung up on the terminology – just write down what you feel about the statement, and we can go from there."

This is going to be brilliant.

"I'll give it a go."

Statements:

1. Every day my best friend reminds me of what a great life I have.

SID: *Ten*
Me: Four
SID: *Why four?*
Me: When was the last time you reminded me?
SID: Yesterday?
Me: No way! It's me who gives thanks every day.
SID: And who do you think prompts you to do that?
Score: TWO

2. I enjoy meeting up with old friends, and making new ones. I always have something interesting to say and my best friend helps me to feel confident with people I don't know.

Me: I enjoy seeing one friend at a time. I can't really say I enjoy it if there's a large group of us.
SID: Because you're scared of being put in the spotlight.
Me: Anyway – I'd rather be dancing than talking.
Score: ZERO

3. I believe I am worthy of love, and my best friend helps to reinforce that belief.

Me: Complete opposite.
SID: Dangerous – not your favourite subject is it: love.
Score: ZERO

4. When my partner and I are out socially, my best friend helps me to feel confident and radiant. If I start to feel insecure she comforts me, telling me I am pretty, intelligent, and fun, and the only woman my partner will ever need.

Me: No chance! SID convinces me my partner would rather be with every other woman in the room, making me feel boring and insignificant. 'Watch him looking at her', he'll say; until my scalp shrinks and burns, my throat blocks, and I couldn't hold a conversation with anyone if my life depended on it! It's hideous. Going out anywhere is a total nightmare.
SID: But I'm usually right, aren't I? They ARE looking at other women.

Me: Everyone looks at other people, for goodness sake!

SID: But not in the way your partners do. Imagine if I didn't say anything, and you thought you were going out with a man you could trust!

Me: I'd rather think that than feeling constantly paranoid.

SID: No you wouldn't. All I'm saying is, forewarned is forearmed.

Me: Oh right: so you're protecting me?

SID: Of course I'm protecting you! That's all I've ever done.

Me: Rubbish.

Score: MINUS FIFTY BILLION

5. Through re-assurance, my best friend helps me to trust my partner.

SID: You! Feeling safe enough to trust! Fat chance.

Me: Because of you! SID clamps himself around my ribcage, crushing me until I can't breathe: I can't sleep: I pick my fingers till they bleed. He goes on and on about how it's impossible for a man and woman to be just friends, how there'll ALWAYS be sexual innuendo and flirting. It's a fact. Apparently.

SID: Well, it is a fact!

Me: According to who?

Score: ZERO

6. My best friend has always supported me in my career choice – she encourages me to network, and to develop into the best journalist I can be.

Me: You are generally positive about the articles I write, SID, I'll give you six points for that.

SID: I enjoy them.

Me: Networking, however, is a different nightmare. I'm nul at it. I never feel confident.

SID: *Well, there are better writers than you out there.*

Me: So?

SID :So, I don't want you to be rubbished.

Me: By who?

SID: Editors.

Me: They're professionals – they wouldn't do that.

SID: How do you know?

Score: THREE

SID: You said I'd scored six for supporting your articles.
Me: I've deducted for not helping me to network.

7. I trust my inner voice and I believe we make a brilliant team. She helps me to be the best person I can be.
Me: Sadly, very sadly, not.
SID: Not true! We do make a brilliant team.
Me: Brilliant at what? Insecurity? Fear? Suspicion? Failure?
SID: Well yes, we're brilliant at all of those. Not everyone can say that.
Me: And what if I don't want to be brilliant at them? What if I want to live life positively, and love everyone unconditionally?
SID: You? Love unconditionally?
Me: What if I want to be brilliant at trust, at self-belief? What if I want to be brilliant at feeling peace, to fall deeply in love and live happily ever after?
SID: Boring! You thrive on emotional turmoil.
Score: ZERO

I re-read my answers before handing the screen back to Sally. She skimmed over it.

"Five out of thirty-five," she said.

I laughed nervously.

"That's obviously not including the minus fifty billion."

We looked at each other.

She read my comments following each statement, taking way longer than I imagined they could ever merit.

Again, we looked at each other.

"So, Nell, I have a question for you." She looked at me intensely. "Based on what you've just written, what is it exactly you would like to achieve by the end of your time here?"

"That's easy, Sally. I'd like to achieve peace."

That's a good one, that'll give her a laugh.

"Inner peace," I added.

Even better!

"I would like to trust and love without question, and never feel suspicious."

Bit ambitious.

"For years I've felt like I've got a massive pile of congealed spaghetti instead of a brain, and I can't see clearly through any of it. I can't be calm and peaceful because everything's too jumbled up. And SID makes it worse. I've never known how to differentiate between intuition and emotion, Sally. Is intuition the buzzing and churning in my solar plexus, or is it the fire and fear in my head? I just don't know. I don't know which controls which. I don't know if I make my decisions based on my stomach, or my head."

I do not make it worse!

Sally listened, watching me.

"So, what would I like to achieve, Sally? Untangled spaghetti. A peaceful inner world, and a SID-free head."

ALICE AND MY SCORE

"First session over with," I said, walking into the kitchen.

"How did it go?" Alice asked, looking up from her charging platform.

"Five out of thirty-five."

"Is that good or bad?"

I showed her a copy of the exercise on my roamer.

"I hope you don't mind me saying, but that is pathetic."

And none of your answers were true.

"What did Sally say?"

"Nothing really. She just said everyone does a similar exercise relating to the reason they're on therapy, so it gives her an idea of where we need to get started."

"And after she'd read yours, did you remind her we've only got eight weeks?"

"Alice!"

Her ears flattened backwards.

THOUGHT-PROJECTION – JUPITER

Mara wore a black miniskirt, which I thought ambitious considering how difficult beanbags can be, but she did seem to manage it with dignity. Her pale blue shirt was again buttoned tightly under her 34Ds. She wasn't the type of woman I imagined Ty Martins to be married to. Not at all. Just the amount of make-up she wore seemed in contrast to the life I imagined they led on the farm in Argentina.

More your type, is he?

"Greetings, one and all," Sally said. She had arranged our seating into a shallow semi-circle. "Please relax into your beanbags, facing that wall." She gestured towards one of the glass walls.

Hah! I hope she's going to share everyone's scores from the exercise yesterday. They'll think you're a right nul.

"Screen opaque!" Sally said, and the glass transformed itself to solid white.

With Alice against my ankle I reclined nervously back into my turquoise island.

"Today we're going to do a thought-projection exercise. I'll need each of you in turn to rest your head against this electronic pad, and close your eyes," Sally said, holding up a flexible sheet the size of my palm. "You'll hear a faint bleep once it's acclimatized to your individual brain patterns. From there it will project your thoughts onto the screen opposite."

"What?" Mara said. "The thoughts I have are private. Why should other people see them? I'm not sharing what's private with people I don't know. Or with people I do know. I don't accept." She stared at Sally.

"I will guide your thoughts to a particular situation before projection, Mara, so don't worry."

"Don't worry! You guiding us isn't going to dictate what we're thinking, is it? There's no way you can control our thoughts. I don't accept. It's totally wrong. And how do we know you haven't set the sensor to steal our information, or alter our identities."

Mara could be in meltdown. Our 'information' is stored on microchips, and there's no way Sally could tamper with them, even if she wanted to. The chips are implanted into our hands at birth, and they're exclusive to us. Each chip holds our individual code, notifies us of incoming communications, they unlock our houses, pay for our shopping, and store all our personal data. Our units are credited monthly onto our chips.

Mum and Dad were both born in the survival parks in 2046, years before microchip implants were introduced, and Mum hates them. She and Dad think it's just another way of the System controlling us. But the Silvers aren't capable of controlling us – it's their programming team she needs to worry about. And Mara, for example, obviously thinks we can be turned into braindead monsters by anyone manipulating our chips. That makes me laugh. The chips aren't capable of controlling our minds.

Yet.

"Jupiter, would you calm Mara by going first?" Sally said.

Don't like the sound of this, it's way too intrusive.

Mara looked at me nervously.

Just refuse to do it.

"Jupiter?" Sally said, "ready to go?"

"Yep," Jupiter said, relaxing into his black beanbag until he practically disappeared.

Sally placed the sensor-pad behind his head.

"You are on this course, mainly because of your polydrug addiction. I believe you are currently injecting three times a day, and gaming for eleven hours," Sally said.

"Up until three days ago, yes."

"Okay. What I'd like you to do is close your eyes and try to relax."

He did.

"Take three deep breaths with me...and now try to picture yourself just before you inject. Take your time. Hold onto the image, and breathe into it. Pay attention to any feelings you may be experiencing. For example, anxiety, calmness, fear. Keep breathing, and focus on the feelings as they appear. The pad will do the rest."

I watched the screen – a blur of wiggly lines appeared for a while, then it cleared.

"Try and relax, Jupiter. Keep taking deep breaths. I know it's tricky. Take your time. Do you have any images associated with how you feel before you need to inject? Any feelings in your heart?"

Suddenly, there on the screen, was an image of, ME! But not me as I am now. Me when I was, what – thirteen? Fourteen?

I was wearing my ed uniform, standing with my back up against a beige wall in a room I didn't recognise. I was holding my hands out in front of me, and they burst into flames. I screamed and started beating them against my hips. I was scraping them up and down my thighs, scoring tracks with my blackening fingernails. It looked like I was trying to beat the fire out against my legs, which started dripping blood. I rubbed my fingers into the blood covering my legs, turned around, and wrote on the wall: I WOULD RATHER BE ME THAN ANYONE ELSE.

Alice rubbed up against my calf, and I rested my right hand on her back. I took some deep breaths and looked at Sally, who mouthed 'you okay?'

Back on-screen, the backs of my legs were running with blood, and my fingers were, one by one, melting into charred stumps. Then the wall caught fire and I threw myself at it, clawing my head and banging my fists into the flames. I turned and fell to the floor, mouthing, 'Don't Go. Don't Go."

The image cleared.

Wow. Not what I was expecting!

Thankfully, a gang of scantily clad worm-headed warriors replaced me. They carried swords and spears and violently slashed one another, and themselves. They tore limbs from bodies and slumped next to one another, writhing in pools of green blood. The pile of bodies grew, whilst more warriors appeared out of nowhere, slashing and stabbing, adding to the pile.

Then a small round pond with a grassy island in the middle, and mossy rocks all around the edge appeared. Over to the right edge of the pond stood the most spectacular wooden and glass treehouse, towering upwards into a magnificent Baobab tree, and out of the treehouse window, Jupiter looked, his lank black hair covering his eyes. He smiled.

The screen cleared.

Silence, followed by a heavy, communal breath.

"Great work, Jupiter," Sally said. "You can open your eyes when you feel ready."

Jupiter slowly opened his eyes and looked around.

Mara was still staring at the clear screen, Ty was looking at Mara, and I was looking at Jupiter.

"Are you alright?"

"Now *that* was different. What did I project?"

"You'll look at your images in a couple of days, Jupiter. This afternoon is all about recording."

"That's nasty," Jupiter exclaimed.

"It's necessary – you need time to digest this," Sally said. "You would be overloaded if I played the recording straight back."

We all groaned.

"There is no way I'm doing this!" Mara said. "No way. What's the point? Why does everyone else need to see what's going on? It's nobody's business."

"It's proven group projection therapy is many times more successful than individual therapy, Mara. Don't worry, if you find it too difficult, or stressful, we can come out of the projection at any time."

"It'll be fine, Ems. It might even be fun," Ty said, patting her on the knee.

"Fun? A complete waste of my time, is what it is," she snapped back, moving her knee out of his reach.

"Nell's up next," Ty said. "So you've got time to get used to the idea."

Mara scowled.

I felt sick.

THOUGHT-PROJECTION – ME

Sally put the pad behind my head.

Oh shit, oh shit, oh shit.

Ready to bare your soul?

I heard the faint bleep.

"Nell, I'd like you to recreate the feelings you had towards the end of your last relationship. Think of things that were said, and how they made you feel."

I didn't really want to think about Youssan, it was over months ago.

Three!

"Close your eyes and try to relax. Take three deep breaths and focus inwards."

Stuck in my mind was the image of my bleeding legs and burning hands. I felt under pressure to concentrate on Youssan, and the more pressure I felt, the more impossible relaxation became. My ears rang with concentration, and all I could hear was the squelching of my Adam's apple, up and down.

"Take your time," Sally said. "Try to clear your mind, and then focus the feelings you were having before the relationship ended."

I forced my thoughts to our first week together, how much we had laughed together, and how passionately we had kissed. I missed him.

My heart started pounding. I thought of him with S and P. Something was crushing my ribs.

"Stay with it," I heard Sally say.

I was kissing him... Who is S x?

He's lying...

Why won't you tell me?

He's a liar...

Tell me!

End it.

Water welling up behind my closed eyelids.

Working late...sunflower vase...

Who from?
S gave it to him…
…they're having an affair
Me, quizzing him...
Chest pounding.
Heart-beat in my throat.
Getting angry …Who's P?
Only trust me.
Heart splitting.
Don't trust this man.
Palms sweating.
Never trust any man.
Breathe.
Never trust anyone.

Alice rubbing against my leg. Counting my breathing: in, one, out, two, in, one, out, two … I started to feel my heart calming. SID's voice faded.

"When you're ready, Nell, open your eyes – take your time – there's no hurry."

But when you've got four other people in the room waiting for you, you feel there *is* a hurry, don't you? I opened them.

"Great projection, Nell."

"It felt awful."

Nobody said a word. Mara stared at her knees, Ty stared at the ceiling, and Jupiter squeezed my hand.

"Do we *really* have to wait for a couple of days to see?" I felt desperate.

"At this early stage of the therapy you need to have time to process the emotions you've just experienced," Sally said. "Trust me."

Why was everyone looking at me!

THOUGHT-PROJECTION – TY AND MARA

Mara grabbed the pad from Sally's hand as she tried to put it behind her head. "I can do it myself, thanks."

"It's better if I do it, Mara, to make sure I get the sensors in the right position."

Mara let Sally position the pad as she leant backwards.

"You know the format by now, Mara," Sally said. "I'd like you to think about how you feel just before you reach for the bottle of whiskey in the morning."

Mara stiffened, dislodging the pad, "I don't drink whiskey every morning!" she shouted. "You say it as if I'm some sort of addict, which I am *not.*"

"Sorry Mara, I just think the whiskey would be a good place to start – unless you can suggest something else you'd rather concentrate on?"

"Life once I'm out of here, maybe?" Mara snapped.

Mara begrudgingly let Sally replace the pad and then closed her eyes. Jupiter seemed transfixed by Mara as she sat there, rigid.

A dark-haired woman appeared on the screen – in her late thirties at a guess. She was dressed in a sky blue knitted sweater, way too big for her, with a dark blue skirt flowing downwards, covering her feet. She stood quite alone in the middle of a massive expanse of concrete. She walked with her head tilted forward and her eyes fixated on the concrete ahead of her. Then suddenly turned at ninety degrees and set off in another direction, with no more purpose than before. She changed direction several more times. Not once did she take her eyes away from the concrete.

Then suddenly, she lifted her head and sprinted in a straight line, her skirt flowing out behind her. For the longest time she ran, her breathing getting heavy. She looked up at the vast expanse of nothing in front of her, and then lowered her head, and slowed down to a stroll. Then once more, she started walking and randomly changing direction, as she had done before.

Was she looking for a way off the concrete? Whatever she was doing, she cut a sad and lonely figure.

No other images appeared on the screen.

Mara opened her eyes, and sat there, staring out of the window into the afternoon sky.

Ty reached over, took her hand, and squeezed it. She didn't move.

"Are you okay, Ems?" he whispered.

She pulled her hand away.

"Why shouldn't I be – it was easy enough."

What did that mean! Had she managed to trick the pad?

Sally said, "And so, to finish off the day, it's over to you, Ty."

"Try not to fall asleep, everybody. I bet this will be about as exciting as watching mud dry," Mara said.

Bitch!

Ty didn't respond.

He's not even going to say anything?

"Right, Ty. I'd like you to focus on your feelings when you think of playing with your two sons," Sally said.

"Oh *p...... lease,"* said Mara.

Why doesn't he stand up to her? They're never going to save their marriage if he doesn't.

"Ty? Do the best you can, and put Mara's unhelpful comments out of your mind. Mara, we all have the right to project, please show some respect," Sally added.

For the longest time the screen remained clear. Sally talked Ty through the process, asking him to relax and focus, and then an image appeared of the biggest plateful of bananas, chocolate, and ice cream I'd ever seen. It was starting to melt in the sun. Then two spoons started tucking in on either side. There were no hands holding the spoons, they had a life of their own, massacring the plate full of goodies. The slurps and laughter of children could be heard, along with excited screeches as the spoons took bigger and bigger helpings. As fast as the spoons raced out of the picture, only to come back again empty, so the plate replenished itself.

The scene zoomed out to show the plate sitting on a wooden trestle table in front of a lake. The invisible owners of the voices were shouting at one another to hurry up and eat before the ice cream went runny. The image of the sun on the screen invaded the lounge, bathing us all in golden yellow.

I looked over at Ty, his eyes shut, with a smile soaked in sunlight. He looked so peaceful, and I wished he would love me, not Mara, forever and ever.

For goodness sake. You are ridiculous.

"I'm going to be sick!" one of the invisible spoon holders shouted. "Me too!" said the other. This was followed by manic giggling. Instantly the spoons stopped moving, the voices stopped squealing and the screen focussed, in silence, on the sun-soaked lake.

The screen cleared, and Ty opened his eyes.

"Thank you, Ty that was a wonderful way to finish the day," Sally said.

"Was it? I can't wait to watch it then. I must say, it felt nice."

Did I see Mara wipe the corner of her eye?

Doubt it.

"Thank you all for being so cooperative," Sally said. "You all have a free day tomorrow to take in what we've done so far. Then we'll meet back here the day after to review your projections."

DAY FOUR

"Thought-projection is exhausting, Alice. Last night I thought I'd get up early this morning, and we'd head into the meadows to think through the last three days."

Three days? Is that all?

"But I don't feel like getting up." I lifted Alice onto the bed next to me. "How about we spend the morning here on the sleeping platform, watching the clouds and the birds pass by."

Boring!

"Sounds good to me," Alice said, looking out through the rooflight.

"So what do you think of the first few days then, Alice?"

"Hooded crow!" she said, just as its tail feathers passed out of sight. "I like Shilly. And Ty is far more handsome close up than in his Farming First bulletins."

"I agree."

"Why not see if you can do an interview with him for Earth Matters."

"He wouldn't want me interviewing him, Alice – he's way too famous."

"Jupiter hadn't heard of him. And how many people actually watch the farming bulletins? He can't be that famous. I think he'd agree – he sounded pretty impressed to be sitting in the Lounge with you – you're more famous than he is anyway."

"No I'm not. People who don't follow Earth Matters wouldn't have a clue who I am."

"Well, you're both famous in your areas of expertise, Nell. No harm in asking him."

"Maybe. And why do you think his housebot is a sheep, Alice? Wouldn't a humanoid robot be more helpful on the farm?"

"He's got Mara for that!"

"Hah, can you picture her scrubbing muck off his boots?"

"There is a limit to my programming, you know! Anyway, Ty's fit enough not to need a humanoid. It's like someone asking why you've got a Friesian cow."

"I spose. Mum freaked when she discovered they'll be getting a humanoid for their seventieth birthdays because they're considered in need of extra help."

"Ridiculous – your Mum's the fittest woman I know."

"Anyway, Alice. I need to concentrate on sorting my head out, not interviewing Ty. Do you think eight weeks of soul-searching can change thirty-five years of habits?"

Massively doubtful.

"Who knows unless you try it."

"I mean, how can raking up a load of old memories and hideous emotions help? And how will I know I've changed until I get into another relationship?"

You'll never change.

"I can't answer that, Nell," Alice said, "but I think you're in the right place to try."

As if her opinion is worth anything. She's an ashing robot!

"I also think that when you've left here, you'll need to keep practicing whatever it is you've learnt about yourself."

Get her and her wise words!

"You're right, Alice. I should start a reminders file on my roamer. Or maybe I'll write in one of my notebooks."

I reached over to the bedside unit and took out a small, square, rice-paper notebook with a forest green cover. "I like this one," I said, writing *My Little Book of Help* on the cover. "I name you, *Little Book of Help,* 'Greenie'."

How original!

"I'll write a sentence, phrase or word on each page and use the pages to remind myself of ways to reinforce what I've learnt."

"Brilliant idea," Alice said, her head tipping downwards.

"Are you due a re-charge?"

"I am – a full – so you'll have to switch me off."

"Okay. I'll just write my first entry in Greenie – 'Sit quietly, breathe deeply, and listen'."

That'll be a first.

It's a start.

SCANNING

I put Alice down on her re-charging platform, switched her off and plugged her in.

I dressed, made a coffee and sat on the sofa. I tapped Mum.

She appeared on my wall-screen, sitting at her office desk in Cassava.

"Hi, Mum."

"Nell, it's lovely to see you. How's the therapy going?"

Her lapwing-grey hair was tied back off her tanned and wrinkly face – her laugh lines looked the deepest as she smiled out at me.

"It's different. You'll never guess who else is on the course."

"Go on."

"Ty Martins – from the Farming First stream. Can you believe it?"

"I can't. What's he like?"

"He is lush."

"Remember why you're there, Nell!"

"I know. I haven't forgotten. How are things with you?"

"It's all good here. You?"

"It's our first free day today, so Alice and I have been enjoying a lie-in."

"And very nice too! I wish I had that luxury."

"How's the new irrigation system working out?"

"Amazingly. The germination rate is excellent. The years of pathetic scraggly trial-crops are finally over. By the time you get back I'm hoping there'll be dark green leaves for as far as the eye can see."

"Sounds really promising. Dad must be proud of his system, and you must be really happy with the plant nursery."

"We are, Nell. It's taken a long time, but it's been worth it."

"I'm looking forward to seeing it, Mum. There's something I want to ask you. Do house-bots have any sort of emotional programming?"

"Not generally. Why?"

"Well, Alice is still saying funny things."

"I thought she'd stopped once you contacted GreenWaters."

"So did I. But since we arrived she's started again. Like, for example, she loves moss! How can she love moss?"

"Oh, it's just Alice, being enthusiastic, Nell. Where's the harm in her loving moss?"

"No, I know there's no harm in it, but if she doesn't have any emotional programming then she can't love anything, can she?"

"She's just copying words you use, Nell."

When have you ever used the word 'love'!

"It's not that, Mum. There's something different about her – I can't quite explain it, but she's not the same."

"Can you think of any examples? Other than loving moss!"

"There's a sheepbot here called Shilly, and Alice is behaving as if she likes her. Is that possible if she hasn't had EP?"

"You could always send her for a scan if you're worried."

"Really? How easy would it be?"

"From Scandi? Not easy, but nothing's impossible."

"Can you find out what would be involved?"

"I will. I'll let you know. Say hello to Ty from us. Dad sends his love."

YELLOW RICE PAPER

"I'm so very, very sorry, Nell," Jupiter said, after the replay of his projection. "I *remember* when you made all those little yellow sticker things to try and feel better about yourself. We made so much fun of you and you burnt them all. We were jealous, Nell. I am so, so, sorry."

"Don't be daft, Jupiter. I'd forgotten all about it."

Liar.

I *was* lying. I'd *never* forgotten about it, and never forgiven any of them.

You don't know the meaning of the word.

It had all started shortly after I won a credit voucher in the ed-unit talent competition for my rendition of Ring My Bell, by Anita Ward. I'd spent weeks learning a dance routine. I'd made a sparkly-silver body suit, and frizzed my hair to the point of no return, which you wouldn't think is the way someone who doesn't really like herself would behave, but that's the fascinating thing about humans. It worked too – the judging panel gave me the highest score of the year. They said they didn't recognise the music, but they'd never seen footwork like it.

I spent my voucher on a positive self-talk program, and shut myself away from my ed friends for a weekend to work through it. The program began by giving examples of negative self-talk. I was horrified at how many of them I could relate to:

She ignored me today. I think she hates me.

I hate talking when everyone is looking at me.

I feel so insecure about my future.

No boys ever fancy me.

I'll never be as interesting as she is.

I spent the weekend paying attention to what was going on inside my head, and I wrote all the negativity down. There, captured in my art book, in black and white, I had everything associated with my Sinister Imagination Disorder. I ripped the pages of negative words into shreds, and burnt them. With guidance from the program I thought of positive words, and with my favourite pen, I wrote them onto primrose-yellow squares of rice paper.

I am unique and have my own style.

I am secure. The future will be what it will be.

I would rather be me than anyone else.

I love who I am, I am interesting, and I am proud of myself.

I control my emotions, they do not control me.

I wrote the sentences over and over, and pinned the squares onto my bedroom walls, and glued them into my books.

I inwardly repeated the phrases to myself, many times every day, and for five weeks primrose-yellow squares brightened my room, my books, and my inner world.

Didn't last though, did it!

Disastrously, Fran and Sharna found a couple of the squares. "Who else would rather be Nell than anyone else?" Fran had asked the class room.

"Look at Nell, isn't she unique." Sharna had added. I remember the humiliation. Jupiter had just sat and laughed.

I mean, real friends don't do things like that, do they? They weren't friends at all of course, but I couldn't see it at the time. With hindsight, I realise they felt threatened by me. With the help of my primrose-yellow affirmations my inner light had started to shine too brightly for them.

I should have stuck with my faithful yellow squares. I should have let my light carry on shining. I would have attracted new friends, whose lights were also shining – we would have been beacons signalling to one another.

But I didn't. Friends are important at that age, and I cared what they thought of me, and I cared about being alone. I cared about not having to sit on my own in the refreshment facility, and I cared about being snubbed every time our paths crossed, which was every day.

So I dimmed my light. I destroyed all my little squares of primrose-yellow, and my positive self-talk faded away. I returned to SID, and to my old ways of negative thinking, and I kept my friends.

Once I left education I didn't stay in touch with any of them.

***

Jupiter was totally spaced out by his worm-headed, murdering warriors, and tearful at the sight of his tree-house – his Dad had built it for him and he used to spend most of his ed breaks in there. He said it was where he had lived some of his happiest moments – he had proposed to Fran in there, and they'd camped in there for two weeks after the wedding.

"Note how the treehouse came after the warriors, Jupiter," Sally said.

"Well obviously," said Mara. "It shows he feels desperate before he injects, and totally at peace afterwards. No surprises there."

"Thank-you, Mara," Sally said.

Friction. Exciting.

"Right, Jupiter," Sally said, "your challenge for the final thought-projection session is to feel only the calmness of the tree house. No more Nell, no more worm-headed warriors."

Jupiter winced. "That's going to be a tough one," he said. "I am an addict, don't forget."

"Ex-addict," Alice said.

SPAGHETTI AND SID

Attention turned to me.

Terrified? Ready for total exposure?

On the screen appeared a heaving, tangled mass of cooked spaghetti. Each strand was interwoven, squirming and pulsating, in, out, and around the others. I watched the strands expanding and contracting, slithering from side to side. And then, as they continued to writhe and twist, words started to form along their length. Some words were faint, others were BIG and BOLD. Sally paused the recording every time a big, bold word emerged, and I noted it on my roamer. This is the order in which they appeared:

LOVE. TRUST. KV. CONTROL. REJECTION. LITTLE NELL.

One strand kept breaking free and bending over the entire heap, like a kind of protective band. In massive bold letters, the strand named itself.

FEAR

I noted it.

Now and again, the spaghetti tried to straighten itself into an orderly pile, just how uncooked spaghetti looks. But right at the point of order, FEAR would burst out of the pack and try to strangle the others, re-starting their squirming and writhing.

"KV?" I asked Sally, as the image faded.

The spaghetti was replaced by a horizontal pile of black, oily, railway sleepers. They sat in the middle of a disused quarry-like place. There were heaps of dirty, wet gravel everywhere, and large potholes filled with muddy brown water. The sky was grey and depressing.

A massive, rusty, iron portcullis appeared at the top of the screen and started to creak and groan its way downwards. It came to a stop on the gravel with a thud.

I tilted my head as I heard a woman whisper, "Don't *ever* trust this man." And again, getting louder, "He's lied once, he will again." "Don't believe him." "He's lying!"

I strained my eyes searching the screen for the owner of the voice, then, very slowly, out from behind the railway-sleepers crept...something. It was speaking, and every time it did, it jabbed an overly long index finger towards the portcullis, and straight towards my chest. "You'll never survive this therapy. You'll never bare your soul." A big blob-shaped woman with massive hair crept towards me, growing larger with every step. She stopped against the portcullis, gripping onto the rusty iron bars. She stared menacingly into my eyes.

I pressed back into the beanbag.

Her intense blue eyes were abnormally large and bulbous, with jet-black pupils marooned in the centres. Her black, matted curls launched themselves up and out, making her entire head look enormous. She tightened her fists around the rusty metal bars and started to rock her head back and forward, slowly at first, then getting faster. Then she started to laugh, and jab her finger at me, "I'm your best friend now. *I'm* your best friend. DON'T YOU FORGET IT."

My heart was pounding. Alice rubbed against my leg.

"You need me. We're a team, you and me. You can't live without me. I can't live without YOU." she shouted, glaring straight at me. Her filthy black clothes stretched to tearing point.

"Never trust a man. You don't need them. I'm all you need." she shouted. "Never trust anyone. They're all liars."

Suddenly, her head spun round to her left, as if she'd heard something. She stood perfectly still, listening. Then she stared back at me, beat her forehead against the grill, mouthed something I couldn't hear, and let go. She turned her back to me and started to creep back towards the railway-sleepers, looking quickly to her right and left as she went. She turned her head towards me one final time, and then disappeared back behind the sleepers.

"Who the hell was that?" I asked the room, once the screen had cleared.

Apologetically, Jupiter said, "If we hadn't made you destroy your stickers, Nell, I bet she wouldn't exist."

Alice headbutted my knee. "I can't believe you're being so dim!"

Everyone stared at her.

"That was SID!"

I stared at Alice until she threatened to charge my knee again.

"SID? But SID's a man!"

"Well, apparently not!" Alice reasoned. "Which is perhaps why he's been so horrible to you, because you've always thought he was a him, not a her."

At least someone round here is vaguely intelligent.

I looked towards Jupiter, and Sally. "Maybe SID is KV – from your spaghetti strands?" Mara suggested.

I looked at her, my mind racing. SID is a *woman?* That's why she's always hated me, because I thought she was a man?

I've never hated you. I've always been on your side.

"SID's a woman!" I said.

Hallelujah!

"Will this change anything? Will her poisonous chatter in my head sound any different?"

"Hopefully it will, Nell," Sally said.

Even though I doubted it, I couldn't help but feel a tiny bit excited. I leant over and fluffed up Alice's face. She squirmed away from me, ears flattening.

"I can't believe it. So what should I call her, Alice?"

"Evil?"

Nasty!

"Not SID?" I asked.

"Nell," Sally said, "by the end of therapy you need either your head free of images of spaghetti, or, peaceful strands lying motionless, side by side. Also, SID needs to have either gone, or she needs to be a positive influence."

I've always been positive – you're the negative one!

I stared out through the glass wall. Was there hope, now I knew the identity of the person behind all of the horrible thoughts I had? A robin, outside on the moss, looked up at me. "Another load of screwed up humans," I imagined it saying.

It flew away just as Mara's 'woman in blue' faded from the screen.

Ty held her hand. I wondered why he bothered when she was so foul towards him all the time.

That's what love is – something you wouldn't know anything about.

"Your task, Mara, is to have eradicated your woman in blue," Sally said.

"Don't really care if she's still there or not," Mara replied.

"Give it a try, Mara, or eight weeks is going to seem a very long time – for all of us," Sally said.

Ty watched his dancing spoons, ice cream, and sunshine with tears gently cascading down his cheeks. Mara didn't make any attempt to comfort him.

I wanted to go over and wrap my arms round him.

You think that would be comforting?

Not SID! Go away.

I couldn't figure out why Ty was being so pathetic, not standing up to Mara.

It's not a question of being pathetic, Nell, it's love. When you love someone you stick by them, through the shit times, hoping the good times will come back.

What, and all of a sudden, you're an expert are you?

"Ty, you need to have some bodies on the end of your spoons for our final thought-projection session," Sally said.

He didn't say a word, didn't even look at Sally. Mara didn't say a word either, and I wondered if it would be possible for them to fix a relationship that appeared to have broken down beyond hope.

"That's it for our first week of group meetings," Sally said, "I hope you're enjoying it so far. I have you all individually for a while, which I'm looking forward to."

"I'm having a great time," Alice said.

"Me too," Shilly added, fluttering her dark brown eyelids towards Alice.

DREAM

I dreamt I was awake. I heard voices. I looked over my sleeping platform, and Alice was pressed up against my wall-screen, whispering with Mum. Alice told her SID is a woman. She told her my head was full of writhing spaghetti covered in ice-cream, and that it loves to dance, with spoons, to robo-techno.

Morning came. I got up, but the dream wouldn't leave me. I checked Alice, and the screen.

"What's up?" Alice asked.

I told her.

"Oh I'd *love* to be able to communicate. How did I do it?"

"You were touching your nose against the screen."

"Do you think it could *really* work? I could message with Shilly and see her black woolly nose anytime I liked. That would be fantastic," she said, excited.

"Then absolutely *no* cleaning would get done," I said, as I scooped her up onto the kitchen units.

NOT SID

"We're going to try something a little more challenging this morning, Nell," Sally said. "We'll watch images on the wall-screen, like before, but I'll be using a different pad. This one works with thought-communication. So, for example, if you want SID to come out from behind the sleepers, you have to think it and feel it rather than verbalise it. However, if SID appears and starts to communicate with you, you will hear her voice. But if you want to ask her a question, you'll need to think it, not say it."

"Sounds complicated."

"Most people get the hang of it quite quickly once they concentrate," she said.

"Let's give it a try." I rested my right hand on Alice's back. Sally placed a small sensor pad behind my head.

"You can do this with your eyes closed or open, it doesn't matter. Focus on wanting to meet SID. Try to hold it as your only thought."

"I think I'll close my eyes to get into it."

"Fine."

I relaxed into my beanbag. I would like to meet you, SID... Not SID... Where are you, Not SID? Okay, how about going back to SID? SID, are you there? SID, I'd like to see you...Whoever you are who was behind the railway-sleepers, I would like to meet you... please come out.

Nothing.

"Think back to Youssan, and see if that can bring her out. Focus on him lying to you."

I opened my eyes. "Not sure I really want to."

"I think it may be the only way to get her to surface."

I took a deep breath and closed my eyes again. I thought about The Award and immediately my stomach was churning. It was scary how quickly my mind could hook me into a state of anxiety.

Your churning stomach started it off, nothing to do with your mind.

"Great, Nell, I have an image," Sally said. "You can open your eyes, but you need to stay focussed on your thoughts. If you can, without being distracted by what you're seeing, you should be able to keep Not SID on-screen."

The same figure as before crept out from behind the railway-sleepers, and slowly walked towards me. Her eyes darted left and right, and then she stopped abruptly, and looked up. She quickened her pace towards me, looking upwards. I could see the portcullis dropping down to the ground. Though she hurried it slammed into the ground in front of her, spraying her with muck. Her eyes followed the perimeter of her iron prison, before they darted straight ahead, directly to mine.

The pile of railway sleepers were the same, the brown puddles, the heaps of gravel – it was all as it had been on our initial meeting.

Are you SID?

She grabbed hold of the metal; her matted black hair framing her terrifying eyes. She smirked.

Now I see you're a woman, would you like a new name?

She stared at me. Her eyes looked upwards to the left, and then the right, then back to me. She let go of the grill, turned her back and hurried away, then turned and hurried back. She did this six times, looking to her left, then right, the entire time. Filthy water splashed up her legs as she stamped through the puddles along her way.

She stopped just short of the grill, stood upright with her hands down by her side, puffed out her enormous chest, and said, "Karensa Veeolay."

"Wow!" said Alice, "not exactly what I was expecting!"

She turned her head in Alice's direction. "Well, that is my name."

Can you spell your name?

She scurried off, back behind her sleepers, and re-appeared with a long, pointed stick. In the mud she scrawled K A R E N S A V I O L E T.

"Pronounced, V E E O L A Y," she said.

I laughed at the ridiculousness of it.

She threw the stick at the portcullis. "That's it! I'm off. It's Karensa Veeolay, or nothing. I've waited twenty-five years for a name, for you to realise I'm a woman, and you can't even take me seriously. Fine. I'll go back to the days of being SID, and stuff your stupid therapy course. You're never going to get anywhere with any of it unless you've got me on your side."

Hang on, don't go, not yet. Veeolay is ridiculous... No... It's maybe possible?... Don't move. Look, I'm sorry I thought you were a man. How about I still call you SID, but spelt Cyd. There are lots of women called Cyd.

"Karensa Vee-o-lay," she said.

No.

"Tough!" She spat at the grill.

It's not tough, actually. I'm on this course to sort my head out and once that's done, I won't need 'Karensa Veeolay' ever again, so it doesn't really matter what you're called.

She marched up to the portcullis.

"You really think it's going to be that easy? YOU! PATHETIC, INSECURE, BORING, YOU!" She jabbed her index finger straight towards my chest.

Sally removed the sensor pad, freezing the image of Cyd on the screen.

"Okay, let's pause there a moment. There's no point in you two stressing. How about if you tell her you will think differently about her if she's called Cyd. Try giving her a bit of love, or kindness. You'll probably receive the same in return. She is in YOUR head, after all."

"And what if that doesn't happen? What if it makes her worse?" I said, looking at the image of a deranged Cyd, frozen on the screen.

"That's just you resisting change, Nell, which is completely normal, change is scary. But you're forgetting one thing: You control your mind, not the other way round. You have to stand your ground, otherwise you are admitting you have lost control – and I'm afraid that goes into a whole other realm of mental therapy techniques, which can't be dealt with here at GreenWaters."

I took some deep breaths and played with Alice's ear before agreeing to continue with the projection. Sally replaced the pad.

I concentrated my thoughts on Cyd.

Cyd. Are you still there?

"It's Karensa Veeolay," she said, appearing instantly, still looking violent. "And yes, I'm here. Where else would I be? Your dysfunctional group of so-called ed-friends are the reason I'm here. I've been your only true friend for years. Supporting you. Helping you. Warning you. And what do I get in return? This," she said – sweeping her arm out behind her.

Think. Think fast.

"All the years I've helped protect you. You need me. I've been right so many times, and what do I get? This ashing portcullis, trapping me in this filthy hole, no chance of ever bettering myself. No wonder I'm like I am! And look at my clothes! Have you noticed how disgusting they are? And my hair. It's a travesty!"

Focus. Concentrate. No confrontation. Think.

SID, as a name, is nice and snappy, don't you think?

"But SID wasn't me."

I know, and I'm not proposing to call you SID, S.I.D, how about Cyd, C.y.d.? There have been famous women called Cyd. I am asking you to be Cyd, a woman, who is kind and helpful, and in return I'll give you somewhere nice to live and we can be real friends.

Alice bumped into my shin. I ignored her.

SID glared at me. She glared at Alice, and back at me. She turned her back and leant against the portcullis.

I would love you to be a real friend. After all these years I can't imagine life without you, but I want your constant chatter to change. Please? Cyd? Kind, helpful Cyd? Cyd. Kind, loving, Cyd. Wouldn't that be great?

I started to feel a buzz of excitement, rather than fear.

I heard a massive sigh as she turned around, scowling.

There's no chance of you ever changing, is there.

Her face looked sour. But then, she smiled. "Cyd, I believe, would be most acceptable."

I don't believe it! Amazing. Thank you, thank you, thank you. New beginnings. Cyd, Alice and Nell.

"Goodbye SID, S.I.D," she said, then she took a step back, raised one arm out to the side and bowed. The portcullis jolted upwards twenty centimetres, scaring her, then she smiled and held her hands to her heart. As she stood smiling, her hair started to tidy itself, and lighten in colour. Her clothes too: the filth seemed to be somehow evaporating. The darkness was lifting. She looked at me, hurried a wave, turned and ran back behind the sleepers.

The screen cleared.

"That…was… AMAZING, Sally," I said, almost too excited to breathe. "SID's been in my head so long, I can't imagine life without him. I'm terrified, but excited."

"Remember, you're only swapping one version for another," said Alice. "You don't know the newly spelled Cyd will be any better."

She can at least give me a chance!

"I have a feeling Cyd is going to be quite different to the old version."

Me too.

"She will be whatever you make her, Nell," Sally said. "Your whole projection was fantastic, and if you make a commitment here and now to break the old SID, and you stick fastidiously to that commitment, which will be difficult at times, then there'll be change. It's all in your mind, you can do whatever you want with it."

"Just like that!" Alice said.

"How about writing out some affirmations and sticking them around your livingspace? Like you did with your yellow stickers at ed. Repeat them to yourself every day. It will help you keep on track. As you repeat the affirmation, picture Cyd looking clean, and living somewhere nice."

"Right, Sally," I said, "I am making the commitment, right here, right now." I shook Sally's hand in confirmation, picked Alice up, planted a kiss on her nose, then put her back down.

I took Greenie out of my bag and wrote: Cyd is a Woman. She is pretty. She is my friend.

Hooray. I'm your friend. I will try.

"That notebook is a great idea, Nell," Sally said.

I rolled my shoulders back, and took a deep breath. "Ready for change, Alice?"

"Ready, Nell."

MARA

"Guess who I had a 'sort-of' conversation with yesterday," I asked everyone when we met up for our evening social in the lounge.

"The King of Scandinavia?" Mara said.

"There isn't one," Jupiter replied.

"I know."

"Karensa-Veeolay," I announced, ignoring Mara's lack of wit.

"Shit!" Jupiter said, "who the hell is *that*?"

"SID," I said. "She wanted to be called Karensa Veeolay – KV for short, Mara – remember? It was one of my spaghetti strand names. I managed to get her to settle for Cyd – c.y.d. in the end."

"How?" Ty asked, quartering an apple with his pocket knife.

"Just asked her nicely, and she agreed. Smart, eh?"

"Cool."

"Do you fancy getting some air out on the terrace, Nell?" Mara asked me.

I raised my eyebrows to Jupiter.

We slid open the transparent double doors and moved out into the fresh May evening. Mara closed the doors behind us, and I zipped up my sweatie. She lowered her voice. "I need to tell you something, Nell. I've got to tell someone, I can't keep it a secret any longer."

Her eyes shot over to where Ty and Jupiter were chatting. "The two boys aren't Ty's," she said, keeping her voice low.

"What? Whose ..."

"I had an affair with Ty's best friend, Rod, and he's the father."

"Shit, Mara. Are you sure you want to tell me this?"

"The farm was like Rod's second home. He'd come up to help Ty with the animals. I'm not even really sure how it all started. One evening I went to fix dinner, and Rod followed me into the kitchen and made some comment about what I was wearing and patted my bum. I didn't really think anything of it. But then he engineered ways of being near me more and more often and I started to enjoy his company. Then a kiss on the cheek, then an arm around my waist, and then, of course, the kisses started to become more intimate. I was flattered – it was so exciting."

"Ty didn't suspect anything?"

"Apparently not."

"Why didn't you end it?"

"I couldn't, I was caught up in the buzz of it all. It became more intense, and then I got pregnant. I told Rod Ty was the father, but he wasn't, I knew by the dates. Rod didn't care Ty and I were still sleeping together. He loved me. And then I got pregnant a second time, and I told the same lies."

Ashing hell! This is a bit extreme!

I looked through the glass doors at Ty. Had he deserved it?

No-one deserves that.

"I know you like Ty. You must think I'm horrible, but the affair became an obsession. If I walked into another room, and Rod didn't follow a few seconds later, like he had in the early days, I'd think he didn't want me anymore. And I was jealous of their friendship. I had two men on the go, for God's sake, and I *still* felt insecure. How nul is that?"

Totally nul.

"I took it all out on Ty," she said, "my guilt, my lies." She looked down at her hands. "I've been foul to him for years, Nell, it's the only way I can cope with it all. He doesn't deserve any of it. I was so happy when we first met. He's such a kind man, I just couldn't make it last. And so here we are, in this big, horrible mess, and I'm supposed to try and sort it."

"And I thought I had problems!"

You have.

"What did you do?"

"I dumped Rod. He wasn't really a nice person. He didn't take much interest in the kids – why would he? He had an amazing body and he was fantastic in bed, but I started to wonder what sort of person would do that to their best friend?"

What sort of person would do that to their husband!

"I drink because of the guilt. The trouble is though, Ty *has* to know the truth. I received a communication explaining anyone who wants to end a marriage has to attend therapy to talk through their feelings with their partner so they can separate on peaceful terms. What's the point? If the marriage is over, it's over – Ty knows how I feel. But because of the rules I have to go through the therapy and tell Ty the truth about the boys. I mean, can you imagine how it will help? They're mad, these silvers. And once the therapy's finished and our marriage is officially over, I'm going to be reallocated. I mean, I understand the theory behind everyone living happily ever after in a functional family unit, but what if that just doesn't work for some people? We're human, after all, Nell, not robots."

"Wow! I thought the two of you were here to save your marriage, not end it!"

"God, how could you think that with the way I treat him?"

"I did wonder. But will Ty accept your reallocation?"

"Of course he won't accept it. I should have walked away from Ty the moment I started the affair with Rod. But I didn't, I wallowed deeper and deeper in a whole pool of shit, and look where it got me."

"But surely marriage and a life with your children is better than reallocation?"

"Not to me. What can be worse than stuck out on a farm in the middle of nowhere at twenty-nine?"

"Mara, it would be my idea of heaven."

"But it's not mine, Nell. It's so boring. We never go anywhere, I never get the chance to dress up, I live permanently in sloppy trousers and gardening shoes, for fuck's sake."

You'd love that.

"What's your reallocation assignment?"

"Election monitor. The System are starting to train monitors in time for the global voting results. Can you believe there will be Committees *and* four human candidates? This is history in the making, Nell. No one ever thought we would be trusted with leadership again. But here we are, after seventy years there's belief in us humans after all. I'm excited to be part of the process."

"You say after seventy years there's belief humans can lead without fighting – but humans have always been leading, Mara, because we're the ones programming the Silvers."

"But psychologically we don't think of it like that, do we, Nell? We see peaceful, calm, emotionless leadership by robots."

"My Mum and Dad hate robots governing – but, obviously, being born in the parks, they were too young to vote."

People in the underground survival parks were worried men would start warring again once they returned to the surface, and so everyone (from about aged ten upwards), across all of the parks, was involved in developing a plan for governance of what was a hugely diminished population.

The parks were organised into groups: Gov – which housed political leaders, the exceedingly wealthy, and the world's religious leaders: Civi – general members of the population: Preservation – documents, media, flora and fauna, and Research – which was a dedicated research and development park. Research was busy developing new technologies, whilst spirituals and women in the Gov parks were relentless in highlighting the importance of peace after surfacing.

Finally, after all the debating, voting was held for what system of governance should be put in place. People concluded men and money had created the near-global state of war before the Disaster. Seventy-eight percent of the population voted for women to take ultimate leadership.

There was, however, a twist. Research had been developing their robotics programme and suggested a team of women, voted for by the population, would program female-looking robots – who would govern through a system of Committees. The robots were physically designed so as to eliminate any discrimination with regards to race, colour, religion or status. Hence, the nick-name Silvers.

I think it works, plus, it's all I've ever known – and it must have been a great moment for women. I said that to Mum once and she laughed. She said however a Silver might look like a woman, or be programmed to act like a woman, it is not a woman. She wants the women programming the Silvers to govern. The Silvers, to Mum, are a waste of time and resources.

She's got a point.

"Anyway, your reallocation sounds dire," I said. "I cannot believe you think sitting in front of a screen all day is going to be better than life with Ty. And what happens to him, is he going to be re-allocated?"

"I don't think so. He said he'd received a message from the Personal Development Committee saying we had to come on this course to see if there was any chance of saving our marriage, or to end our marriage amicably. I think he's realised for a while that there's no chance of the former."

Maybe there's hope for you yet!

"And he has no idea about your reallocation?"

"None," she replied. "I don't mind the idea. At least as a monitor I'll be in a community of people who I can hang around with. Hopefully some will be my age, and hopefully I can have some fun. I'm twelve years younger than Ty you know – it matters."

"Reallocation, fun! What about your family? Okay, you're not locked up or anything, but you're not free either. Don't you even have to earn leave passes?"

"I'm not sure, Nell. We all voted for the re-allocation system to be implemented by the Silvers, so it can't be that bad, can it? I think everything is up for review before the elections, anyway. All I know is that I've been trapped for too long, and I want to feel free again – at least to have a social life. Don't get me wrong, I did love Ty before our wedding day, but the moment I uttered the words of commitment I felt as if my soul had been pulverised into dust."

You two will be best friends, for sure. So much in common.

Watch it!

"And your two boys?"

"I can never go back to a married life, Nell. And if it hadn't been for emergency surgery I would have died having my first boy anyway – so naturally I should never have been a Mum. I do love them both, massively, and I'll miss them, but I just can't live like that anymore."

"Well at least you know your future."

"You don't?" she asked.

"I've been given the Award."

"Wow. That's pretty amazing, Nell."

"But I don't have a partner! And if I refuse the award I will be subject to a 'status review', which, I imagine is the same thing as reallocation. Society's all about benefitting one-another, right,

Mara? And if I don't contribute to the population, then I'm failing society."

"Take the status review, Nell," Mara said, looking directly into my eyes. "Don't give up your freedom by having children at any cost."

CORN-FLAKES

Affirmation for Today: All is as it should be.

"Ty and Nell, I'd like you to work together please," Sally said.

Hah! He'll run a mile when... Brilliant, is what I meant to say. What a great time you'll both have. See? I'm trying to change.

Thank-you, Cyd.

On the ground, in the middle of the lounge Sally placed four mini-screens, four styluses, white paper, four marker pens, flame providers, incense, empty bottles with lids, string, a bag of flaked corn, two flat metal trays, candles, two gongs with beaters and an assortment of crystals.

Mara took a photo with her roamer.

"The aim of this exercise is to rid yourselves of emotional baggage, negative thoughts, or both," Sally said. "I'd like you to go off somewhere private in your pairs."

Time to bare your soul. And, what a shame it's with Ty! That'll be the end of that little fantasy.

Not helpful. All is as it should be.

Of course. Quite right. Just make something up.

"I'll give you an example," Sally continued. "I'd like to rid myself of ..." She closed her eyes and sat in silence, "my attachment to being bullied at the ed facility," she said.

She opened her eyes, took a sheet of paper and pen and wrote BULLIED in the centre. Around it she added: Victim, Unhappy, Ugly, Dull, Sad, and then she scrunched the paper into a ball, and held it up to her mouth.

"I am going to burn you, BULLIED, because I have carried your energy around for far too long. At the time I thought I deserved you, I thought I'd done wrong. I believed I wasn't as nice as everyone else, and that's why I was being picked on. But I realise now that's waste, and I don't want to carry around those negative emotions associated with your memory anymore. They're not helpful. I'm ready to forgive the people who bullied me. They didn't know the effect they had on me. I forgive them.

But more than them, I forgive myself for listening to them, and believing I was at fault. By burning this paper, I am freeing myself from feelings attached to your memory."

She closed her eyes.

Jupiter twirled his index finger round in a circle, whilst pointing it at his temple.

Sally took a few deep breaths, and slowly blew into the paper. She opened her eyes, placed the paper ball on the metal tray and promptly set fire to it.

I winced at the idea of her burning emotions, as they became no more than a tiny pile of ash, which Sally promptly brushed onto the lawn.

Alice whizzed behind me.

"Won't your emotions just seep into the ground and then come back in the grass?" I asked, confused and horrified.

"Man, that's a crazy thought," Jupiter said.

"The earth is the greatest cleanser, Nell, so don't worry," Sally said. "Plus, every night I perform a ceremony to rid the space of any harmful energy."

"God Sally, you sound just like Ty," Mara said. "That's all he ever used to go on about: how I should walk barefoot on the farm more often. It would help me feel the energy of the planet, soften me, help me to feel more peaceful."

"And let me guess, Em," said Jupiter, "you completely ignored him."

"Right! Ty and Nell, Jupiter and Mara, into your pairings please," Sally said, raising her voice a little.

Why didn't Ty ever rise to her challenges?

Weak, is what I believe you called him before.

Ty and I shuffled our beanbags towards one another, smiling.

"Decide amongst yourselves the method you'd like to use," Sally said.

"I don't really fancy burning anything, Ty," I said, once our beanbags were close enough our knees touched.

Desperate, or what!

"I kind of gathered when you were watching the flames."

"I'm not sure I like the idea of setting fire to something that's been part of me for so long."

"Corn-flakes then?" he suggested. "We could talk into them, then crush them and throw them into the bay."

"To drown," I said, looking glum at the thought. "I'm not good at getting rid of things. I mean, we're talking about a woman who's kept her favourite pair of shoes from when she was four because she can't bear the thought of them being separated at the recycling facility!"

Don't admit that to Sally, for God's sake, she'll have you booked in for a brain sweep.

"Well, not really to drown, because they've already been crushed. And it's all symbolic – they're not people, Nell. Crush them, throw them in the bay, the fish will eat them, and everyone's happy: we've got rid of a useless emotion, and the fish get some corn-flakes!"

"They'll be coming round for breakfast if we're not careful!" I said, laughing.

Sally walked over to us, "What have you chosen?" she asked.

"Corn-flakes," I said.

"Really?" Ty asked, "I was kind of joking."

"Why not? It made us both laugh – which has got to be a good sign."

Creep.

"Corn-flakes it is then," Ty said. "We're going to go and sit on the jetty at Deserted Bay."

Good choice.

"Great," Alice said. "Shilly and I will hang out on the moss by the beach."

Jupe and Mara chose burning, and they specifically asked for a fork, which they intended to stab into the ball of paper and then hold over the flame of a candle. Their emotions would thus have no chance of escape.

"They're perfect for one another," Ty whispered.

Maybe there was more to him than I'd given credit.

He'll have you figured out in no time – see right through you.

Sorry, did you say something, Cyd?

Beautiful day for it, the bay will be lovely.

Ty picked up the bag of corn-flakes and we walked out into sunlight. It took roughly four minutes to walk onto the little wooden jetty in Deserted, by which time I'd found out Ty isn't a strong swimmer and doesn't like being cold. Luckily the sun was directly overhead.

The translucent green water of the bay covered a floor of pebbles, seaweed, and lime green moss, and darting through it and around the legs of the jetty were tiny fishes.

"It's the fishes' lucky day," Ty said, as we sat down on the edge of the jetty, side by side, our legs dangling over, our arms practically touching. Ty's shoulders rose about four centimetres above mine, and hardly moved as he inhaled.

"Right, shall we get on with it?" Ty asked, looking sideways at me.

"Shame to spoil such a perfect moment."

He play-punched my arm. "Think of it as an amazing opportunity, Nell. Three weeks ago, could you ever have imagined today: you and I sitting on a jetty in Scandi, with a bag of corn-flakes?"

"Nope," I said laughing, wishing he'd punch me again. Mind you, go back a bit further and I didn't know I was going to have to get pregnant in the next eighteen months – but I wasn't about to spoil the moment by telling Ty any of that.

"If we put some effort into this, who knows what we'll get in return. Trust me, if I'm ready to bare my soul in front of a woman I hardly know, then it'll be a doddle for you. And anyway, the tiddly-fish are looking hungry."

Trust him? A smooth talker like...

Cyd.

What I meant to say was there's nothing lovelier than tamarind trees in flower.

I thought back to my commitment to break old habits, and knew this was a chance to try it out. Otherwise what was the point? Change has to start somewhere, right? And when would there ever be a more perfect setting than this?

All is as it should be.

"Tiddly-fish?" I said, liking Ty more by the second.

"My eldest boy called his first goldfish that," he said, "and I thought it was so lovely I've used it for every fish I've met since."

"You've met a lot of fish, have you?" I asked him, smiling.

"Only tiddly-ones," he replied. We laughed and I felt my face warming up.

"Right," he said, rubbing his palms together. "How about we kick off with a little declaration."

Is he being serious?

"Declaration?" I said, making a face.

"I used to ask Mara to declare confidentiality and respect before we started counselling a few months ago, but she wouldn't, saying she hates all that 'inner searchy shit'. Somehow, I get the feeling it'll be different with you, Nell. Could we stand up and hold hands for it?"

Cringe. Bit too close for comfort, I'd say.

Me, stand, holding hands with Ty Martins, on a wooden jetty, in a deserted bay, in the sunshine, in Scandinavia? I'd ashing love to! And if I have to make a declaration to do it, who ashing cares!

"Come on, let's get into this good and proper," he said, smiling and standing up.

I joined him, and we stood facing one another. His warm, rough-skinned farmers' hands reached over and held mine as if they were precious. I didn't know where to look. Into his eyes would have felt like we were sharing wedding vows. Out to sea would have seemed I didn't care. At his chest and he might think I was fantasizing about him naked. Finally, I settled for alternating between his eyes and his left shoulder.

We both took a deep breath.

"Thank you for bringing Nell and I together in this wonderful place. Please help us to feel safe with one another, and to work together in confidence and with respect. Please help us to see unhelpful emotions, and give us the strength to ask them to leave. And please could you render the corn-flakes void of any harmful emotion before they are eaten by the tiddly-fish." He smiled and squeezed my hands.

Oooh, that was a bit good!

I looked straight into his deep brown eyes. Was I blushing?

Oh, go for it. Give it a go, you never know – you could be pregnant by the end of the day!

"Thanks, Ty, that was lovely," I said, as he let go of my hands.

"Shall I start us off then?" he asked, as we sat back down, our arms gently brushing one another's.

We sat in silence looking out over the bay, then Ty closed his eyes. I couldn't help but look at his weathered skin, the smile wrinkles starting to form at the edge of his eyes. His long, dominant nose. And those deliciously soft lips.

Oh p... lease. I'm going to be sick!

"Right," he said, opening his eyes and turning his head to look at me, "the word 'regret' keeps repeating itself."

He knows you were watching him, fantasizing about his lips.

I passed him a corn-flake.

REGRET

He smiled and cupped it in his hands in front of his chest. "Is this mad, or what?" he said. We laughed. "A month ago I was home, running through the lambing procedure with Rod, my mate who helps me look after the farm, and now here I am, sitting next to the one and only Nell Greene, caressing a corn-flake!"

"Yep, you'd never have predicted that one!"

"It's Ems," he continued, seriously, "I regret marrying her, and I've never seen the point in feeling regret."

I studied his face.

"I knew before we got married she'd struggle, and I should have said something. I knew my lifestyle wouldn't be enough for her. But she was crazy about me, and I thought I'd break her heart if I stood her up three days before our wedding," he continued – focussing on the corn-flake.

Crazy about him? Get him and his ego. Typical man.

"Don't get me wrong – I did love her – I still do, just not in the same way, and I know Ems feels the same about me. I want her to be happy. We used to have so much fun. But she's not the same Mara anymore – and now here we are on this therapy course. I keep telling her to put some effort into it, so we can move on in the best way possible for the boys, but whenever I talk about it with her she just starts to cry."

I felt terrible knowing what Mara had told me.

"I can't find anything to say to her, which is the saddest bit of all. I'm so sorry that our marriage hasn't worked out. I know Ems is foul to me, but she doesn't mean it, she's just angry and doesn't know how to express herself. She hates herself for it, and there's nothing I can do to help her."

Well isn't he just Mr Confident.

"Which makes me regret it all even more. Why do I still want to help her? Why can't I let go and move on?"

"Is it that easy?" I said, "I mean, I'm no expert, but I doubt it. Look at my thought-projection. I'd only known Youssan a few months! You and Mara have been together for years."

No expert is right.

Cyd!

Relapse.

"Well, Nell," he said, "this corn-flake and I are about to find out just how easy it is."

He cupped the corn-flake to his mouth.

"Regret. You are not serving any worthwhile purpose, and it's time for you to move on. Thank you for whatever it is you've shown me, but I don't want to feel sad anymore. Regret – I am asking you to leave."

He looked at me and raised his eyebrows before breathing into his hand, then placing the flake against his chest. I watched as he closed his eyes and jolted his hand out in front of him, as if he'd ripped out a piece of his heart. Slowly he returned his hand, cupping the corn-flake to his mouth.

Five months has passed since I got the message about my Award, and here I am, watching a grown man whispering to a corn-flake.

Just goes to prove, you never know what life has in store.

He screwed his right hand into a fist and I heard the corn-flake crunch, then he ground his palms in circles. He leant forward, opened his palms, and tiny crumbs of corn-flake wafted down onto the water.

I leant over with him, and as the tiddly-fish rose to savour their first taste of regret we smiled like five-year olds.

Ty stood up, inhaled half of Scandinavia, and shook his body from head to toe.

"Fan…tastic," he said, looking down at me. "I actually do feel a lot better! Maybe it *is* that easy."

I doubt it very much.

He put his hand on my left shoulder as he sat back down.

"And now, Spaghetti Head, I believe it's your turn," he said, smiling.

Ready?

A COUPLE MORE CORN-FLAKES

I closed my eyes and they started flitting from side to side behind my lids, searching for an image, or a thought.

You're trying too hard.

Go away. All is as it should be.

There's no rush. You're feeling you have to hurry. Breathe. Slow down.

I tried not to think. That was even *more* difficult. I took deep breaths and tried to calm my mind.

"Don't panic, Nell, we've got all afternoon," Ty said.

Had he been studying my face, like I had his?

Doubt it.

"Ruby," I said, without having seen any image at all. I opened my eyes.

"Ruby?" Ty asked.

"We grew up together. If you saw Ruby, you saw me, and vice versa. Her parents work on Feed the Soil, Feed the People, in Mali, along with my Mum and Dad"

"Which zone?"

"Cassava."

"And how's it going?" he asked. "I hear they're starting to get some half decent harvests."

"They are. I spoke to Mum a couple of days ago, and she said the germination rates are the best ever."

"That's good news," he said, his eyes locking into mine. "But we've got distracted, Nell."

"Yeh. Right."

"Ruby?"

"Ruby. Yes. Well, basically, I don't trust her. I had a mega-crush on someone at ed. I talked about him so much Ruby nearly asked to change bedrooms! Then before I realised what was happening, she was going out with him! I couldn't believe it. I cried for two days. And she was still pretending to be my best friend. I didn't understand what was going on."

"It sounds horrible."

You haven't mentioned how much it all hurt.

"I tried to get away from her. I changed rooms. I started hanging out with Jupiter and his little gang, hoping she'd get the hint. But even now she still tries to be friends with me. After Youssan and I had been together a month I introduced them, at Ruby's request may I add, and she smooched all over him."

"What did Youssan do?"

"He lapped it. She even gave him her contact number!"

"For what? And why did Youssan take it?" he said. "Can't you just ignore her?"

"How? I'm rubbish at stuff like that. It makes me feel bad," I said, looking him in the eye.

Like she's made you feel bad for years.

Ty looked down and snapped off a splinter of jetty. He threw it into the bay, and followed it with his eyes as it bobbed around below us.

"Okay," he said. "If you can't physically get her out of your life, what is it you need to change about you and her?"

Tricky. You need to deal with the fact you don't trust her with anyone you go out with. And, if you were going out with Ty, you would NEVER EVER introduce them.

I started examining my fingernails. "I feel anxious with her."

And scared.

"Well I'm not surprised."

"I don't want to introduce her to any of my friends, or a future boyfriend. It sounds so childish, but I just don't trust her."

"It sounds like you've never met the right man, Nell."

Well you've worked your way through a few trying.

"Just ignore her. No decent man would lap your best friend flirting with them. Personally I'd be horrified," he said, holding my eyes with his.

He probably has lots of women flirting with him, so that's a lie. No. I'm wrong. Hang on – is there something 'going on' here! Is this 'a moment'? Has he just offered to be your man?

I brought my hands up and rested them against my forehead. Ruby, short, slim, permed red hair, lowcut top, was floating around my mind. I shoved her out in front of me. My heart was pounding. I felt anxious and vulnerable. Ruby was standing, her legs astride, with her hands on her hips, in front of my forehead, laughing. She had a cord coming out of her chest attached to something I couldn't see. I bent an imaginary foot up to her stomach, and kicked her backwards. As she fell, the cord pulled Youssan out in front of me: the two of them were attached.

"Are you okay, Nell?" Ty asked, rubbing his hand up and down my arm. I kept my eyes closed, breathing heavily.

Breathe. All is as it should be.

"How about saying something out loud to her?"

I couldn't.

Youssan had one cord attached to me, and one to Ruby. I chopped Youssan's cord with an enormous pair of gardening shears and he vanished into thin air behind me. I slashed at the cord attached to Ruby with a massive, silver sword and she fell backwards, into my hand. I closed both hands around her and moved her away from me. My breathing slowed, and I started to feel calm.

"You okay?" Ty said. "Ready to get rid of her?"

"Ready," I said.

I opened my hands just enough for Ty to poke the corn-flake inside, and I cupped my hands tightly around it and Ruby, as if I had a rare insect I didn't want to escape until I'd shown it to Granma.

"Did you know my Granma's favourite living thing is a silverfish?"

"No, I didn't know that, Nell," Ty replied, smiling.

Get on with crushing Ruby! I can't wait!

I surprised myself at how much I enjoyed pulverising Ruby. For all the boys she'd stolen off me, I crushed her into my palm. For copying me in everything I did I rubbed her into fine dust, and for her behaviour with Youssan, I drowned her in the transparent green waters of Scandinavia. I washed any remnants of her off my hands and stood up.

I ran to the end of the jetty. Alice and Shilly looked up, startled. I circled my shoulders and took some deep breaths. I shouted, "I'm free."

"Well go and be free back there," Alice said.

I walked back towards Ty, feeling lighter.

He smiled, and gave me a standing ovation.

IMAGE

"Image," Ty said, moving onto his next corn-flake.

Surprising! The first time I saw Ty I thought how refreshing it was to meet a man who seemed imageless.

"No, I'm not sure image is the right word," he said.

Phew!

"Okay, forget image. Soapbox – is what I want to say."

"Bit of a drastic change," I replied, as he opened his eyes. I'd missed them.

We sat down.

"This is the weirdest thing to do – I had one thought, and then a completely different one barged out through my mouth before I could do anything about it."

And what a beautiful mouth to barge out from.

Get a grip, for God's sake.

"I talk a lot about my lifestyle, Nell."

"As well you should."

He smiled. "I think some people, especially Mara, are bored to death of listening to it all."

"I know I'd never tire of listening to you."

Cheesy. No, it was good – who doesn't like some flattery?

"But it's your subject, Nell, isn't it   so it interests you. I get such a buzz out of the way I live – just the fact I don't need to rely on anyone other than myself for my family to have everything we need to survive. I want others to feel that buzz, I'd love to be an inspiration to everyone."

"I think you already are, Ty," I said. "You certainly are in West Africa, anyway. And Farming First has quite a following."

"Maybe I should move up there then. Where I am, all I need to do is talk for a couple of minutes and people's eyes glaze over!"

We laughed.

Did he just suggest moving to West Africa?

"I love the farm, Nell, don't get me wrong, but I'm exhausted, especially with a wife who'd rather be anywhere than there with me. This is the first break I've had since I came out of ed."

"And so where does the soapbox fit in?"

He stared at the water.

"I'm bored of just talking about living self-sufficiently – which, by the way, we could all do if the System would let us."

"Amen to that."

"I'd rather be dumping rubbish from the old landfill sites outside the System's environment centre to force them to act. I'm bored with my voice. I want to fight for what I believe in – not literally, of course, but be more of an activist. If I don't have to worry about how Mara would take it, it doesn't matter, does it? I mean, how much trouble could I get in?"

Quite a lot if his wife being reallocated is anything to go by.

"And what about the boys?" I said.

"I'll just have to protest whilst they're away in ed. No more lecturing, Nell, I'm going to fire up and give the System something to think about."

I punched my fist in the air. "I'm with you all the way, Ty. Ready for a corn-flake?"

"Yep Siree."

He held the corn-flake and clutched it close to the bottom of his ribcage, falling silent for the longest time.

Silence. Comfortable, meaningful silence with another person can be a most powerful thing.

"I'm ridding myself of my old approach. I'm gearing up for action," he said, directly to the corn-flake. "God, we must look insane."

He pulled the corn-flake away from his chest, pounded it against the jetty, and threw the tiny pieces into the bay. The tiddly-fish took an age before they appeared.

"They're full!" Ty said, laughing.

God, I wish he'd fall in love with me.

Oh shit.

He stood up, stretched his arms away from his broad, muscular torso and strolled back to the shore. I watched as he walked along the beach for a while, gently tapping pebbles with his feet, before turning and walking back towards me.

Beautiful. Beautiful casual, confident walk.

Snap out of it.

"Look out world, here I come!" he said, as he took my hands in his and pulled me to my feet.

Palpitations.

"Thanks, Nell," he said, "for letting me ramble on."

We looked out across the bay.

The portcullis is moving! It's gone up another twenty centimetres – that's forty since I became Cyd. Brilliant. I'll be out soon. It's working, Nell. The therapy's working!

Out?

I focussed on our hands touching, and pictured myself wearing a flared, silver bodysuit, belting out, 'I feel love', by Donna Summer, and the crowd going mad.

Here we go – don't let yourself get carried away. He's still married to Mara.

Not for much longer!

CONTROL

"Had enough of corn-flakes yet?" Ty asked.

I'd had enough of soul searching, but I hadn't had enough of sitting with him on the jetty. I didn't want the afternoon to end. When would I share time alone with him again?

Probably never.

"I think there's one more in me," I said.

We sat back down in silence.

"It's something about me in relationships."

For God's sake don't tell him any of that! He'll run an ashing mile.

"It's about how I try to control the relationship. And manipulate. I control where we go and who my partner talks to."

"Why?"

"To control the threat." I said, picking at my fingers. "I can't believe I'm telling you this – it sounds ashing ridiculous."

Totally ridiculous. And childish.

"It's not ridiculous, Nell, we're cleansing!" he said, laughing. "And anyway, I'm enjoying getting to know you."

Take it.

"But control the threat from who?" he asked, looking like he was interested.

"Other women. If I can control the women my partner meets, then I can control the threat," I said, looking down into my lap.

Talk about scare a man off!

"Radical," he said, lifting my chin to look me in the eyes.

God he's beautiful.

"So you think every woman your partner talks to is a threat to your relationship?"

"Yep."

"But if your partner prefers someone else, no amount of attempts at control are going to stop him."

"Ah, but if I control who they see, then I could prevent them from ever meeting that person in the first place, couldn't I?"

He studied my face, puzzled, "It wouldn't work, Nell, you'd be paranoid every time they were out of your sight!"

Yep, describes you pretty well.

"Maybe this still has something to do with Ruby," he said, "After this session today maybe things will feel different the next time you're in a relationship."

Nice if he'd offer himself as a guinea pig.

"But that was only Ruby, Ty!"

"Well, Nell, I don't think this bag of corn-flakes is big enough to crush and drown every woman but you on the planet!" he said, smiling.

Funny!

"I know it's ridiculous. I sound so pathetic, but it's what happens and I hate it."

He shuffled closer, held my hand and rested it on his thigh.

God, please don't let this moment ever end.

"And then, of course, because I've controlled our relationship to the point where we don't have any social life left, I get bored. Through my stupid fears I've ruined it," I said, swinging my feet.

"I don't know what to say. I think everyone's probably got issues with relationships – I mean, I never believed I could be enough for Ems. But I think you're wasting your life feeling threatened by other women – what's the point? You're afraid of something that might never happen. I wish I had some magic sensory pad I could whip out to take fear away for you," he said, squeezing my hand between both of his.

Now there's an offer!

"And don't forget Cyd is now different. She can help too."

I definitely will.

"I need to crush control, Ty," I said.

I closed my eyes and imagined Youssan and I standing at a bar, surrounded by women I didn't know. He was talking to one of them. I felt my chest tightening and the anxiety building. I pictured a field of dandelion flowers, but a massive fist swung forwards and ripped them all out. Youssan reappeared with his arm around one of the women.

Ty put his hand on my back and gently rubbed. I felt the warmth of his hand, and I felt cared for. He put a corn-flake in my hand.

I brought it towards my chest and returned to the image of Youssan. He was still there in my solar-plexus, laughing with the woman. I focussed on the warmth of Ty's hand on my back, and imagined it as a yellow light. I moved the light towards Youssan, and as it covered him he took his arm away from the other woman and came over and kissed me. I blew the woman out into the corn-flake, and crumbled it into nothingness. I breathed yellow in and out before opening my eyes and scattering the flake onto the water.

"You alright?"

"I just need to try something," I said, closing my eyes and thinking of Youss talking to Ruby: calm: silence: yellow: Ty.

Wow! This is a different feeling! It's really rather nice.

I took some deep breaths, celebrating the calm. "Thank-you," I said to Ty, opening my eyes.

We stood up, and he looked so handsome with the sun low behind him.

Don't make a pass at him, for God's sake.

Then he embraced me. His strong arms were around me, cementing our new-found bond of secrecy. If I never felt this again with any man I ever met, I wouldn't care, because here in Scandi, in May 2116, I felt safe, equal and cared for. He kissed my forehead.

***

Jupiter and Mara turned up the next morning with burnt finger tips and eyebrows, and from then on spent an unnatural amount of time smiling at one another.

Entry into Greenie: Crush a corn-flake.

AN AMBASSADOR

Affirmation for Today: 'Now' is all there is.

"Brain journeying?" G said, horrified. "With what? Have you never seen the film *One Flew Over The Cuckoo's Nest*?"

"No, I haven't, G. That one can't have made it onto the entertainment cloud before the disaster!" I replied.

"Can you refuse it?"

"I don't want to – nothing awful's going to happen, I'm quite looking forward to it. I've won the Award, remember? The System wants me to reproduce."

"And do you want to, Nell? You haven't until now, why would you just because the System say you must?"

"G, I'm tackling one thing at a time. I'll sort Cyd out, then we'll see what happens."

"Anyway, I've heard the Award isn't just about having children. Apparently you are also made an Ambassador of something or other."

"Who told you that?"

"Evie, a friend of mine down here. Her daughter got the Award last year."

"Can you find out more?"

"I'm seeing Evie tomorrow, I'll ask her."

"Thanks, G, and don't worry about the brain journey exercise, it'll be fine. I'll message you the minute I'm finished."

"Mind you do, or I won't sleep," she said, blowing me a kiss.

No pressure there then, as she'd hardly slept since Granpa died. He had a massive heart attack and there was nothing anybody could do, and believe me, they can do something about most things these days. Every five years us humans are hooked up to a health prediction computer, and any signs of future issues are noted. Those who show any problems are regularly monitored and cared for throughout their lives. It prevents surges on the Health Committee's resources. The first check is when you're ten, and it's also when you're registered for all future checks. Granpa was forty-nine when the checks were introduced, thirty years after the Disaster, and somehow he slipped through the net.

'Health checks are just another way of invading our privacy', Mum reckons, but I disagree. We do still study history during our ed years. It tells us good health care used to be a service provided only for the wealthy, rather than for everybody. How can that be right?

LILY

I met Sally in a new hexagonal cabin. It was cozy, burgundy in colour and welcoming, with small windows and a deep wool carpet. Sally was sitting on a chair next to a treatment table. Opposite the table was a wall-screen, and hanging over one of the corners a leopard print cap with ear flaps.

"No Alice?"

"I can't tear her away from Shilly these days – she seems to have found her soul mate."

"And how about you and Shilly's owner?" Sally asked, raising her eyebrows. "You two seemed to spin it off with the corn-flakes."

"We had a great time, Sally. If only!"

"Stranger things have happened," she said, plumping the pillows on the treatment table. "Okay, Nell, let's get going. Make yourself comfy on here, and I'll give you the hat to put on. We're going to try and get the picture of your spaghetti up on the screen, at which point the hat will literally take you on a journey inside the strands. Once you understand why the strands carry the names they showed in your first projection, I'm hoping you'll be able to straighten them. Your mind will take you into whichever strand it wants you to see."

Exciting!

"And understanding the strand will straighten it out?"

Ever hopeful.

"That's the theory. Today, for example, you'll see images and memories you'll recognise, and hopefully acknowledge as being a part of you."

What, acknowledge you're not perfect!

Cyd.

"Then you can decide whether they are images and memories that are still helpful to you, or not. Once you attach no more importance or emotion to the unhelpful ones, I believe the spaghetti will straighten."

I love her optimism.

"We'll complete the burrowing, and work through what it all means over the next few weeks. Some days we'll work together, and other days you'll be free to go over it all in your own way. It's perfectly safe, it doesn't hurt, and most people enjoy travelling around their own minds."

Most people haven't got a mind like yours!

I put the hat on, feeling small metal pads against my temples. I closed my eyes and felt as if I was crouching, motionless on a cold damp floor. I was breathing in cold, rancid air. I felt around me for a wall, a door, something other than darkness, and my hand knocked against metal. It felt like some kind of railing, and I decided to follow it into the blackness. I strained my eyes and ears. I shuffled along for a few minutes, until, way off in the distance, I spotted a tiny, downward shining beam of light. It grew brighter the closer I got. It shone down on what appeared to be a giant gourdcup. I walked closer, and whatever it was got hairy! I reached the edge of the light which was, in fact, shining down on an enormous, garish pink, half-coconut shell. I stood examining it. I looked back into the darkness, and as I did a tiny convex door in the coconut's side opened towards me.

Shit. What. I'm supposed to get in?

The door flapped, which I took to mean, yes. I looked around. It flapped again. I stepped in, onto a cream carpet. A dark brown cushioned bench ran around the inside, and a highly-polished silver handrail circled the shell's rim. The door closed. I sat on the bench. The light went out.

My heart started to pound. I put my hand out in front of my face and couldn't see any sign of it. The coconut started to silently move. It picked up speed, tilted forward and started to head down. I grabbed out for the handrail and hung on tight as we hurtled downwards, further into darkness. At a sicko fast speed, we jolted left, then right, then up, left, and down. "STOP!" I screamed, as the shell took a sharp right, nearly throwing me out.

"You're totally safe, Nell." I heard Sally say off in the distance. "Try and enjoy the ride if you can."

Enjoy it! Coconut's insane!

We started to slow and level out, thank God, until we were merely floating alongside a dimly lit platform. I sat back upright and loosened my grip on the rail. A drip of water from overhead broke the silence. Glossy red tiles covered the floor, and the walls and ceiling were black and wet. I took my hands away from the rail and zipped up my jacket. The platform was just about light enough to see my breath.

The coconut had stopped parallel to a large rectangular sign: FEAR.

Was I in my fear spaghetti strand?

The door opened.

I didn't move. Who in their right mind would want to step into fear?

I shut the door. Again, it opened.

"Move," I whispered. "Move. Coconut shell, MOVE!" My words echoed around my dank surroundings.

Nothing.

Try naming it. I changed after you re-named me.

Naming it? I could barely think, let alone come up with a name for an ashing coconut shell. My eyebrows started feeling tight. I rubbed by palms up and down my trousers.

Lily the Pink? Granma's favourite song?

Try it.

"Coconut Shell, I hereby name you, *Lily the Pink*, and I thank you very much for the interesting ride. I am looking forward to us becoming friends. Now, please, *MOVE.*"

The door stayed open.

FEAR

I stepped onto the wet tiles and *Lily the Pink's* door closed behind me. Across the platform, above a rusty door, a sign 'Welcome Nell' started to creak back and forwards.

Run, Nell. Now. Run.

Where. Remember your affirmation for today? 'Now' is all there is?

I crept across the platform, and pushed the door open.

I was in a brightly decorated livingspace. A younger version of me rushed towards the door, carrying a tall-backed chair. She slammed the door shut and wedged the chair up under the handle. Shouting and gunfire came from outside, and she ran and crouched beside the wall, staring terrified at the flimsy barricade.

"Shut up, SID, he's not out there," she said, frantically tapping her roamer, which didn't respond. She stared at the door. The gunshots got louder. She belly-crawled to behind the sofa.

"Leave me alone, SID, no-one's coming to get me, just shut up," she said as the memory faded, and changed to a sandy track out in the Malian bush, and to a different me, with short, red hair.

She walked quickly, nervously looking over her shoulder. A twig ahead cracked. She stopped. Listening. Looking.

"There's no-one there, shut up." But she turned around, and ran.

Again, the memory changed. A 'little me' – was I ten? – with long curly hair and an elephant print pyjama shirt on was lying in bed, lights off, but with the door open. Her head was propped up on a stack of books, and she was staring at the reflection of the hallway in the window.

"Why would he be hiding outside," she whispered. She moved her head higher onto the books, and stared more intently.

"He can't get me because Mum and Dad are here, so go away."

The memory disappeared, and was replaced by a 22-year-old me, sitting on one of the dining chairs at home in Cassava, staring at her roamer.

"Shit. Mak's just said he loves me."

"That's nice," Alice said.

"He wants us to live together," she said, picking her fingernails. She got hold of a piece of skin on her index finger and pulled until it bled.

She picked up the roamer, "I can't," she wrote, but didn't send. She closed her eyes and turned her face to the ceiling, then looked down and sent.

The roamer started to ring and she ignored it.

"Answer it," Alice said.

"No."

"That's not fair."

"I can't talk to him – he'll ask me."

"What?"

"Why I don't love him."

"And?"

"I can't say it. I've got to get outside – go for a walk. I can't breathe."

LEAVING FEAR BEHIND

The room vanished and I was back out on the platform. *Lily the Pink* was flapping her door. I was breathing heavily.

As I passed the FEAR sign, a card flew out at my feet. I picked it up:

> You are never alone
> because you are loved

I stepped in to *Lily the Pink*. A CARDS pouch, which I hadn't noticed before, opened under the handrail. I put the card inside, and sat on the bench. The platform seemed lighter, and I unzipped my jacket.

I must have been talking to SID in the first few memories, and he was making me believe that I was about to be physically attacked.

I've changed.

But that last image with Mak messaging me? Have you made me believe feeling emotions towards someone is as terrifying as being attacked physically, Cyd?

Maybe.

No wonder you're classed as a Sinister Imagination Disorder!

Not anymore.

I took in a deep breath and tried to calm myself.

An image of Granpa suddenly appeared, surrounded me, and tried to cuddle the life out of me. Granma appeared and joined in, Alice, my old sunbike, Dad, an old pair of dungarees, my old cat, Mum, Dad's parents, my childhood riding-centre pony, a sunny field full of daisies, Ty, and my fluffy birth-dragon. All of them cuddling me, one another, and *Lily the Pink*. Granpa and Granma cuddled and stroked one another's hair. Even my sister appeared and joined in. The platform grew lighter and lighter.

"Breathe us all into your heart, Nell," Granpa said.

A compartment sprung open in *Lily the Pink's* bench, I looked in and took out a tissue.

"Keep us here, in your heart, Nell. We are always here. Always. Never forget it," he said, smiling.

I miss you, Granpa.

"I know, Nell, I know. I'm here, I've never been anywhere but here. Dry your eyes. We all love you, never forget that. Breathe us into your heart, Nell. You can visit us anytime you like."

I put the tissue into my pocket, and inhaled the hologram into my heart, like Alice hoovering dust up into her undercarriage. I breathed their love in, and out, in, and out, until I thought I'd burst.

The platform became warm, and bright. I felt happy. 'Now' is all there is.

Thank-you Fear!

Lily the Pink set off into the darkness, meandering up and down gentle slopes, around long sweeping bends – even along some flat stretches. I suspected we were travelling along my fear strand, and it was beginning to straighten out.

Lily passed a sign saying 'Thank-you for the visit, and good-bye from your spaghetti strand, Fear'.

CARDS AND PASSES

We came to a T-junction, and *Lily the Pink* turned left. We plunged almost vertically down, into a new strand. We whizzed left and right, through tunnels and over bridges, up and over in a circle and I hung on for my life.

Finally, we started to slow. We approached another platform – which was as bright as sunlight and decorated in green and white swirls.

'LOVE', read a massive oval sign hanging over the platform.

Lily didn't stop, but inched along slowly, and as we reached the end of the platform a plump, Pomeranian Goose waddled over. I cowered down on the bench – I don't trust geese.

Not surprised after one chased you round the educational farm.

"I'm rather a friendly goose," it said, before bending its neck down towards the platform. It lifted its head and pointed its beak towards me – holding out a card. I took it:

Understand the others and
love will be your home.

I just managed to put it into the CARDS pocket before we zoomed off again.

With a renewed grip on the handrail we sped straight into a massive domed hall where we came to a halt.

Transparent walls, exquisitely decorated with shimmering daisies, curved endlessly upwards towards a white and gold filigree ceiling. Huge pearl coloured eggs hung serenely on long golden ropes from the centre of the dome. Each egg had a daisy-chain circling around its middle.

"Welcome, Nell," a calming female voice said, from the peak of the dome.

I looked up, feeling as tiny as an ant.

"Welcome to Rejection," the voice said. "We've been waiting for this visit for thirty-five years. We knew one day you'd make it."

"How can rejection be this beautiful?" I asked, staring upwards.

Soft laughter washed down over me.

I reached for the tissue in my pocket.

"The eggs hanging above you, Nell, are your memory pods. There are thirty-four."

I counted.

"We are offering you two pod-passes, Nell, for you to discover the truth behind your memories from two specific ages, and the emotions you've attached to them. We will give you some moments to think about which age-pods you would like to visit. Everything you are shown is relevant to understanding your rejection strand. It is alarming how much damage can be done by carrying a distorted memory. Humans seem to be good at remembering what they want, rather than what really happened – we can only assume it is some kind of protection mechanism."

Just randomly pick any age.

"I'd like to visit them all please," I said.

Her laughter warmed me.

"I'm afraid you can only visit two, Nell. They will provide you with all you need."

"That's cruel! And the problem is, I don't remember when I first felt rejection."

I felt the woman behind the voice smiling.

"We thought you might say that, most people do; you humans are appalling when it comes to matching a 'happening' to a time or an age. In your case, the pods that will be of most help will choose you."

That's a relief.

"All you need to do is look up at the pods," the voice said, soothingly.

I looked up. Nothing happened. Then a tiny slot on the undercarriage of a pod opened, and something dropped out. It floated down onto the tiles. I leant out and picked up a beautifully hand-written pass, read it and put it in my lap. I looked up again and another pod opened, dropping down a typewritten card.

"Thank-you," I shouted up to the pods.

"Thank you, Nell. We will see you soon."

Lily started to move forwards, and I absorbed the energy of the dome.

"Start to bring your attention back to the room, Nell," I heard Sally say. "Wiggle your toes and fingers and bring your awareness back to lying on the table."

Sally lifted the hat off. "Take your time, Nell, brain journeying can be exhausting."

I opened my eyes. "Exhausting and terrifying. Why was the ride in Lily so violent?"

"Your mind took you directly inside your spaghetti strands, and because they are so tangled the ride was extreme. Hopefully as you progress with therapy the strands will start to straighten themselves out, and the ride will be more gentle. It's only a theory – I could be totally wrong. But you just need to know you can't come to any physical harm – so if you can, try and enjoy it."

"At the moment I don't feel like I want to do it again."

"You've experienced an advanced therapy technique, and mentally they can be exhausting. But I'm confident you'll feel fine again after a rest. If you need help with anything related to today's session, just message me, and don't forget your cards and passes."

"Yeh, right," I laughed. "They were all in my mind."

She didn't laugh, but her eyes moved to the end of the table.

Uppermost was a white card, trimmed with gold, bearing the typewritten words:

Nell Greene,
You are hereby invited to visit memory Pod Seventeen.
I look forward to seeing you soon.
X

THE ORIGINAL HUMAN FOUNDATION (TOHF)

Founded in 2072, The Original Human Foundation (TOHF) have this as their, very short, manifesto:

Life is for living. Live it. Feel it. Honour your right to live freely on this planet as a human. Join us on our peaceful and democratic journey to keep the human voice heard, and in allowing us to live with respect and in harmony with the System. We believe humans are ready to lead once again.

I saved the message on my roamer, just as my wall-screen lit up:

To Nell Greene
In reply to your enquiry as to what a 'status review' entails, I am happy to tell you it would mean you being reallocated to the highly sought-after position of Livingspace Monitor. You would be under the Health and Safety wing of the System. We receive very positive feedback from our existing Monitors who tell us it is a very rewarding post. Your housebot, Alice, would be allowed to accompany you in this post.
The Livelihood Committee

"So it's not a status review at all, Alice. It's reallocation."

"Just under a different name – sold to you as a 'very rewarding post'."

There was a knock outside. I walked over and opened the door to Ty.

Flip. He didn't waste any time!

"Ty!" I said.

"Hi," he replied.

"Are you coming in?" I asked.

"Fuchsia pink: my favourite!" he said, smiling, as he and Shilly walked in.

"Fancy a drink?" I asked, diverting him from the kitchen, where I had lots of my affirmations stuck all over the cupboards.

"I'd love one," he said. "Freedom from Sally's house-visiting rules, at last."

I made us a rum punch each and we sat at opposite ends of my L shaped sofa.

"'I forgive myself for the mistakes I've made'," he said, reading one of my stickers out loud.

My face felt hot.

"I don't suppose you agree with that one, because, as you said to a corn-flake not so long ago, there's no point in regret, and mistakes are in the same category as regret really, aren't they?"

"Technically I suppose they are, but it's good to forgive yourself for them, and to learn from them. Ems would have freaked if I'd had stickers like that around our house – good for you for…" Ty's head spun round towards Alice and Shilly, over in the corner. "What did you just say, Shilly?"

Silence.

"Shilly. What did you just say to, Alice?"

"Sally's an active member of the Original Human Foundation," she muffled into the carpet.

"No way!" I said, looking to Alice. "In such a high-profile job? She can't be."

"I think anything's possible with this new Director – especially since she's announced the elections. Have you heard what TOHF have been doing?" he said.

"I don't really follow them, though I did just receive their election manifesto on my roamer. Mum and Dad are always trying to get me involved, but I'm not around often enough to join any of the groups. Mum signed me up as a life member the moment I was born – which is as far my involvement goes. Mum and Dad met at one of TOHF's first meetings. Though they've never said so, I think they're disappointed by my lack of enthusiasm."

"I'm not sure it's a lack of enthusiasm – it's just because we've grown up in different times to our parents, Nell. But apparently some TOHF members have been replacing their livingspace bots with humans," he said, "and handing out credit units to them, and of course The Livelihood Committee is absolutely furious. There's no law against having a human working in your house, but bots are cheap, faithful and last forever, so why would you?"

"So why are TOHF members doing it?"

"I'd like to see humans iron three shirts in two minutes," Alice said.

"Sadly, Alice, people are losing faith in their bots," Ty said. "One couple wanted to change living communities in Venezuela. They were about to contact the Housing Committee, to request a swap, when a news bulletin appeared on their screen informing them that the exchange programme in their area would be closing for three years. They became suspicious of their bot and removed its chip."

Alice and Shilly raced under the dining table, ears flattened.

"Don't worry you two," we said, laughing, as they cowered together. "We trust you."

Shilly bumped Alice with her shoulder.

"And now TOHF are using that incident as part of their election campaign, which I don't think is entirely the right direction to be taking, but there you go," Ty said. "But about Sally. Should we be worried?"

"I don't see why."

"It's rather curious as to why a therapy centre would have a Foundation member as its director, don't you think?"

"Maybe she's simply the best there is, Ty. If anything odd starts happening I'll ask Mum – she may still have some useful contacts."

TY MARTINS

Affirmation for Today: Love is all around.

Ty's small bio-dynamic farm in Argentina, it turned out, wasn't far from where my career as a journalist started. I was writing an article about a farmer who was using the long-rooted dock plant to aerate his compacted soil, and help bring minerals up through the roots to the soil surface. As the leaves of the plants died, the farmer left them in place – providing a brilliantly nutritious mulch. The quality of his soil improved drastically over a period of a few years.

"I remember the article," Ty said, "because I know the farmer, and I used his surplus dock leaves to wrap our sheep's cheese in, he was a nice guy. To be honest, Nell, I remember most of your articles."

Lovely thing to say.

Ty's Grandparents had settled on the land after the survival parks.

"Dad died when I was fourteen, leaving Mateo, my older brother, and Mum, to run the farm. Mateo hated the cold and mud and moved on to electrical engineering at the first opportunity. So I stepped in to help Mum. I struggled, at first," Ty said, sipping his rum punch. "The farm was just so expensive to run, there was no profit in it at all. And yes, it may be a way of life, and yes, I may be custodian of a part of the planet, but I'd still like to be able to afford to go to a rock concert, or take the boys on a sunbus holiday, or buy Ems a new jacket. People around me seemed to think I had no right to want to make a profit. God, that used to vex. So, I studied the farm's accounts and soon saw the biggest drain on finances was the machinery – so, out it went! First to go were the tractors. Mum tried talking me out of it, but I couldn't see any other option."

"But how were you going to farm the land without machinery?"

"Well, luckily our old tractors were collectibles by then, and worth a bit, so I exchanged them for six grass-powered heavy horses – two Suffolk Punch and four Shires, along with all their equipment, and a lifetime supply of winter feed. I couldn't believe my luck. It was really tough at the beginning, but I love my horses and wouldn't be without them. Working with them is good for the soul, Nell. As I felt more connected to the land, minus the noise of the tractors and the smell of the fuel, I started to think about becoming self-sufficient. The farm already had two wells, and so over the years I've built a couple of windmills and installed solar panels, and now I guess the farm's as close to self-sufficiency as it'll get."

"Please don't be offended, but in our introductory session, before I knew you were Ty Martins, you didn't strike me as a farmer."

"You didn't take a good look at my hands, then," he replied, smiling.

I hadn't done. I'd been too busy admiring his jawline, and listening to his deep, husky voice – letting it filter down through my body whilst fantasizing about spending the rest of my life with him.

Don't tell him that, for God's sake!

He held out his thick, broad, callused hands: palm up.

"Stay there," I said, and ran up to my sleeping platform, picked up my lavender oil and rushed back down. I moved over to Ty's end of the sofa, took his hands and put them on my knees, and started to massage the oil into the cracks and calluses.

Not a word passed between us.

My screen burst into life, making us both jump.

Granma, dressed in a pale pink shirt smiled out at us. In her hand she waved a huge, red rosette. "I won the ladies over-nineties eight-hour walking tournament, Nell, darling. Isn't it great?"

"Wonderful G. I'm proud of you," I said, smiling back at her.

"Ooh, I see you've got company."

"Yes G, meet Ty Martins. Ty, say hello to my Granma, the best in the world."

"Don't say that, Nell – Ty may have grandparents still alive."

"Sadly not," Ty said. "They didn't live long enough to get to Australia."

"I'm sorry for that – it really is lovely here."

"Ty's on the course with me, G."

"Well no wonder we never hear from you!" she replied, whooping with delight.

I blushed.

Ty laughed.

"You have a lovely rugged look, Ty," G said, "reminds me of your Granpa, Nell."

Ty blushed. I laughed.

"I won't keep you then, just called to let you know I won. Message me when you're free, there's things I need to tell you about the Ambassador scheme."

"Ambassador scheme?" Ty asked.

"Will do. Well done on the walking tournament. Alice sends her love," I said, clearing the screen.

"Ambassador scheme?" Ty asked.

"Oh, it's some new project the System are introducing, to do with my work," I said, focussing on his left hand.

Liar. You're here to change your behaviour – so STOP LYING!

"She's a hundred and six. Not bad, is it? I think she looks great. Granma gave me Alice," I said to Ty, returning to the hand massage.

"I got Shilly for my twenty-first birthday. She's been a lifesaver for me really, the farmhouse would be totally neglected if it wasn't for Shills."

"And what about Mara – doesn't she help?"

"Ems! Cleaning, or wearing a pair of wellingtons? You must be kidding."

He still calls her Ems, still loves her.

"So why a sheepbot, and not a humanoid? Wouldn't a humanoid be more helpful?"

"It's not all about help, is it," Alice said from under the table.

"No, it's not, Alice, you're quite right," Ty said. "I love my Dorset Down sheep, so I wanted one that would last forever. And Shilly is brilliant around the house. Between Ems, Shilly and I, we manage well – having a humanoid seems like a step into old age somehow."

"My polishing brushes are state of the art you know," Shilly said.

"Look, I'd better get out of here, Nell," he said, softly squeezing my hands, "before we're branded adulterers and sent to the reallocation chamber!"

Alice's ears flew back against her head.

"Sorry, Alice, not a nice word is it?" Ty said, apologetically.

Now was not the right time to tell him.

When ever will be?

I saw him to the door and we hovered closely for a moment before he stepped out into the cool, dark night. I could smell him, and feel the warmth of his stubbly cheek close to mine.

"Thanks for the hand massage," he said, "sleep well."

He kissed my forehead.

"Night, Ty."

Love is DEFINITELY all around.

The portcullis is right up – it's nearly gone. What's going to happen when it crashes down? It can't work with Ty. It's way too complicated. He's married. It's all going to come crashing down.

Don't panic, Cyd – anything is possible. He doesn't love 'love' Mara, does he? And remember Ty appeared when I was sitting in *Lily the Pink*? He made up part of the group I breathed into my heart? And he just kissed my forehead. Surely that's got to be a good sign.

Let's hope so.

It'll work, I know it. We'll run away from here together. We'll live the rest of our lives on his farm. I'll grow vegetables and make chutneys and jams for units. I'll wear my floaty lime green skirt every day and walk barefoot behind his Suffolk Punches, as hand in hand, he and I work the land.

Barefoot, ploughing with heavy horses – have you lost your mind?

***

I left the thousands of stars in the Scandinavian sky and walked back into my livingspace. My roamer bleeped.

Somehow TOHF engineered Sally specifically to lead your group. Why, I don't know. How, I don't know – they must have some Silvers involved. I'll find out. Keep your wits about you.

Also, Award Ambassadors work for the System. I'll tell you more when you're alone. G x.

"That's weird, Alice. Why would G send a message to my roamer?"

"So it's not so easy to trace?"

"Surely it would be easier to trace on my roamer than on-screen. And why should I need to keep my wits about me? And anyway, why would anyone want to trace a message from Granma?"

"Delete the message," Alice said, "and check it's not been registered on your wall-screen."

"How could it be? Alice you're starting to worry me."

"Well it is weird that she should write. Delete it, so at least it's not easy to find."

"Not easy to find! By whom?"

"I don't know," she said, whizzing off to re-charge.

POD AGED TEN

Affirmation for Today: I am me, and proud to be.

"Did you remember your passes?" Sally asked, as I walked towards the treatment table.

Does she think you're nulbrain, or something?

"Yep, right here." I tucked them into my pocket. "Is it okay if Alice joins us?"

After Granma's message, I decided Alice should keep an eye on Sally.

"No problem," she said, "I'm happy to have company. You know the routine, Nell, make yourself comfortable. How are you feeling about travelling through your spaghetti strands again?"

"Slightly anxious. I just hope the ride's not as violent as last time."

"You'll be fine. When you put the hat on the only place you'll be taken will be your memory pod dome. You need to show the pass to whichever pod you would like to visit first. You're totally safe, you're the only one in there."

Oh no you're not.

I put the leopard print hat on and closed my eyes. *Lily the Pink* appeared in front of me and her little door opened.

"You're looking lovely, Lily," I said, as I stepped in. I sat down, grabbed the rail, and off we sped – almost vertically downhill. I screamed. We careered around some hairpins, so violently I almost got thrown out, before we screeched to a halt in the middle of the beautiful opaque dome of rejection.

"In a hurry, Lily?"

"Hello, Nell." Came the dreamy voice from the dome. "Lovely to see you again. Please hold up the pass for the memory pod you would first like to visit."

I breathed in the energy of the shimmering daisies and the peacefully hanging pods, before holding up the handwritten, lime green card:

Nell Greene
You are cordially invited to visit your
memory Pod Aged Ten.
I look forward to seeing you soon x

I stepped out of Lily onto the platform. A handrail rose up around the tile on which I stood, and then I slowly and smoothly started rising, into the dome. I waved to Lily. At the same time one of the pearly eggs started to drop. An undercarriage opened, and a wooden staircase spiralled downwards out of its middle. I stepped onto the staircase and walked up, into rejection.

The lemon scented egg-shaped room had clear sides so I could look out over all my dangling memory pods. Soft fluffy cushions were scattered over the floor, and dotted randomly in amongst them were boxes of tissues.

"Hello, big-me-Nell! You look…big! With very red hair."

"Hello, Ten."

I bunched up the cushions and sat down.

"I've wished for this visit for loads of years. Now you're here. So it worked. And I'm going to play you some of your memories on the screen. Things you need to see. It'll be fun."

"Thank-you, Ten."

"This whole pod is a screen. It's so clever, you'll love it. You can ask me stuff if you like. I can stop or pause the recording too, if you want. What's supposed to happen is I show you a memory and it makes you understand something about the way you are."

"As easy as that, Ten."

I was just thinking the same!

"Well why not? Unless everything gets complicated as you get older. Just enjoy it and do all the serious thinking about it later. Ready?"

I sat cross-legged on the cushions.

The screen flickered into life.

'Welcome to the memories of
Nell Green, aged Ten.'

"I wrote that. Nice writing, isn't it?" Ten squealed with delight.

OH…MY…GOD. I reached for the tissues. Ten-year-old me, standing right there, in front of thirty-five-year-old me. I was so *pretty* – with my mad curly red hair, and my freckly nose that I'd waged a make-up war on when I was sixteen. They were beautiful freckles, why had I ever tried to hide them? I wore my patchwork dungarees Mum had made for my ninth birthday. I'd lived in them until they fell apart.

I watched Shoo, my sister, and I, attempt the high jump out in the garden. We ran, turned sideways and did a scissor jump, more often than not knocking the bar off, and always arguing about who had jumped the highest.

We laughed and chased one another, me pretending to run really fast, but always letting her catch me. God, I wanted those days back. I grabbed a tissue from in-between the cushions.

Then my 'Yellow House' class-room at ed fac came up, and I was standing by the window with Ruby.

"Look, look at this message," I said to Ruby, taking my roamer out of my pocket:

Hello Nell
Will you please marry me one day?
Josh xxxxxxxxxxxxxxxxxxxxxxxxxxxxxxxxx

She laughed, and grabbed the roamer. "Are you going to write back?" she asked.

"Deffo."

"When?"

"In class later."

"What are you going to say?"

"I'm going to say, yes please, Josh, I'd love to."

"How pathetic," she said.

"Ruby!" I looked shocked, and as I stood staring at her, Josh walked into the room.

We both looked at him, and then at one another. He walked over to his chair, ignoring us as he passed. We giggled – annoyingly.

Then the image changed and I was walking into the reading room where Josh and Ruby were huddled in a corner, giggling together and looking into a bag.

I walked towards them, smiling.

They looked up. Ruby's smile dominated her face. Josh started blushing.

"Josh has just given me his 'promising artist' prize," she said, taking a silver plaque out of the bag. "He's only just got if from the office and he's giving it straight to me! Isn't it pretty?" Her eyes sparkled. I looked from Ruby to Josh, and Josh to Ruby. Josh looked at his shoes. Ruby stood there beaming.

Silence.

"Congratulations, Josh," I said, turned, and walked out of the room. Out in the corridor, I sprinted to the toilets and locked myself in one of the cubicles. I cried and sobbed, making the toilet seat rattle.

As I watched, I saw a tiny flash of light, like a glitter-star, rush into my ear.

"Don't worry," came a voice from the screen. *"It'll never hurt this badly again, I won't let it. I'll protect you."*

"SID? Can you pause it, Ten?"

"Of course."

"How can I be hearing SID, if this is a memory from when I was ten?"

"I have, on record, everything, Nell, including thoughts. Clever, isn't it? SID is part of that memory, so that's why you can hear him."

"Very clever, Ten. Okay, you can continue playing the memory, thank-you."

"I'll look after you," SID was saying. *"Love me, not anyone else. Listen to me, I'll be your only true friend."*

"I'm never going to love anyone, ever again," Ten-year-old-me said, through the tears and saliva. "I will never ever trust Ruby, or Josh, or anyone, ever again, as long as I live."

"You can trust me. I'll protect you."

I rose, shakily from the toilet seat. I rubbed my eyes on my sleeve, held my head high, puffed out my chest, and moved towards the toilet door.

"Come on – it's you and me now – we don't need anybody else," SID said.

The screen cleared.

"So that's when SID came into being," I said into the pod. "But I don't remember it. I remember Josh giving Ruby the plaque, but I don't remember crying in the toilets. And Ruby and I carried on being friends – so I can't have thought it was too bad."

"Completely normal. But don't think about why you don't remember it. It's all true what I'm showing you – a memory is a memory. This one is showing you where you first felt rejection. I've got an idea. Want to know what it is?"

"Of course."

"I'm going to re-play the image of you crying in the toilet. Then you can imagine yourself going and sitting with ten-year-old you. Give her a cuddle. Tell her it'll be alright. Tell her she won't even remember this when she's old."

"Old*er*, cheeky!"

"Want to try it?"

"Sure."

The image re-appeared. I closed my eyes and imagined myself walking into the screen to join ten-year-old-me in the toilet. I put my arm around her, and I could feel the betrayal like it was yesterday. I imagined ten-year-old-me resting her head on my chest. I kissed the top of her head and told her it'll be alright. I picked her up and sat on the toilet with her on my lap. We rocked backwards and forwards until she went to sleep.

I opened my eyes.

"How will that help, Ten? The damage was done a long time ago."

"It just will. It's about changing the link to it, or something like that. Just get on with life, that's what I say, Nell."

"The sad thing is Ten, every relationship I've ever had has been affected by those two minutes in the classroom – because that's what triggered SID into appearing."

You created me. I didn't just fly in your ear from nowhere.

"Because of a silly silver art plaque too!" Ten said. "Josh was just being a 'boy'."

"Yes, thank-you, Ten."

"Go and have some fun, and ignore SID."

Ten cleared the screen and I sat in silence.

"Is that all you're going to show me? Granpa was still alive when I was ten. I'd love to see him. And my Siamese cat."

"You can see them anytime you like, all you need to do is think about them."

I reached for another tissue.

"I don't want to leave, Ten," I said.

"I don't want you to either. Twenty-four years waiting, and over in a spark. But we did it, Nell. I got my wish. I showed you what you need. All your memories love you. They don't want you to feel bad, they love being your memories."

"Thank you, Ten. I shall cherish you forever," I said.

I wanted to have a ten-year old kicking fit on the floor and refuse to go, but before I knew how I'd got there, I was standing back on the platform.

The dome started whispering.

"She's doing well, Jenny. She's in her memory pods at the moment."

That's Sally's voice.

"Can you screen in on her?"

That's Mum!

"Too risky."

"How do you think it's going?"

"She's doing well – she should be ready by the end of the course."

"You'll be on for a promotion, Sally."

"Not interested, I just want to make sure she's ready for the job."

"Did you manage to set up the com modification?"

"Yep....... Listen, I've got to go, I think Nell is picking us up."

"Mum?" I said, looking up and around the dome. "What modification? Is my Mum in here?" I asked into the dome. No reply. "Sally?" I asked. Silence.

"Rejection, did you just hear my Mum and Sally whispering?"

The silence rang in my ears as I strained to hear more whispers – but none came.

POD SEVENTEEN

"I trust you enjoyed Aged Ten, Nell," the voice of the Dome said.

"It was certainly interesting, thank-you. Did you just hear people whispering?

"No, Nell. Pod Seventeen is ready for you now."

A pod moved overhead, its undercarriage opened, and a chrome, spiral staircase dropped down to meet me.

I wound my way up onto a luxurious pale green carpet, and walked the two paces across it to sit on a black leather bench circling the pod's middle. Pale green cushions matching the carpet were scatted all along the bench, and again, the entire pod was a screen.

"Hi, Nell. Great to see you," Seventeen said, "I'll activate the screens in a moment. You know how it works, just sit back and enjoy. My hope is what I show you will help you understand your relationship with rejection. Recognition first, understanding second. I play you the bit you can recognise. Then you need to do the understanding. Then you can change the relationship."

"Thanks, 17."

"Everything that happens in our lives forms a memory. Everything. Most people file many of these memories away at such depths they're never found again. But they're still there. I'm going to show you memories maybe you don't consciously remember. You can stop me anytime, ask questions, pause, rewind etc. There are tissue pockets on the front side of the bench, should you need them."

"I think I'm all cried out, 17, but thanks."

On came the screen.

WOW! How someone can change in seven years! Plaits tamed my red curls and I wore flared blue hemp trousers and a tight red sweater. I was completely flat-chested, and as thin as a planting rake. My eyes were surrounded by dark-green eyeshadow, black liner and heavy black mascara.

I sat remodelling a pair of trousers, singing along to Michael Jackson, "Don't stop till you get enough..." I stood up and disco-danced around my bedroom with my sewing – how I didn't stab myself with the needle, I don't know.

The image changed to Fran and I sitting in the college canteen. I was wearing the same red jumper.

"You should have come to the ragga session last night, Nell. It was tops."

"Was Rupert there?"

"Yep."

"Shit. I didn't get out of my writing class till late. Did you talk to him?"

"No, but Sherri did."

"Oh."

"They were dancing and chatting all night. And they left at the same time."

"Sherri and Rupert? Didn't think he even liked her."

"Sharna said she saw them kissing."

"Oh."

"Never love anyone, then you'll be fine." SID's voice filled the pod.

The screen switched to the music lounge. Rupert and I were standing face to face. His shoulder length blonde hair curled past his big green eyes. He was looking straight into my seventeen-year-old eyes.

God how I had loved Rupert. I thought we would spend our whole lives together.

"Nell, are you going on the end of year weekend trip?"

"Not planning to, Rupe. Are you?"

"Only if I can persuade you to come with me," he said, pulling one of my plaits.

"WHAT?" I shouted into the pod, "NO WAY! Rupe asked me on the trip with him? He never did! I'd always dreamed he would, but he never did! This can't be true, 17."

17 paused the memory. "I carry a true record of your life, Nell," 17 replied. "But as I said earlier, sometimes memories are filed so far away you don't remember."

"But I wouldn't have wanted to file this away. I absolutely idolised Rupert. I would have killed for Rupe. It doesn't make sense."

"Patience, Nell. Patience," 17 said, playing the memory from where she'd paused.

"It'll never last – he'll hurt you in the end, just like Josh did." SID's voice came out of nowhere.

"Go away, SID!" I shouted at the screen.

"They're all the same. Don't trust any of them. He asked Sherri out just two days ago."

I watched myself smiling at Rupe. And then my eyes changed from excitement to emptiness as I listened to SID's words.

"Sure, Rupe, I'd love to," I said, looking into his heavenly eyes. "Does Sherri know?"

"Why would Sherri need to know?"

I turned and walked away from him.

"Tell him! Tell him!" I shouted, from the bench. "Tell him you adore him. Tell him you have a pain in the arse living in your head. Tell him you've loved him ever since you first spoke."

But as I sat on the bench watching, on-screen I carried on walking away from him.

"Well done. You could never trust him if he likes Sherri."

The image showed me walking into my bedroom. I slumped down on my bed and started crying. The screen cleared.

I sat in silence, looking out over my other pods.

"Can I say something?" Pod 17 asked.

"Go ahead."

"Rupe chose *you*, Nell – not Sherri."

"But why would he have asked Sherri out two days before if he was serious about me?"

"Do you even know he did? Wasn't it just SID, manipulating you? You need to believe people like you, Nell."

"I can't believe I don't remember that moment with Rupe. I mean, he was the only boy I ever wanted to be with, ever."

I slumped back into the bench.

"All these years, all the men I've chopped because I never believed they loved me. All because of SID. Rupe, my soulmate had asked me out and SID ruined it all."

I felt numb.

"I felt a connection with Rupe I've never felt since. I can't believe I let SID destroy it all."

I tore a tissue.

"There's nothing to say you won't feel a connection like that again," 17 said. "You just need to believe it can happen to you."

"Ty," I whispered. "Ty Martins, on the course – I feel a connection with him."

"Well then, Nell, now's your chance to see if you can change your behaviour."

"Such a waste," I said, snivelling into the tissue.

"Sit a while, Nell, and whenever you want to leave, the stairs will open and help you back onto the platform. Remember two things for me. First: you can visit your memory pods anytime you like – if you sit peacefully, relax, breathe, and think of a place or image associated with a certain age, then the answers you're looking for will come to you. All you need to do is sit and connect. Second: above all else, Nell, remember – *Rupe asked you out*. That is the important thing to take away with you. He wanted you, Nell, not Sherri, not anyone else – you. It was SID who manipulated you."

I sat on the bench for the longest time. How different would my life have been if I'd said yes to Rupe? I threw away the love of my life because of you, SID.

All is as it should be!

***

"How was it?" Sally asked, looking down at me.

"Brilliant and horrendous."

"And tiring, I expect. You need to get a good night's rest."

"Sally, were you talking to my Mum, by any chance?"

"Your Mum?"

"Yes."

"When?"

"Then, when I was in the hat."

"Have you given her my chip number?"

"No."

"Then I couldn't have been."

"Weird," I said. "I could have sworn I heard the two of you whispering when I was in my memory dome."

"It would be impossible, Nell. There's only you in there, all alone, that's how it works."

WE NEED TO TALK

I looked into the bathroom mirror: "I am me, and proud to be," I said to my reflection.

I heard a bleep.

To Nell Greene
Congratulations, we hear from Sally you are making good progress with your therapy. As you are aware, time is marching on, and we believe to give you the best chance of finding your life-partner, and avoiding reallocation, it is necessary for you to start a new relationship. This will give you the chance to put your therapy into practice. We have, therefore, selected a perfect match for you. His name is Derek Raud, and he's a Geologist, you can look at his profile on our site. He is arriving in five days' time on the 16h15 boat from Sassnitz. Please collect him from the Port at Trelleborg. If you have any objections to meeting Derek, please address your concerns to Puter 2.

Good luck!
The Dating Committee

"Derek, a Geologist, is my perfect match?"

"Bit extreme, I must say," Alice said.

"Extreme! Five months ago my life was my own. Now I'm not even sure if I'll be able to choose my own colour of underwear tomorrow morning!"

"I can choose it for you if you like."

"I need to go and see Ty, Alice. You coming?"

"No, I'll stay and polish – I haven't done it in days."

"I've got to tell him everything, Alice: pod 17: the messages from the Dating Committee: The Award: my reallocation. I don't want Derek, a Geologist. I want to put therapy into practice with Ty."

He's still married remember – forbidden fruit.

Oh hi, Cyd. I wondered when you'd surface. Now go away. I don't want anything to do with you, after seeing what you did in the pods.

You're making a mistake. Please, be careful with Ty.

Now's my chance to change my behaviour – just like Pod 17 said. I'm not listening to you. You're were the liar, not them.

I admit I wasn't the most supportive at times.

At times!

But I always thought it was for your best.

That's rubbish. You just wanted me to yourself. All is as it should be, Cyd, and I am me, and proud to be. Leave!

I'm trying to change. I'm not SID anymore.

Well, whoever you are, I control my mind, and you are now eliminated.

***

Ty opened his door and kissed my right cheek so tenderly my skin tingled.

See? He definitely likes me too.

Portcullis: gone: out of sight. I'M FREEEEEEE!

"We need to talk."

"I know," he said. "Come on in. Jupiter and Ems are already here – they didn't get one."

I followed Ty.

"One what? Hi, you two. Haven't seen you for ages, how's it all going?"

"One of these." Ty held out a piece of rice paper covered in very large, dark blue, inked handwriting.

"What's that?"

"You haven't received one?"

"No."

"Then what is it we need to talk about?"

"What?"

"At the door. You said, we need to talk."

"Did I? – oh yes, it's Alice and Shilly – I think they've fallen out."

Shilly looked across at me.

"Oh right," he muttered, frowning.

'Later', I mouthed at him.

He read the letter to us:

'Dear Ty Martins,

This letter is being sent to you in strictest confidence. Your participation on the therapy course, along with your wife, Mara, has been brought to our attention. We cannot tell you who by. We are aware Mara needs to tell you something before your marriage can successfully end, and it is absolutely critical you find out what it is as soon as possible. We are fearful that you, like Mara, Jupiter, and Nell, face reallocation. We are sorry if this comes as a shock to you, but we know you are in good company, and will be able to talk things through with your therapy colleagues.

We are worried all of this may have something to do with the upcoming elections, and we would like to invite you to become an active member of The Original Human Foundation (TOHF). We need people like yourself, who are committed to a peaceful and pure planet. We will get in touch with you as soon as we have any more information regarding your possible reallocation.

If you would like to contact us in the meantime regarding membership, please enter one number, any number, three times, in three seconds into your roamer. At the end of the communication, the number will be automatically erased. If you use the *same* number for a second communication it will not work.

Please destroy this letter, preferably by burning, rather than crumbling it into little pieces and feeding it to the tiddly-fish!

Yours hopefully,

The Original Human Foundation'

Jupiter, Mara and Ty all looked at me as I stood there.

"How did they know about the tiddly-fish?" I asked, trying to cut through the atmosphere.

"Is it true, Mara? Do you have a reallocation assignment?"

She nodded.

"And you, Nell?"

"Yes."

My heart was trying to make a rapid exit out through my chest.

"Why haven't you mentioned it?"

He turned to Mara, "Why haven't *you* said anything? You're my wife, for fuck's sake."

"I couldn't, Ty. One of the conditions of therapy was I had to keep the reallocation assignment a secret."

"Same for me," Jupiter said.

"Why?"

"Because you'd have freaked and refused to come," Mara said, looking at her high-heels, "and because I need to tell you some things while we're here that are going to hurt you."

"You're right, Ems, I would have refused to come – but why are Nell or Jupiter's reallocations important enough for secrets?"

A fist reached in and ripped my insides out.

Shit! The Portcullis: it's bloody plummeting!

Ty turned towards me.

"Sorry, Nell, that didn't come out right."

Didn't come out right? That's an effing understatement.

"No worry," I said, as the fire in my head took over. "Like you say, our reallocations are of no importance to you."

"That's not what I meant. Nell, wait..."

I turned and walked. I would have collapsed on the floor otherwise.

"Nell. Really, hang on."

I held my head high and carried on walking, just as I had walked away from Ruby and Josh, all those years ago.

LOOKING ON

I wobbled back to my livingspace. I felt sick.

Don't say I didn't warn you.

But he'd come over to mine about five seconds after Sally lifted the visiting ban – why would he do that if he didn't like me? He met Granma. He kisses me every time we meet. I oiled his effing hands! I can't believe I got it so wrong.

It'll be okay. Go and have a cuddle with Alice. I've got one hell of a mess to sort out here – the ashing portcullis smashed back down and shot stuff everywhere.

Sorry.

I'm sorry too. And I'm sorry for how I was as SID. If you let me....

"Alice! What the hell are you doing!" I shrieked.

She spun around, ears flat, stock still in front of my screen, which showed Jupiter, Mara and Ty, exactly where I had just left them.

"What are you doing!"

Silence.

"Are you watching Ty's livingspace?"

"It would appear so."

"How?"

"I don't know."

"Don't know? Of course you know. How long have you been watching?"

"A while."

"Did you hear him read the letter? Did you hear what was said after?"

"Yes."

"How? How did you access the screen?"

"I didn't – it accessed me. I heard this bleep when I was over there polishing under the table."

"At which point?"

"When Ty opened the door to you."

"How did it do that? Does it mean our spaces are bugged?"

"I think someone has activated the surveillance devices."

"What surveillance devices?"

"Up there," Alice said, pointing her nose upwards to the underside of my sleeping platform.

"Where?"

"That tiny black square. It looks like an environmental monitor. Shilly and I researched it."

"Have all the livingspaces got them?"

"Ty's definitely has. Shilly checked."

"Why hasn't she told, Ty?"

"She hasn't had time."

"So who do you think has activated it?"

I cleared the screen. The image re-appeared.

"I've no idea. Possibly someone who wants you to be able to keep an eye on what's going on elsewhere."

"*Me*? Don't be ridiculous." I put Alice into a kitchen cupboard and cleared the screen. The image came back.

"It's nothing to do with me, Nell!" Alice cried from the cupboard. I let her out.

"Why on earth would I need to see what's going on elsewhere, Alice? It just doesn't make any sense. I think I need to have you scanned."

"I can't believe you think it's anything to do with me. I can't believe you don't trust me, Nell." Her ears flattened back, her head lowered and she rolled herself over to her charging platform. "I suppose they're installed in case a suicider is on therapy."

"I've got to tell the others."

"Why? Think about it – there's something you're supposed to see."

"Don't be ridiculous," I said.

Out of the corner of my eye I looked at the screen, and straight into Ty's eyes. "And you're telling me he doesn't know the camera's there?"

"He doesn't have a clue."

MARA'S SECRET

"So, Ems, what's the big secret you've been keeping?" Ty asked.

"You'd better sit down."

"And what the hell's all this reallocation crap?"

"It's more just a change of lifestyle really."

"To what?"

"First you need to sit down and listen," Mara said.

Ty sat down on his sofa, next to Jupiter and opposite Mara.

"This therapy is supposed to help me to summons the courage to explain to you why I drink."

Ty studied her face, watched her lips.

"He still bloody loves her, Alice," I said.

Jupiter started fidgeting.

"Maybe this would be easier if it were just Ty and myself," Mara said, looking at Jupiter.

"Listen," Ty said, "Anything I need to know, I'm sure Jupiter can know too. In fact, I'm sure he already knows, Ems."

"Look, Ty," Jupiter started, "I never meant for any of this to...."

"Jupe, don't bother. Ems and I haven't been living as a married couple for years – it was only a matter of time before one, or both of us found someone else."

Did he mean anything by 'both of us?'

Possibly. Why not? It's such a beautiful time of year for it, why not indeed.

"The boys aren't yours," Mara mumbled into her palms.

"Pardon?" Ty said, moving forwards to the edge of the sofa.

"The boys aren't yours, Ty," she repeated, looking up at Ty, tears streaming down her face.

I picked Alice up and cuddled her as my eyes filled with water.

"That's what goes through my mind before I drink whiskey – not that shitting woman in blue trying to find her way out of a car park!"

Ty stared at her.

"They're Rod's," she mumbled. "We didn't have a short fling like I told you; it went on for three and a half years. I got pregnant with both of the boys by Rod. I'm so, so sorry."

"Man," Jupiter said. "Listen, I'm going to leave you two to sort this one out."

"DON'T YOU MOVE!" Ty shouted.

I jumped, Mara jumped, and Jupiter looked decidedly worried. Alice and I looked at each other.

"Don't like the sound of this," Alice said.

"Do you think I should go over there and break it up?"

"No, give them some time."

Ty moved over to beside Mara. He held her face up to his.

"He's going to snap her neck!" screeched Alice.

I doubt it.

"I'm serious, Ty," she said. "I wish I was making this up. I'm so sorry."

Ty wiped her tears with his thumb and kissed the top of her head.

My ears started ringing. "How did I ever get the impression he likes me, Alice. Look at the way he is with at her. I've been a total idiot."

"No you haven't, Nell," Alice said.

He's your therapy guinea-pig, remember?

Jupiter was looking on, wide-eyed.

"Ems, I know you're sorry, and you're possibly not going to like this next bit, but did you really think I didn't know?" he said calmly. "I've always known. I knew the first night you spent with Rod. How? – by the way you treated me the next day. You hadn't been so loving and attentive in months. Also, I had a call from one of Rod's friends who was supposed to be meeting him in a bar, and he hadn't turned up."

"What?" Mara said.

"I know it went on for three and a half years, again, because of the way you always behaved. I could even tell you the date it all finished if you gave me a while to remember."

"Why didn't he say anything?" Alice asked.

"Beats me," I replied.

Bit twisted, if you ask me.

"I've also always known the children aren't mine. There isn't a nose that huge in either side of our families – but have you ever seen Rod's grandfather? I knew the moment each of them were born."

"WHAT?" Mara hollered, turning to face him. "WHAT ARE YOU TALKING ABOUT? WHAT DO YOU MEAN, YOU KNEW?"

Her tears dried and her face turned white.

"WHY THE FUCK DIDN'T YOU SAY ANYTHING? WHY DIDN'T YOU TRY AND STOP ME FROM SEEING HIM? WHY DIDN'T YOU REACT? THROW ME OUT? STOP ROD FROM COMING TO THE FARM?"

Ty smiled.

"Oops, he shouldn't have done that," Alice said.

Mara leapt to her feet to tower over him.

"AND WHAT THE FUCK ARE YOU SMILING ABOUT? WHY DIDN'T YOU SAY ANYTHING?" Mara screeched.

Ty stood up and held her shoulders. She ripped them away. "Where would it have got us, Ems? You'd probably have run off with Rod. Then when you'd realised you'd been wrong, you would have come back, begging for forgiveness, which, I'm sure, would have been worse. I knew it wouldn't last with Rod."

"You conceited BASTARD," Mara screamed, and pushed him backwards.

He stayed upright.

"Hey!" he said, raising his hands in surrender. "Slow down a minute, Ems."

"You BASTARD. SLOW DOWN?" she shouted, picking up a handful of snacks and throwing it at him.

Jupiter dodged an apple ring.

"Hold on, you two," Jupe said. "That's enough now."

"ENOUGH?" screamed Mara, swinging round to face Jupiter. "Have you any idea how I've felt for the past few years?"

"And what about how Ty's felt, Em? Stop thinking about yourself for once," Jupiter replied.

Mara looked like she'd been slapped in the face.

The room went silent.

She slumped back down into the chair.

Ty sat down on the sofa, removing a pineapple chunk before he did so.

Shilly started cleaning up the snacks from the floor.

"I know you're angry, but imagine, on the other hand, if I'd confronted you and we'd decided to stay together. You would always have worried I wouldn't bring the children up as if they were my own. You would have been paranoid about Rod coming to the farm. Whenever we'd had an argument, out it would come, used as our favourite and most painful weapon. You know it's true. One day one of us would have said something in front of the children, and then the mess would have been twice as big."

"Fucking hell," Mara said, looking down at her knees. "Now what the fuck do we do?"

"Well, Ems," Ty said. "You stop drinking, because now you don't have any reason to. We tell Sally you've achieved what you had to on the course, and we're going to go home and try to rebuild our marriage. You write to the Livelihood Committee and tell them you've confessed to me about Rod and the children, our marriage is healing, and you no longer need to be reallocated, thank you very much."

"My God, he still wants her, Alice," I said. "After all that – he *still bloody wants her!* How could I have been so totally and utterly wrong about him?"

Mara looked up at him.

Jupiter turned to Ty and then to Mara, blinking furiously.

"You are joking…right?" Mara said.

WHAT NEXT

"Yes, Ems, I'm joking. Of course I'm fucking joking. I've been living a lie for years too, thinking we might be able to make it all work somehow."

"Shit, for a moment there I thought you were going to take all that crap, and *still* try to work it out," Jupiter said.

"No, Jupe. I think it's time for all of us to have a new start. And after I've had time to digest all this, I think I need to go and apologise to the woman I'd like to make a new start with," Ty said, standing up, "I hope you're okay with it, Ems."

"Of course I'm okay with it, Ty, you and Nell are made for one another – don't know why it's taken you this long to figure it out."

"That's YOU!" Alice shrieked, "He wants to make a new start, with you, Nell!"

I grabbed Alice. "Oh my God, Alice! I WAS right. See, Cyd? Oh my God, can you believe it?"

"Do you two mind leaving now?" Ty said, "I'd like some time alone."

"Can we not sort all this out once and for all, Ty – whilst we're here. There's the slight matter of reallocation."

"That can't be serious...can it? We've got two healthy boys for goodness sake."

"Mateo is to adopt them."

"*Mateo?* Why on earth would he adopt them? He doesn't want kids. Why can't they stay with me?"

"I have no idea, you weren't mentioned. The communication I received said the children would be looked after by your brother and his wife – family unit and all that."

"Does Mateo know?"

"I doubt it or he would have contacted you."

"Don't like the sound of it," Jupiter said. "Something they're not telling us, me thinks."

"Don't like the sound of it? That's my fucking children we're talking about. No-one's looking after them, apart from Mara or me."

"Hey, maybe you won't have to have children if you can get together with Ty, and have his," Alice said.

"Why didn't you say anything to the Committees, Ems?" Ty asked.

Silence.

"Does anyone know what Nell's assignment is?" he asked.

Nobody spoke.

"And Jupiter – what's yours, and why are you being reallocated?"

"Because of my addiction, Ty. Once an addict, always an addict. But my assignment is top – I'm going to be developing ed games to try and prevent young people from wanting to try drugs in the first place. I get to live in a town built especially for ed creators."

"Are you even allowed to leave the town you're reallocated to? Can you see your family? Do you go to Australia with everyone else when you're over 85? Are you free to live your lives as you wish?"

"We don't know any details, all we got was the initial communication," Jupiter said.

"And you didn't challenge it?"

"For what? You know what the Committees are like – once they've made a decision, it's made," Jupiter replied.

"But it's worth fighting. With the elections coming up, everything could change, surely it's worth a shot. Go public saying you don't agree with it. There's no way they're taking my children away."

"Look, Ty, all the election monitors are under 35 at the moment, because it's a new scheme. It'll be fun – I can reinvent myself, be whoever I like. Get off the whiskey once and for all," Mara said.

"And never see your children again? Can you even communicate with them?"

She looked away.

"I can't believe you're just taking this shit. This is the lives of your children you're screwing up, Ems. Right here, right now, you are choosing, as their mother, to desert them."

"I'm really sorry, Ty."

"And Nell, is she fighting?"

I looked at Alice. "Why aren't I fighting, Alice?"

"You've been too busy trying to figure out how to get pregnant?"

Ty leant forward and put his hands on Mara's knees.

"We'll get an official end of marriage certificate, Ems. If you're in the front line for a failed marriage, I figure I must be too. I'm going to clear up this reallocation nonsense once and for all."

"How?"

"Leave it to me."

Ty kissed Mara on the cheek before she and Jupiter left.

"Are we going to let the System give the boys to Mateo, Shilly?"

"No way!"

TY'S APOLOGY

My screen cleared, just before my roamer bleeped.

Nell, I hope you're not angry with me! I'm sorry for what I said earlier – it isn't what I meant at all. I'd come round now to apologise, but I've just had one shit of a confession from Mara and I'm going to take myself out for a long walk to think everything over. Are you around for breakfast tomorrow? 8am? I'll come to you. I'll tell you everything then. Ty xx

Ty, 8am is perfect. Nell x

TY'S PLAN

"Forgive me?" Ty said when I opened the door to him, at 07h59.

"Maybe," I said, smiling. "Is toast and yoghurt good with you?"

"Great," he said, following me over to the kitchen worktop.

"Nell, your reallocation *is* important to me, which I know isn't what I said yesterday, but the letter from TOHF completely freaked me, and I didn't really know what I was saying. After you'd left, Ems told me what she had to so that we can end our marriage 'amicably' – so now we're both free to get on with the rest of our lives. Well, Ems isn't free, because she's chosen reallocation, but you know what I mean – we are free from one another. Well anyway, I went out for a really long walk after the two of them had left, and I was planning how I'm going to fight against all your reallocations…"

"…is that wise?"

"And I was also thinking about my life from here onwards…"

"Raspberry or cloudberry yoghurt."

Stop interrupting!

"Cloudberry. So anyway, yes, I was thinking about life – and about how I'd like the rest of mine to include you, if poss. But obviously, only if you want the same thing."

I launched the yoghurt spoon and threw my arms around him.

"Watch it!" Alice said, as the spoon hit the floor.

I had an image of myself, sunlit, with my eyes closed, my arms reaching upwards, and my palms touching the rays, singing 'Can You Feel The Force', by The Real Thing.

Alice and Shilly spun round in circles.

We've done it. We're in love! The portcullis is up.

He pulled back from me, "shall I take that as a yes?"

We laughed, and cried, and he wiped my cheeks with his thumb. Then he leant forward and kissed me.

His beautiful soft lips against mine – please let me feel like this for the rest of my life.

Deal.

"You knew what Ems had to tell me, didn't you?" he said, once we'd come up for air.

Oh shit.

I nodded.

"Why didn't you say anything?" he asked quietly.

"Ty, you know it wasn't my place."

"It wouldn't have mattered anyway, Nell. I'd always known."

"I'm so sorry. Why didn't you ever do anything about it?"

Brilliantly convincing. He'll never know you've just watched all of it unfolding.

"It's a long story, for another day," he said, stroking the back of my neck.

We cuddled and kissed. Delicious, soft kisses. Warm, big hands holding me. My 34 A's pressed up against his hand knitted sweater.

"Let's go and sit down," I said, taking his hand. He sat on the sofa and I laid with my head in his lap. He stroked my hair and I kissed the fingers of his other hand.

"Ems also told me yesterday, that my boys are to be adopted by my brother, Mateo, and obviously, I'm not going to let that happen. I assume it means I'm up for reallocation too, and I need to tell you this, Nell, because I have a feeling it's not going to be a smooth trip for us."

"Now you sound like you're trying to put me off!"

"Far from it," he said, leaning over and kissing the top of my head. "By the way, what did you come to see me about yesterday – you said we needed to talk?"

I let go of his hand, and sat upright.

"Not a good sign," Ty said.

"I guess the best thing I can do is start from the beginning," I said, my hands feeling clammy.

Breathe. All is as it should be – remember that.

"OUTRAGEOUS!" Ty shouted, once I'd finished. "You can't be reallocated just because you haven't got any children. I've got two, and no wife, you can have those. Why didn't you tell me? How come none of this came out in our chats?"

"I couldn't tell you. I would never have been able to convince you I was falling in love with you for you, not because I needed to have children."

"Shit," he said. "that was quick! I think I only realised my feelings for you when you walked out yesterday."

Bit of a put down, but don't focus on it.

"I knew the moment you crushed your first corn-flake," I said, laughing.

"So you didn't get a letter from The Original Human Foundation?"

"No."

"Odd."

"I did get something else though."

"Go on."

"I'm being sent a perfect match. He arrives on Tuesday."

"A what?"

"A perfect match, Ty. A blind date. Someone I'm supposed to fall in love with, accept the Award, have children with and avoid reallocation. Derek, a Geologist."

"From where?"

"Central America."

"Freaky: why would someone come all the way from there?"

"It is odd."

"Tuesday is five days away, Nell."

"I know."

"Who's sending him?"

"The Dating Committee."

"And what if you like him?"

"Ty, I've waited 18 years to feel like this about someone again. Derek, I'm afraid, is somewhat doomed before he's even set off!"

"I'm going to contact TOHF," he said after a long silence.

"Is that wise? If anything happens to you, then where will I be?"

"What's likely to happen to me for contacting TOHF? If I don't do something I'm going to lose my children and you, which, I'm afraid, just isn't going to happen. Don't they expect people to object?"

"Well no, they run a peaceful planet, Ty."

"But none of this is fair. What can it achieve?"

I shrugged my shoulders. "If there were no limits or boundaries wouldn't it be total chaos?"

"Anyway," Ty said, "I'm not having everything I love taken away from me without making some sort of protest. You remember the corn-flakes. You were with me when I fed my soapbox to the tiddly-fish and chose action."

"Let's message the Dating Committee," Alice said.

To the Dating Committee
I am very pleased to inform you Ty Martins and I have, quite unexpectedly, fallen in love. He and Mara (his wife) have already ended their marriage, which was unrelated to Ty and I. I am looking forward to practicing my therapy on Ty. Please could you cancel Derek's arrival.
Nell Greene

To Nell Greene
I am sorry to inform you Ty and Mara will still be officially married up until the end of the therapy course. I think therefore, you should not get too excited about the prospects of any future together. Derek has resigned from a very good service provision role to come to Sweden, and so I am unable to cancel his arrival. Please meet him at the Port as mentioned in our previous message. He is a nice man, please try and spend some time with him.
The Dating Committee

"That's ridiculous," Ty said. "I'd guess they don't even know Derek. You'll have to tell him about the situation."

"There's no way I can trust him, Ty, I don't know anything about him."

"We've got five days before Derek arrives, and four more weeks at the centre. I don't really have anything more to achieve through therapy, seeing as Mara and I have agreed to split 'amicably'. So, I imagine she'll spend as much time as she can with Jupiter, which frees me to work out what this is all about, and to spend every possible moment with you."

Swoon.

"Should we mention anything to Sally, seeing as she's a member of TOHF?" I asked.

"Not yet."

He took my hand and led me to the sleeping platform, and we stayed there for three days. We surrounded ourselves with stickers on which was written 'Love is All Around'. We chatted, laughed, exchanged planet-saving techniques, and loved one another like I had never loved before.

The portcullis has just blown off its hinges. Gone – for good. Ce...lebrate good times, Come On....

Ty was the only guinea pig I needed:

Insecurity? I know he loves me.

Jealousy? Still need to test it.

Fear of rejection? None. He's not the type to muck around.

Love? Most definitely.

Let's hope he's ...

Cyd!

How beautifully blue, the sky today.

CONVERSATION I

Affirmation for today: Love is all around.

I knocked on Jupiter's door, the day before Derek's arrival, and thank God, he answered.

"Jupe, hi. How are you getting on?"

"Hi, Spaghetti Head. I'm great. Come on in. Life is cool – so much better than when I got here."

"Anything to do with Mara?"

He smiled. "Mara, and forgiveness. I've forgiven people, I've forgiven memories, and I've forgiven objects. Forgiving myself though, Nell, has been the biggest trip. I've spent hours up on the rock you can see from the lounge. I ended up exchanging marriage vows with myself yesterday! Bloody powerful stuff that is. You should try it, Nell. I feel like a new person."

"Sally does have some interesting techniques."

"She knows about my reallocation assignment, so she's suggested we work on preparing for the change in lifestyle, which sounds like a breeze compared to what we have been doing. And you, Nell, are you okay?"

Alice and I followed him into his bright sunny livingspace. "This is the first time you've been round since we got here! I was beginning to think I smell, or something."

"Time's gone so fast, Jupe, plus I've been a bit busy the last few days...."

"With Ty by any chance?"

I smiled.

"Good on you, Nell. Fingers crossed the System doesn't come up with some plan to ruin it all for you."

"What, apart from sending me a Perfect Match?" I said, explaining my messages from the Dating Committee.

"I swear these Committees are insane."

"It's the first time I've felt this way since, Rupert – remember him? From ed days?"

Good idea to openly admit the way you feel – that'll reinforce it.

"God, you loved him," Jupiter said, looking out of the window. "I'm so happy for you, Nell."

"Thanks, Jupe, I'm happy for you too."

"So, Nell, what's up?"

Alice whizzed over to his sleeping platform. She nodded to me.

"There's something I need to run past you – in strictest confidence."

"Goes without saying."

"Right. Well, basically, everyone's livingspace has a surveillance device. Did you know?"

"No."

"Up above my head," Alice said.

"Isn't it an environmental monitor?" Jupiter said, walking over to join Alice.

"When you were all round at Ty's, when Mara told him about Rod, I watched it all on my wall-screen."

"Cool!"

"Not really. I have no idea how my screen managed to pick it up, and I've no idea why I should need to watch it, or who may be watching me in my space, or you in yours."

"Odd Sally didn't mention them in our introduction session, but surely she has to be the first person to ask. I imagine she has the power to activate them, so maybe she thinks there's something you need to see regarding Ty – things that'll help straighten your spaghetti strands out?"

"Sounds like a risky way to achieve that," Alice replied. "And is it not also rather massively unethical?"

"Yes. But if it's valid as a therapy tool, is it then justified?" Jupiter said.

"But if I can watch, then so can Sally, and so can the System."

"My guess is they won't – why would they?" he replied, waving his hand in front of the device. "I'm going to put tape over the lens."

"I don't like it, Jupe," I said. "Things seem to be changing since the System announced the elections. People are behaving differently. Do you think they're wrong to give humans back the hope of leadership?"

"Man, who knows. I guess only time will tell. I can't imagine what will happen. All we've ever known is governance by Silvers. They've kept the planet peaceful and healthy, so I don't really get why anything needs to change."

"Quite," Alice said.

"I don't even have any clue which human organisations or individuals are going to stand for election, do you?"

"No idea," I replied. "And talking of organisations, didn't you think the letter from the Foundation to Ty was odd?"

"Very weird. Maybe they're hoping to get Ty involved with leadership – if they're even going to stand. Back to the device, though, Nell – when you watched Ty's livingspace, was it helpful?"

"Well, yes, because I watched Ty tell Mara how he feels about me."

"So, there you go," he said. "Wasn't the thought-projection image of your spaghetti strands all about fear and rejection?"

"Yes."

"And hadn't you just stormed out of Ty's space because he said something or other about you not being important to him?"

"Yes."

"Well, there you go. I think it's been set up as part of the therapy. I'd ask Sally if I were you."

"Do you think I can trust her? She's with TOHF, you know."

"I'd trust Sally with my life, Nell. You're starting to sound slightly paranoid!"

CONVERSATION II

"Hi, Sally," I said, "Oh, sorry, Mara, I didn't know you were in a session."

"Don't worry, Nell, I'd just finished, hadn't I, Sally," Mara said, looking very happy I'd appeared at the lounge door.

"No, not really, Mara," Sally said.

"Well, Nell looks like she's in need of you more than I am, so I'll leave the two of you to it. Message me if you want me to come back in later, Sally," Mara said, climbing out of her beanbag and squeezing past me through the door before Sally could reply.

"What can I do for you, Nell?" Sally asked.

Alice and I stood on the grass carpet, across from her.

"I hope I can speak to you in total confidence, Sally?"

"Of course."

She's bound to say that! You've just got to take the risk.

I told her about the surveillance devices, and being able to watch Ty's livingspace.

"Oh God, I'm so sorry, Nell, I should have warned you. I programmed the devices as part of your therapy. I was going to prepare you for it when I next saw you."

"And the others, were you going to tell them?"

"It wouldn't work if they knew, Nell."

"I'm afraid Jupiter knows – I talked to him about it earlier."

"Oh, that's…"

"It's a complete violation of privacy, Sally!"

"Try not to think of it that way, Nell."

"Well how should I think of it?"

"I had a feeling, after your corn-flakes exercise, Ty was going to become important to you, and so I had the idea of activating his surveillance device. I thought there may be a chance of you seeing something that could help you."

"How could you know that?"

"It's my job, Nell."

"I don't feel comfortable with it, Sally. What if Ty finds out?"

"Is Jupiter likely to tell him?"

"He promised he wouldn't."

"Then, hopefully he won't."

"What about confidentiality, Sally? It's totally mashed."

Sally looked at Alice.

"I even got shut in a cupboard because Nell thought I was controlling her screen!"

"Did what you see help though, Nell?" Sally asked.

"Yes, but that's not the point. I appreciate the theory behind it, Sally, but really, it's not right. And how do I know no-one's activated mine and is watching me?"

"Why would they?"

"Who knows."

"No, Nell, it's only the Director, that's me, of the therapy programme who has surveillance rights. If I have participants who are mentally unstable, or suicidal, then I activate the cameras to keep checks on them. Every new therapy centre has them."

"You should have told us at the start of the course, Sally."

"Yes, I should have. I will add it to the introduction session in the future."

"You must deactivate them, Sally. It is completely wrong."

CONVERSATION III

I walked back through a drizzly afternoon to my livingspace, and twisted my surveillance device around to face the wall. I messaged Jupiter to tell him about my meeting with Sally, and asked him again not to mention it.

"African sunset!" I said, and the glass changed, blocking out the wet and uninspiring dusk. Ty would be over soon, so I had just enough time to have a chat with Mum and Granma.

Alice rolled to her recharging platform and switched off.

"Spaghetti Head! Lovely to hear from you – it's been ages!"

"Sorry, Mum, I've been a bit busy. How's it all going?"

"Pretty well. We're planting a new variety of cassava in the east of Zone D, directly into the sand, before any soil improvement. It's all very exciting."

"Listen, I want to ask you something: Sally has activated a surveillance camera in Ty's livingspace. She reckons it's part of my therapy, which seems extreme. We know she's a member of TOHF, and I was just wondering if it has something to do with them, rather than with therapy."

"I can't think why it would," Mum said.

"Do you know Sally?"

"I don't. How are you and Ty getting on?"

"We've got together. Can you believe it? He's amazing, you'll love him."

"I don't know if I can believe it, Nell. Who would have thought you'd meet someone during therapy? That's fabulous news."

"He's received a hand-written letter from TOHF, asking him to become a member. They told him they thought the System may be planning to reallocate him. He had no idea what they were talking about. It'll be disastrous if he's re-allocated – he's the one, Mum, I know he is. I can't have him taken away from me. We can accept the Award together."

I think you may be getting a little ahead of yourself.

"Are you still involved with TOHF, Mum?"

"I am, Nell, though more on an editing level these days – with regards to publicity for the election campaign."

"Could you find out anything, especially with regards to him being reallocated?"

"I'll find out who I can talk to about it."

"So they're definitely entering the election?"

"I believe so."

"Do they know who's going to lead them?"

"I think it's all being kept secret until they're obliged to declare a leader, which is in about six months."

"They wouldn't by any chance have their hopes set on Ty, would they?"

Mum laughed. "I thought you said TOHF had only just contacted him about becoming a member – they're not likely to promote him directly to leader!"

"No – it was just a mad idea of Jupiter's. Anyway, you haven't forgotten about having Alice scanned, have you? She's still acting weird, and she was alone in my livingspace when Ty's surveillance camera first connected to my screen. I wondered if she'd activated it at first."

"She wouldn't be capable, Nell. I've looked into scanning, and it's going to be difficult having it done in Scandinavia because she's such an old model. Can it wait until you come home? If she gets worse, or violent, just close her down."

"Alice, violent! No, I'm just worried the System might have got to her somehow."

"I wouldn't worry about Alice, Nell – just concentrate on your therapy, and everything else will fall into place from there."

"I love your optimism, Mum."

CONVERSATION IV

"G!" I said, smiling at her tanned, round face, "have you got a spare five minutes?"

"Of course I have, how are you getting on with Ty Martins?"

"Very, very well. I think he's the one, G."

I think so too.

"That's so wonderful, Nell. It's about time," she said. "I'm so glad you've messaged, because I've been meaning to get in touch with you for a few days. First, I don't think there's anything suspicious about Sally leading the course. As far as I can make out she's been recognised by the System as brilliant at what she does, and they're keen to encourage members of TOHF into high-profile positions."

"Election build-up, no doubt, but that's great – one less thing to worry about."

"On the other hand, if you accept the Award, which I'm sure you will now you've met Ty, you will also become an Ambassador for the System."

"Which means?"

"You and your family are supported financially, receiving payments from the Windfall Committee, for the rest of all of your lives. In return, you will be the first contact point for young people interested in becoming a journalist, for example. Or Earth Matters could ask you to represent them in their publicity campaigns – in photo shoots, or information sharing. That sort of thing."

"Sounds bizarre – they must have people already doing all of that stuff?"

"I guess it's to give a more human face to the System, Nell,"

"So, either way, life as I knew it five months ago, is over."

"How do you figure that out?" she replied.

"The status review, G, haven't I mentioned it?" I asked her, knowing I hadn't.

Coward.

"Status review?" she asked, "what on earth is that?"

"If I don't accept the Award I'll be reallocated to become a Livingspace Monitor."

"Oh no you will not! I'm not having any granddaughter of mine being 'reallocated'. Does Jenny know?"

"No."

"Just as well – she'll freak."

"Once I know if I'm accepting the Award or not, I'll tell her."

"Of course you're taking the Award, Nell, why wouldn't you! The world's going mad, thank goodness I'm the age I am. I don't understand it, I really don't – your life has been reduced to either working directly for the robots as an Ambassador, or working directly for the robots as a Livingspace Monitor."

"It wouldn't be working for the robots, G – that's impossible."

"Well, working for the System then. You know what I mean."

"I've always been working for the System. 99% of what I write has been suggested to me by the Earth Matters editor – a silver."

"Yes, but that's not the same. You're free to live as you like. Earth Matters have helped you develop your career. Whereas the Ambassador scheme or Livingspace Monitor means you are controlled."

"I know. I'm still struggling to understand it all."

"Well, one thing is for sure, Nell – they must really like you."

THE DAY DEREK ARRIVES

Ty and I had breakfast in bed. Well, when I say breakfast, just an apple. He sat next to me, with his legs under the quilt and carefully peeled the apple. Then he sliced it whole, into thin circles. He arranged all of the circles over my chest, and then picked one up at a time. First he fed me a slice, then himself. Our eyes didn't leave one another.

I mean, how's a heart supposed to cope with such romance?

"I definitely love you, Nell Greene," Ty said, feeding me the final slice of apple.

Panic! Nope. No need to panic.

"Well, Ty Martins, I do think I definitely love you too," I replied, smiling like a child.

Well done. Good idea keeping the 'think' in, just to be on the safe side.

"You know you can trust me, don't you, Nell?"

Ruby and Youssan flashed into my thoughts.

Of course you can trust him.

"I know trust's a big one for you, Nell, I just need you to know I'll never let you down."

"I trust you, Ty. And I'll never let you down either." We kissed.

My heart's going to burst. We've done it!

We have, Cyd – apart from the fact today I have to go to the port to collect Derek!

DEREK

Affirmation for today: All is as it should be.

Sally lent me the centre's suncar to drive the two hours to the Port.

Clever; was my first thought when I saw Derek standing in the terminal. Not that he looked clever; but that the Dating Committee had been clever in their choice. He was very attractive in a clean-shaven way.

Fickle. What about Ty?

I'm only saying he's attractive. Calm down!

He held his chin high. His wavy blond hair was swept back off his face and tumbled down around his ears. He was wearing a cream coloured shirt, unbuttoned at the neck, and he had one hand in his jacket pocket. With the other hand he tapped his roamer against his thigh.

Get it over with, Nell.

I took a deep breath.

Be pleasant, but distant.

"Derek, Hi, I'm Nell."

I shook his cold, smooth hand. Not the sort of hand I was expecting from a Geologist.

"Nell Greene. Hello. You recognised me from the photo the committee sent you then."

"Just. But as the only other two people in here are women, I thought you were a safe bet."

"Indeed," he said smiling. "Thanks for coming to pick me up."

"No problem, though I wasn't actually given a choice."

"Ouch!" he said. "Your first time through the Dating Committee?"

"Yep."

"I'll be gentle then," he said, and winked.

I hate winks. Winks belong to men who fancy themselves. A wink is presumptuous. Ty doesn't wink.

"Let Alice take your bag on her tow hitch."

"Alice?"

"Alice: my cowbot. Alice meet Derek, Derek meet Alice."

"Quaint," he said, looking down at Alice.

Her ears flattened back against her head. "Quaint? What sort of word is that?" she said.

"Alice! Don't be so rude." I gave her a nudge.

"Ah. Sorry," Derek said to Alice, "you've obviously had some emotional programming over the years. Please forgive me."

"Sorry, Derek, it's been a tricky few months, hasn't it, Alice?"

Alice didn't say a word.

"Shall we head straight back, or would you like to have a look around?"

"Let's head back, then we can have a cup of tea and start getting to know one another."

Grim.

"What are you going to be doing here?" I asked him

"Don't you know? I'm here for three months. I'm working on new promotional information for the different therapy centres in Scandinavia. I'm spending the first three weeks at the centre with you, and then I shall be travelling around."

"I thought you were a geologist."

"I am. The information I'm gathering is based on geo-thermal energy. The Health Committee is researching the possibility of geo-thermal healing rooms."

"What's that got to do with the Dating Committee?"

"Nothing. The Dating Committee's involvement is purely supplying you with a perfect match."

"Anyway, I'm done at GreenWaters in under four weeks, so you're going to be here alone for a while."

"Hopefully not," he winked.

I felt the muscles of my neck spasm.

"Do you have any music other than ancient disco?" Derek asked as we drove back to the centre.

"I'm afraid that's it," I said.

"Maybe you should start an Original Disco Fan Foundation, in competition with TOHF for the leadership," he said, laughing.

I looked at him suspiciously through a haze of Sister Sledge.

"What!" he said.

"Switch yourself onto solo listening if you really can't stand it."

"How much further is it?" he asked.

"We're half way."

He made no switch to solo.

"How's the therapy going?"

"Really well, it's fascinating how complex the mind is. I've learnt things about myself I never thought possible, and I've made some good friends."

"I thought you were all reallocation cases."

How would he know that?

"Reallocation 'cases'. You make it sound like some kind of mental disorder. And anyway, what difference does that make to friendship?"

"Just not a lot of point I'd have thought if you're never going to see one another again."

"That's a pretty short-sighted reason for not making friends. And anyway, how do you know about the reallocations?"

"The information I was given by the Windfall Committee before coming."

"Windfall Committee?"

"Sorry," he stammered, "the Dating Committee."

"What's your connection with the Windfall Committee?"

"There isn't one – just a slip of the tongue."

His eyes searched the dashboard, as if looking for support.

"How can a tongue slip from Windfall to Dating?"

"What are you, Private Investigator Greene? I was reading the latest committee bulletin before you arrived. The Windfall Committee have been talking about adjusting the one-off payment they give to parents when their children are born. There's talk of splitting the cost with the Health Committee, so, for example, rather than Windfall paying a lump sum until the child reaches seventeen, Health would pay for the first ten years, until after they've done the first health scan, and then Windfall would pay for the following seven years. Reading between the lines, I think they're broke. I've been reading up on you, too, Nell," he said, tapping his roamer.

"Oh yes?"

"I'd just flicked up 'Underground' when you arrived. I didn't get a chance to start it. Off the music and I'll read it out loud now."

"Really? I do remember it, funnily enough!"

"I'd like to," he said. "Anything's got to be better than 20th century disco-shite."

He cleared his throat.

"I love disco music," Alice said.

UNDERGROUND

"Eh hem."

'UNDERGROUND: An Interview with Rose Cherman.

Rose Cherman, aged one hundred and six, is one of the eldest remaining survivors of the underground parks, and recently she shared her memories of those years with me:'

"When I say me, obviously I mean you, Nell, because you are who wrote it."

'Yellowstone is on North American soil, and so obviously the American Government had to announce the possibility of an eruption, Rose, who worked in one of the Preservation parks, says. The problem was the rest of the world didn't trust America by 2036, and most people believed the announcements to be election propaganda – if America could save the planet's population from total disaster, maybe the world would take them seriously again.'

"Like in the old Superman movies."

'And when did that sentiment of suspicion change, Rose?

About a year after the first announcement. Underground transport systems all around the world – mostly in the Southern Hemisphere – were closed for conversion into survival parks. It was total anarchy – there was rioting and businesses closed because their staff couldn't get to work. Armies had to guard the construction teams. Russia refused guidance from the USA regarding park creation. Spain and Italy were the only two European countries to agree to creating parks – don't ask me why. North America was to be evacuated entirely, which was impossible – people wouldn't leave their homes based on a 'maybe'.

And other countries in the Northern Hemisphere?

They were 'advised' to evacuate. With hindsight, more people would have survived if they hadn't been given a choice. But America was covering it's back – I mean, can you imagine how many compensation claims would have been filed if people had left their jobs, homes and animals for nothing?

And if you did evacuate, where did you go?

To pre-fabricated towns that were being built, too slowly, in Spain, Italy and the Southern Hemisphere, Rose says.'

"I cannot imagine how that must have been."
"It is pretty impossible to imagine," I said.

'A friend of mine worked on one of the park construction teams in Sydney. He could not believe how complex it was – communication systems were installed: complex air filtration systems: water storage and filtration: sewage treatment systems: generators: batteries: stocks of fuel. There was a hydroponic farm. There were media rooms, theatres, canteens, and thousands of rooms with bunk beds in. When he told me about it, I knew the threat of eruption was serious.

So you evacuated?

Yes. To one of the make-shift towns in Spain. I'd worked with a wildlife trust, so put my name down for a place in a Preservation park. That's where I met my husband – he was in the aviary section. The bird-squawking nearly drove him mad.'

"Can you imagine? And the smell!"
"He didn't eat an egg ever again," Alice said.

'I was lucky, I worked in the insect park, and I grew to love all of them, but silverfish became my absolute favourite. They are beautiful little creatures. And ancient

– probably more than a hundred million years. They can out run a spider, and live without eating for a year. They kept me company on many sleepless nights in the park, and some of them used to sit on my fingertips quite happily. One, I called Hannah, lived for six years – she almost made it out to freedom.

And what did people think about having different classifications for the parks, Rose?

I suppose they had to sort them out somehow – but the Gov parks were seen as elitist and discriminatory. Then after a year underground something happened: the previously warring religious leaders started to talk to one another. They started to pray together, and they started to discuss how we could all build a more peaceful future. Was the name of their God the most important thing? Or was the most important thing that people live their lives to their highest potential. They decided the latter was the answer. And then, quite miraculously, they decided to unite.

It's hard for those of us born after the Disaster to believe so much hatred existed.

I know – none of you really believe it. But Spirituals (previously known as religious leaders) were serious – and they campaigned the remaining governments tirelessly. They said the disaster had been a gift, giving the population a fresh chance to create a peaceful planet. Neutral Faith programmes were developed and broadcast in all parks at peak listening times for five of the seven years underground. They were brilliant – very entertaining, very interesting and extremely challenging. Park-occupants all over the world were opening their hearts, and healing. Enemies hugged one another. They cried and laughed together. Two old East African men who I will never forget as long as I live – one Tutsi and one Hutu inspired many others when they met and talked and forgave. The Tutsi man's entire family had been massacred – and if he could forgive a man who had helped kill them, then we are all capable of forgiveness. The buzz of hope in the parks was electric. It was an absolute triumph. The underground population was transformed.'

"Do you believe all of that happened, Nell? Young people now have this counter theory that religions were never at war in the first place – but all the unity and forgiveness was staged to create a more generic world, so being ruled by robots wouldn't be so shocking."

"Maybe young people should read some history books," Alice said.

'The eruption was predicted for January 2043, and lots of people moved underground, including me, taking up my job in the insect park.

You were one of half a billion people, according to the records.'

"Imagine the logistics."

'But Yellowstone didn't blow, and people grew fed up of the daily warnings, so lots of them left and went back home. I'd already noticed this rather attractive man who was in the bird section, so I thought I'd stay and get to know him a little better! In April, news channels reported the floor of the Yellowstone caldera had started bulging upwards, and there were lots of mini-earthquakes, so again, lots of people fled underground.

A billion people this time.

Again, a week later many of them left. Not me – I'd found the courage to talk to Rem, and we were getting on really well! I remember watching the news on my phone on the 29th of July 2043. After six hundred and forty thousand years, Yellowstone could hold on no longer, and it blasted twenty-five kilometres upward into the atmosphere. My phone went dead. Everyone ran around the park following the drills we'd been practicing for months. All the entrance doors were sealed shut. And then the piped music started up. I don't think I'll ever experience a more bizarre moment.

Around six billion people (the majority of them in the Northern Hemisphere, despite the evacuation warnings) had remained on the surface, many of them building make-shift fallout shelters and underground bunkers. But hardly any had realised how long they would need to live in them.

Conditions in the parks were cramped, to say the least. But we survived. You are here today, Nell, because of those parks. I'll never forget the moment – about six years after the eruption – the parks started letting non-filtered, fresh air in. People partied for days – hanging around the air vents, gulping in their beloved planet. We were all desperate to leave the parks. But finally, when we did, the scenes were traumatic. The reality of how few people on the surface had survived finally sunk in.

Rose, thank you so much for sharing your memories with us.

Article by Nell Greene'

"Not bad, Nell."

"Thank-you."

"Not bad! What does that even mean," Alice said.

"I've visited the Caracas survival parks memorial. I don't know how people lived down there for years on end. The conditions were so cramped. I think I'd have gone dooloo," Derek said.

"Better than the alternative on the surface. I went to the Government memorial park in Madrid. If you've visited a civilian park, you have to go to a government park – the difference is hard to stomach. The Government parks had private bedrooms, and lots of small dining rooms offering different cuisine. No massive canteens for them."

"Things were so different then, Nell, weren't they? You were rich or poor. Powerful or not."

"Here we are," I said, as we pulled up at the centre.

"Listen, I'm tired," I said, after he took his luggage out of the car. "I've been doing some extra sessions over the past five days, so I'll leave you to sort out your space and settle in. I'll catch up with you tomorrow."

Extra sessions is a good way of putting it!

"Let me treat you to dinner, Nell," he said.

"No, really, I'm exhausted. Treat me tomorrow."

He kissed me on the cheek.

Better than a wink, I suppose.

THE BULLETIN

"I'm proud of that interview, Alice," I said, as we walked into my livingspace.

And so you should be.

"Do you remember how excited Granma had been to have me interview her?"

"How could I ever forget!"

"Are you coming round to Ty's with me?"

"No. I need to re-charge. I'll see you later."

When I got back, Alice was waiting for me.

"I've been catching up on life outside Scandinavia, Nell," she said. "More improvements are being made to the solar parks in the States of America. Chip fraud is on the rise – no surprises there. There's been a protest about the amount of work pupils are being given to do in their breaks. One of the last surviving turtles from the underground parks has died, aged eighty-five, and France beat Spain in the inter-ed sports challenge."

"Great, Alice. Thanks for the update. Couldn't it have waited until morning?"

"I also caught up with this morning's committee bulletin – the one Derek mentioned. He said the Windfall Committee gave out some information," she added, looking at me, "but the thing is, I can't find it."

I streamed the bulletin on my roamer.

She was right, there was no mention of the Windfall Committee.

BALL OF TRUST

As I ate breakfast, my screen bleeped.

Nell, Can't make it over this afternoon, sorry. See you tomorrow, I'll explain all then. Ty

Here we go.

My mind raced back to Youssan's message five months ago. I picked up my roamer and called Ty. No answer. My scalp was heating up.

I'm sure it's nothing to worry about.

"Odd he didn't call, Alice."

"Very unlike, Ty. There's obviously a problem."

"What kind of problem?"

"TOHF?" Alice said.

Or reconciliation with Mara.

No chance.

My ears started buzzing.

Unless he's feeling unsure now Derek's here.

He knows I don't want Derek.

Well then.

Maybe someone else has turned up.

Like who?

Well there must be other women who like him.

Hundreds, I'm sure. But why would any of them be here?

"I'm going over to his and see what's going on."

"I'll come too," Alice said.

We reached his livingspace: empty. My heart beat too fast.

"Bit early for him to have started therapy isn't it?"

"Never too early to start therapy, Nell," Alice said.

Or perhaps he did a sunrise watch.

Or perhaps he didn't stay here last night.

Perhaps.

Breathe, Nell. All is as it should be. Breathe. Now is all there is.

***

"Sally, are you free for the day?" I asked, walking into the Lounge.

"Yep. Why?"

"Can I have a session?"

"Of course. Are you alright?"

"Not really. Cyd's fired up."

I have not! You have.

"Okay. Put your palm on your solar plexus and take some deep breaths. Now, what's Cyd firing about?"

Nothing.

"Trust, as always."

"It's a beautiful day. How about we go outside to work?"

"Love to."

Sally, Alice and I walked up behind the therapy centre into a peaceful, wide open meadow. I could see three hundred and sixty degrees around me.

"PINK CLOVER ALERT!" Alice shouted, whizzing round in circles, "I love pink clover."

How can she? She's not programmed to love.

"And geraniums, Alice," Sally added, pointing to patches of mauve.

"This is going to be the best day EVER," Alice said.

Sally took a blanket out of her backpack and spread it out in full sunshine.

Ty would love this.

But he's somewhere else.

"I thought I was in control, Sally. I thought I'd changed. But everything has been churned up again."

"When you say, everything, Nell, what exactly?"

"Suspicion. Anxiety."

"About what?"

"Ty. I got a message from him this morning, and it was more or less the same as one I'd had from Youssan. It's sparked things off."

"Do you trust Ty?"

I stared at the blanket.

"I know this is one of your main issues, Nell, but, be honest with yourself, do you trust, Ty?"

You told him you do only three days ago!

Alice scuttled over to a patch of mauve.

I stayed silent.

"What do you think trust is, Nell?" Sally asked.

I looked across the meadow towards the bay. "I think it's dangerous, Sally...and impossible.

"Impossible?"

"Well how can you know what someone's up to when they're not with you?"

"You can't."

"Which makes me suspicious."

"And what happens when you feel suspicious?"

You cry.

"I feel anxious," I said, my chest tightening.

"Right, then let's start there," Sally said. "Okay, Nell. Breathe. Take deep breaths, one after the other."

Hey, that feels nice.

"So, can you tell me where suspicion is most intense."

"In my head."

"Where, exactly?"

"Here," I said, pressing my palm up against my forehead.

"Can you vision a colour in that area?"

"Bright red."

"Red? Indigo is the colour for the chakra where you have your hand, so the fact you're seeing red in its place could explain why things are off."

Sally took some coloured paper-balls out of her bag. "Right. Take the red one."

I did. Then she handed me a length of string and some transparent tape and asked me to attach the string to my ball. "Now, hold the ball to the area of your body where suspicion is most powerful."

I held the ball to my head.

"You look mental," Alice said, having returned from her patch of geraniums, "I shouldn't have come back so quickly." She scurried to a different patch.

She does have a point.

"Excellent, Nell. The ball you're holding represents Trust."

I threw it backwards over my head.

Bit extreme.

"My next question was going to be how comfortable you feel with Trust this close to you."

I laughed.

"Okay. You need to go and get hold of the string, Nell, and leave the ball where it is."

"Is this for real?" Alice asked, as we walked up the meadow together.

"Yes, Alice. If this ball and string can help, then I'm willing to give it a try."

"Seems nuts. You can trust Ty, you know you can. In fact, you told him you do! Cyd's still the problem. Get rid of her and you'll be fine."

Oi Fluffy! Watch it!

"I don't know if it is Cyd anymore, Alice. I think it might have been me all along."

"Nonsense," Alice said, as we arrived at the ball. I unwound the string.

"How are you feeling, Nell?" Sally shouted up the meadow.

"Anxious!"

"Oh for ef's sake," Alice said, and whizzed off.

With the string in hand, I walked back down to Sally.

"Right," Sally said. "Imagine if the first time you'd sat in *Lily the Pink* she'd travelled at walking pace, in a completely straight, flat line…"

"…Nice…"

"…For five minutes."

"Possibly boring."

"Exactly. I think after about a minute you would have been bored. As too, I think, if your emotions stayed permanently on one level – you'd be bored."

"I'd give it a go."

"Everyone experiences suspicion, Nell, and most of us have had our trust betrayed."

"I know, Sally. I know none of my 'stuff' is earth-shatteringly awful, but it makes me feel the way it makes me feel. Just because people have similar issues and feel shit about themselves, it doesn't mean how I feel isn't valid, does it? Or are you saying because they're such common experiences I shouldn't let them affect me?"

"No, sorry, I'm not saying that at all."

We both stared out to sea.

"Nell, have you ever heard the tale by the Sufi Sage, Jalaluddin Rumi?"

"No."

"It goes like this," she said. "'A soul was questioned by God at the gates of Heaven, "You are the same as when you left! You were blessed by a life full of opportunity – so where are the bruises and scars left by your journey?"'"

FROM RED TO INDIGO

"You have a choice, Nell: bring order into your inner world – and accept that it may be a little calmer, or forget therapy and embrace the disorder," Sally said.

"I'm sticking with therapy, Sally. Twenty-five years of chaos is enough."

"In that case, Nell, make yourself comfy on the blanket, we're going to bring Trust down the field and out to the front of you."

We turned our backs to the ball.

"Feeling suspicious and untrusting has become a habit though, Sally."

I'm glad you've admitted it. Now you can understand how tricky it is for me to get used to being nice. Can't happen overnight, can it?

"How do I change a habit?"

"Be aware it is a habit, Nell. The next time you feel suspicious, ask yourself for evidence. When there isn't any, ask why you keep doing this to yourself. What is the point?"

That's you I'll be asking, Cyd.

Good. Because I'll tell you you are safe to trust.

"Of course the change may be difficult at first. The mind is clever, Nell, it gets good at what you let it get away with. Remember though, it's your mind – you are in control."

"I got a message from Ty this morning, saying he can't see me this afternoon. Cyd's telling me he spent the night with Mara."

LIAR!

"Their marriage is over, Nell."

"I know, Sally. But I can't stop feeling suspicious."

"Okay, so give questioning a try: What evidence…"

"…do I have that Ty spent the night with Mara? None."

Correct.

"What is the point of me thinking that!" I said.

There's no point.

I picked up Greenie and wrote: Question your anxiety. Ask for evidence.

I took a deep breath in, and pulled the string hard. Trust bounced to a stop, about two metres behind me.

We heard a bleep behind us. I'm sure Sally didn't notice any difference, but I could see Alice's ears twitching, and her wheels wobbling ever so slightly underneath her.

"You alright, Alice?" I asked.

She didn't answer.

"Alice! Are you okay?"

"Everything under control this end," she replied.

Sally and I looked at each other.

"Can Alice send and receive?" Sally asked me.

"I've never had her re-programmed, so, no."

"What year model is she?"

"2089."

"I doubt it then. Anyway, back to business, Nell, how do you feel with Trust this close?"

"Nervous."

Alice joined us on the blanket.

"Right. Let's see if you can turn the colour in your head from red to indigo, and go from there. Why don't you close your eyes. Do you think you can picture something indigo?"

"Yes, easily – I have a flower-patch cushion made from antique Tuareg cloth."

"Perfect. Think about the cushion and imagine indigo filling up your forehead chakra."

I smiled. "Ooh, I feel happy," I said, opening my eyes. I turned around and pulled trust closer. I picked it up. I kissed it, and threw it out in front of me. I shuffled to the edge of the blanket and un-taped the string.

"Is there a firelighter in your bag, Sally?"

I set fire to the red ball, and watched it disappear into the grass. Then I picked up the closest coloured ball I could find to indigo and held it to my forehead. I breathed the colour in, and out.

"If Granma saw you now she'd call the meltdown centre," Alice said.

Our laughter filled the warm, sunny afternoon, and I swore I would take responsibility for my thoughts, and ask for evidence whenever I became suspicious. I felt light and free inside. We stood up, and I rubbed my palms as Sally packed up the blanket.

"Look!" Alice shouted. "There's a boat out in Deserted Bay."

Sally grabbed some binoculars from her pack. "Windfall Committee," she said. "What can they possible want?"

She passed the binoculars across to me.

"Maybe they've come to talk to Mara and Ty about managing their children's units after they split."

"Maybe," Sally said.

"That's why he couldn't make this afternoon," Alice said.

"Right. Focus, Nell. Forget the boat. Let's give one last acknowledgement to what you've shifted today, and leave the old stuff up here in the meadow. You're heading back to the centre with a different relationship to Trust."

Amen to that.

I took a deep breath in.

"Oh God, not another embarrassing moment," Alice said, rolling quickly ahead. "I wish I'd stayed at home polishing."

TY'S STORY

By the time Alice and I arrived back at our livingspace, it was getting chilly. We'd just walked through the door when my wall-screen flashed on.

"Did you do that?" Alice said.

"Just about to ask you the same thing."

We looked towards the wall and saw Ty, sideways on, sitting on his sofa, staring open-mouthed at *his* screen.

"Look at the clock behind him, Nell."

07:15.

"And the light on his trousers – that's morning sun. I think this is a recording."

"Why on earth..."

"...no idea..."

"Shit. Sally hasn't deactivated his surveillance camera."

"Might as well watch it then," Alice said – rushing towards the sofa.

I picked her up and we sat side by side.

A panel of four female Silvers, all with their beautifully chiselled cheek-bones, were on Ty's wall-screen. Each one wore a different coloured open-neck t-shirt. They sat behind a long wooden table with piles and piles of discs lined up in-front of them.

"Hello, Ty," orange-shirt on the right said.

"We are delegates of the Livelihood Committee, Ty," green-shirt said. "We are sorry to contact you so early in the day, but due to the sensitivity of this communication we decided it was necessary to ensure we find you alone. You need to understand however, we are purely serving as a communication panel and what we are about to say has come from the Livelihood committee direct. Their decision is final and we do not have the authority to change anything. Is that clear?"

"Carry on," Ty said.

"Is that clear?" Green-shirt on the left repeated.

Silence.

"Certain issues concerning your marriage and your children have been brought to the Committee's attention, and they have examined your medical records. As a result of that examination, we are very sorry to have to inform you that you are sterile."

Ty burst out laughing.

"We are glad you are taking the news well…"

"What? You're not being serious."

"Do not interrupt us please, Ty…"

"I damn well will interrupt you. I have two healthy children, or have you forgotten?"

"Biologically the children are not yours."

"So I'll have some more."

"And biologically you cannot contribute to the population of the planet."

"I want proof of that. Why would you have examined my medical records?"

Alice and I stared at one another.

"Shit, Alice. Ty, sterile?"

"Something is really very wrong here," she replied.

My heart pounded, my mouth dried.

"Because of these findings, you are to be reallocated."

"NO!" Alice shouted.

"I refuse," Ty said, "if it hadn't been for me, Ems would never have had the affair, and the two children would never have been born anyway, so biologically I may not be their father, but technically I am. And I'm sure you understand *all* about the technical side of things. Plus, I am demanding proof that I am sterile."

"This decision has been taken by the System, and it has been passed down to us to communicate to you."

"You ARE the System; all of the Committees and panels make up the System."

"We are purely communicating the findings to you, Ty."

"I'm not very surprised – the other three participants here on the course have been given reallocation assignments, so I've been waiting for you to make contact. I figured, if they are all re-alls, I must be too."

The Silvers looked at one another and chattered quietly amongst themselves. "How do you know about the assignments

174

of the others? Like this communication, that information is private, and you should not tell anyone."

"I'll tell whoever I choose. I am human, and humans crave friendship and love and company, and in the process of having those things we talk, and trust, and share things with one another."

"It is forbidden to share this information," green-shirt said.

"Why? You've never 'forbidden' anything before. Why now? Anyway, it's too late. We've already shared, and there's not a damn thing you, or the 'Population Committee', or 'Windfall Committee', or 'Dating Committee', can do about it."

"They're not going to like that," Alice said, looking up at me.

"Your revelations will be forwarded to the Director, Ty, and they will be dealt with appropriately. As far as we are concerned, the decision has been taken for you to be reallocated one month after you have finished this course of therapy."

"*WHAT?*" Ty leapt up out of his seat.

"Please remain calm, Ty, or we will have to send a health member to sedate you."

"Sedate me? What are you talking about? You can't reallocate someone because they can't have children. What happened to the System supporting the population in growing into who they strive to be?"

"Times have changed," purple-shirt said.

Did I see the orange-shirt hang her head ever so slightly?

"The programming team have changed, you mean. You wouldn't be giving out any of these re-allocation assignments if it wasn't for them. They're scared of being voted out."

"That is all we can say to you at this time."

"I cannot be reallocated. What about my boys? What about my farm and the example it sets? What about my bulletins and programmes with Farming First?"

"You have been recognised for your hard work in this area, and your reallocation assignment will reflect this. You will, nevertheless, be reallocated seven weeks from now."

I dropped my head into my hands.

"Something is terribly wrong," Alice said. "Do you realise what this means? You've fallen in love with a man who you now find out is sterile, so you wouldn't be able to accept the Award. Isn't that just a bit strange?"

"I can't think about that right now, Alice."

"Well it's exactly what you need to think about, Nell. Not only is he so-called 'sterile', but he's going to be reallocated. That gives you and him absolutely nullo hope of ever reproducing. Which means you and I will also be reallocated."

I looked back to Ty, who moved to the window, staring out over Deserted Bay.

"That's where I fell in love with him, Alice."

"Yes, great. Now is not the time to be getting sentimental, Nell. It's the time to be getting seriously concerned."

"I will not let this happen," Ty said, turning to face the screen.

"I'm afraid you have no choice," yellow-shirt said.

"There's always a choice," Ty replied. "I fear you may have underestimated me."

"No, Ty, we have not. We are sorry for the news, but the decision cannot be altered. We will be in touch with you in writing to inform you of your reallocation assignment in more detail."

And with that Ty's screen cleared. He paced up and down in front of the windows before scooping Shilly up, and tousling her woolly head.

I hugged Alice.

"Why didn't he come over here?" I asked Alice.

"What did you do when you received the first communication about the Award?"

"Talked it all through with you."

"For ages. So that's what he'll do with Shilly."

Breathe. All is as it should be.

He put Shilly back down, went over to the kitchen, and started chopping up a stick of celery faster and faster and into smaller and smaller pieces.

"What the hell are we going to do, Shilly?" he said.

"Fight it," she said.

"*Fight it?*" shouted Alice. "What the hell is she talking about?"

"Okay," said Ty, "you're on."

TY'S BATTLE BEGINS

The recording of Ty's space continued to run. His screen lit up with a written message.

To Ty Martins
To confirm our conversation earlier today.

"You call that a bloody conversation!"

You are to face re-allocation four weeks after you have completed your therapy.

"What was the ashing point of me coming on therapy then? What a total and utter waste of time and resources."

Your reallocation assignment is as follows: you will develop ed materials about natural farming suitable for all fourteen to nineteen-year-olds. You will live with other ed developers, and will be free to travel to farms to give demonstrations.

We hope this has not come as too much of a shock to you.

"As if you really care."

We are sure you will be happy in your assignment, and everyone is looking forward to meeting you.

The Livelihood Committee

Ty collapsed back onto the sofa, with sunlight surrounding him. The clock behind him changed to 09:00 – just about fifteen minutes before he had sent me the message this morning.

He got up and paced around, Shilly following at his heels. He sat down, he stood up, he paced.

"Any of this got anything to do with Derek, Shilly?"

"Shouldn't think so, he looks like too much of a geek."

Alice laughed, and I flicked her with my index finger.

"Well, TOHF sent me that letter for a reason, and I think now is the right time to make my acquaintances."

"No, Ty!" I said to the screen. "He's getting himself into trouble, Alice. He's already been rude to the Livelihood Committee and now he's going to contact TOHF."

"I'll send a quick message to Nell to cancel this afternoon, and then we can crack on sorting this out."

The image of Ty cleared.

Alice looked up at me.

"Don't say it, Alice. Ty's just been given devastating news and all I could think about was whether he'd been shacked up with Mara all night. God, I'm shit."

Correct.

"Don't worry," Alice said. "No-one knows but you and me."

And me! And Sally!

My wall-screen flashed up again. This time I looked in on Mara's space, and the clock said 09:20.

"You got a minute?" Ty asked her, walking through the door.

"How fucked up is that?" Mara said, once Ty had explained the messages. She held him and cried with him.

My solar plexus fizzed.

It's of no importance. She is not a threat.

"Can I use your screen? It'd be better if it couldn't be traced to my livingspace."

"Oh great, but it's okay if it's traced here."

"Well, you've already accepted your reallocation, haven't you? But I'm not accepting mine."

"Why don't I stay with you for the day – you must be feeling terrible."

My head started warming up. Nice try, Mara.

For God's sake, she's trying to help him!

"No. I'm okay. It's given me a focus. I intend to spend every second I have left in the free world fighting their decision."

"But you'll never get anywhere, Ty. Drop it," Mara pleaded. "Drop it, Ty, please, you could make things a lot worse for yourself."

"What, could possibly be worse than having to leave all I love and go and write learning materials with no freedom to move around!"

"They've thought about your assignment, Ty. They've given you a job they think you might enjoy. That's a hell of a lot more than they've done for Nell or me. Maybe they've found out about the letter from the Foundation asking you to join. Maybe they see you as a threat – they know you have a following on the

Farming First stream – maybe they think you'll try and influence your followers to vote for the Foundation."

"Maybe. It's not going to stop me though. And I'll be fighting for all of us, by the way, not just me."

Mara walked out without another word.

Ty sat down at Mara's table and started writing:

To The Original Human Foundation

Thank you so much for your recent letter· I am impressed by how timely it was, because indeed today I have received both a verbal and written communication from the Livelihood Committee···

"I think that sounds a bit sarcastic," Shilly said.

He screwed it up into a ball and set fire to it.

Shilly silently vacuumed up the ash.

He burnt three letters in all, before settling for this:

To The Original Human Foundation

Thank you very much for your recent letter·

I assume by the timeliness of your correspondence, you were aware I was about to hear from the Livelihood Committee·

They have today informed me I am to be re-allocated four weeks after I leave here· The reason given is because I am sterile, and therefore cannot contribute to the future population of the planet· I don't believe that is true, and I am getting more than a little suspicious· There is a woman on the course with me, Nell Greene· She is a non-active member of the Foundation, and I think you know her Mum and Dad better·

Are you aware she received a message five months ago honouring her with the Award? Well, it stated that if she isn't pregnant within eighteen months, she will be subject to a status review· As you suggested in your letter, the status review really means reallocation·

Nell and I have fallen in love, and we hope to marry and have children of our own·

Marriage? When was that ever mentioned?

"What the bloody hell? Alice! Did you see that?"

Three days ago, the Dating Committee sent Nell a perfect match – Derek – a geologist· I assume they are supposed to fall in love· I mean, who names their child, Derek?

As I already mentioned, today, I have been informed I am sterile and will be reallocated – which means there is no hope for Nell and I· I am beginning to think this chain of happenings revolves around Nell· Could you help me investigate further?

I have no intention of being reallocated, and would also like your assistance in fighting the System·

What do you think? Please contact me on my roamer – the code is attached· If I have not heard from you by this evening, I will contact you within the next forty-eight hours·

Oh, and of course I would be more than happy to join The Foundation and help however I can towards the coming elections·

Ty Martins

He photo'd the letter to his roamer, and tapped in a number.

My screen cleared.

"I'm going over to see him."

"You can't, he said he couldn't see you, remember?" Alice replied.

Not still paranoid about Mara, are you?

No.

Sure?
Positive.
Brilliant. There's no need to be.
"I don't care, I'm going over. He must be feeling terrible."
"Don't, he'll know you know what's been going on."
My screen flashed.

Nell, Fancy coming over for a bite to eat? Derek

"That's the last thing I feel like doing."
"I know," Alice said, "but I think it's the one thing you must do. And find out if he's ever got anyone pregnant."
"Alice!"

DINNER WITH DEREK

Derek opened the door and kissed me on the cheek.

"Did you have a good day with Sally?"

"Productive," I replied. "How about your day?"

"Interesting. If, of course, almost drowning can be termed as interesting."

"Drowning?"

"I'd taken a boat to another centre, and on the way back the captain swerved to avoid a rock and nearly dumped me overboard."

"What time was that?"

"Around four."

"We saw the boat from the meadow," I said, studying his face. He maintained eye contact.

"Which centre did you visit?"

"Pine Needles Park."

"And they sent the boat?"

"Yep."

"Then how come the boat had Windfall Committee written on the side?"

"Did it?" he said, surprised.

Impressive eye contact.

I looked over at Alice, whose ears laid tightly back against her head.

"Oh come on, you can't have missed it! We could see it from way up in the meadow!"

"Pine Needles must loan it from the Windfall Committee then. What's your problem with the Committee, anyway?"

Alice started to wander around his space, inspecting the walls and floors.

"After I received my Award, someone mentioned to me the Windfall Committee carry out a 'love-test' on all couples about to have their first child."

"Can you blame them? The Committee credits such a huge number of units to parents for their child, that some couples have been scamming."

"I don't understand why they need to issue the units like that. Why not give parents an annual amount, rather than seventeen-years' worth? It doesn't make sense."

"It's all about budgets, Nell. The System knows how many children will be born each year, and they know exactly how much it will cost to feed, clothe, educate, house, la-la-la, that child. By giving a one-off payment, the units become the responsibility of the parents – which I think is a good idea."

"But not if couples are scamming. Did your parents manage your units?"

"Meticulously. They were so worried the units would run out before I turned 17, that my ed trips were few, we rarely went on holiday, and my roamer was always a hand-on model from my uncle, or nephews. I must admit I was vexed by that – I wanted a modern roamer like my friends had."

"And the units lasted until your 17th?"

"Yes, with a few thousand to spare. Mum and Dad used it to pay for me to go to the best science college in Central America. Did yours last?"

"Just. But I don't know how they think a love-test can prove anything."

"I think it sieves the obvious fakes." He started dishing out a bean chilli. "I'm vegetarian, hope you don't mind."

"Not a bit."

"How about dinner at yours tomorrow night, Nell?" he asked.

Should I tell him about Ty so he backs off?

No. Not yet.

"Tomorrow's no good for me," I said. "How about I message you when I'm next free?"

I doubt he'll give up easily. The only reason he's here is to have a relationship with you, remember?

"Are you with Sally tomorrow?"

"I think so, yes."

"So you'll be free the day after?"

"Give me a few days. I'm trying to put all my efforts into therapy, Derek."

"Well let's hope the Dating Committee doesn't do a random visit," he said.

"Are they likely to?"

"The way things are going recently, I'd say anything's possible."

ACCOUNTABILITY

Affirmation for Today: It is safe to trust.

Just as I was heading out to the Lounge, desperate to see Ty, my screen bleeped.

"Nell, darling. How are you getting on?" Granma said. "Have you noticed anyone acting suspiciously around your therapy centre?"

"No, G, why?"

"I watched a live Accountability Matters two nights ago, and the Windfall Committee were being questioned about their budget – or rather, lack of it. It caught my attention, because that's who you'll be getting your Award payments from, isn't it?"

"It is."

"Well anyway, it appears they're broke. They've squandered millions of units they were given when the Committees were first created, and they've been trying to hide it from the Director."

"How could they do that?"

"Apparently the Programming Team have been funding a secret 'artificial consciousness' trial with Windfall Committee funds. The Silvers have computed something bad has happened and they have suggested deleting the Committee."

"That's funny, I was only talking about the Windfall Committee budget last night with Derek."

"Derek?"

"My 'perfect match', G – the Dating Committee have sent him here, hoping we'll fall in love, and I'll take the Award!"

"Whatever next?!" she said. "Why didn't you tell the Committee about Ty?"

"I did. They said there was nothing they could do – Derek's trip was already finalised."

"What a total waste of resources!"

"I know!"

"I don't know how you're coping, Nell, I really don't. What are they going to throw at you next? Well anyway, apparently, the Programming Team have been 'acquiring' information from meltdown centres and therapy centres to feed it into their artificial consciousness research. Obviously they can't log that in the Committee expenditure, so they've been making up bogus projects – one of which is a promotional exercise based around the love-test at new therapy centres in Scandinavia!"

"Derek is up here doing promotional work!"

"Ashing hell!" Alice said, "he has made a couple of slip-ups mentioning the Windfall Committee too, hasn't he, Nell!"

"But Derek was sent up here by the Dating Committee."

"According to who?" G asked.

"According to him, and the Dating Committee. They gave him the geo-thermal research so he'd have something useful to do here."

"Bit of a coincidence," G said. "Sounds like you need to find out more about him, Nell. I'll see if I can uncover anything. Remember to lock your door at night. Love you both."

THE LOG CABIN

As I walked towards the glass-walled Lounge, I could see Ty massaging Mara's shoulder.

My heart flipped.

It is safe to trust.

Thanks, Cyd. Doesn't really matter anyway does it, if Ty's being reallocated.

I opened the door.

"Nell, oh love of Ty's life," Mara said, smiling.

See?

Ty laughed and blew me a kiss.

"Are you both okay?" I asked, sitting down.

"I've lots to tell you later," he said, as Sally, followed by Jupiter, walked in.

"Right folks," Sally said. "We're more than halfway through the course, so today we're going to check in on the people we saw in our first thought-projection session, five weeks ago. Only the people."

"Coolyoss," Jupiter said.

"Jupiter, you go first, please. Think only of the people who were in your first projection."

"Before I start," Jupiter said, "I'd just like you all to know I haven't touched a drug from the moment I got here. The first couple of weeks was tough, but thanks to you all, and Sally, I am now officially a 'regenerating addict'. And I just want you all to know I'm happy. For the first time in a very long time I'm looking forward to my future – even if it is in re-allocation. So, thank-you all, from in deep."

Our beanbags shook under the applause.

He sat back and closed his eyes.

The screen flashed on, and he was lying next to Fran on the cushions in his tree-house. "How many children shall we have, Franny?" "Three and a half," she replied, and they burst out laughing.

"Why did the Silver cross the road?" Fran asked. "Don't know," Jupiter replied. "It was programmed by the chicken." They laughed hysterically.

The screen died.

Jupiter watched the replay with tears flowing down his face.

"I haven't seen Fran look that happy in years," he said.

"Well done, Jupiter," Sally said. "Both Nell and the worm-headed warriors have gone."

***

My turn. I leant back and closed my eyes. I thought of Youssan, but my inner world remained calm.

Time heals all. Think about yesterday morning, and Ty's message cancelling your afternoon.

No! I focussed on my right hand resting on Alice, and finally opened my eyes to applause and congratulations. Sally hit replay:

Cyd burst out through the door of a small, single-storey cabin made of black, oily railway sleepers. A large wooden veranda ran all the way around. It had two square windows with orange curtains, either side of the wooden front door. In the image, I was standing in front of the cabin.

"What do you think of my hair? Isn't it brilliant? I always wanted to be a redhead...And I never have to comb it, it's so soft and lovely...And my new outfit...I love floaty skirts.... And I love green.... And I've got proper canvas shoes...And no black at all, anywhere.... apart from the sleepers, of course. It's all just so fantastic."

She grabbed my arm. *"Guess what I've named her, my cabin?* Chez Nous. *Isn't that great? Our House. Yours and mine. Mostly mine. Look how beautiful it is!"* she said, dragging me inside.

The wooden floor was sprinkled with green and blue rag-rugs. A wood-burner stove stood over in one corner with a neat pile of logs stacked behind. A pristine kitchen area, with orange curtains on the front of all the units, ran along the wall to my right, with the big open living area in front of me. The cabin smelt of sage. A spiral staircase rose out of the living area to a sleeping platform, where Cyd had a king-size mattress covered in tan coloured cushions.

"Isn't it wonderful?"

We walked out to the veranda. "It's fantastic, Cyd. Where did you get it all from?"

"From you, silly. The sleepers started stacking themselves into walls when you realised I'm a woman, not SID. Then, when you promised to eliminate me after the memory pod visits I realised if I wanted to stay with you I had to change. So that's what I've been trying to do, and each time I say something nice, something new for the cabin arrives, or I wake up in a new floaty skirt, or my hair's a shade lighter. It's brilliant."

"So what about this morning?"

I cringed as I watched the playback.

"Listen, it's a start. We've come a long way in the last few weeks. I'm still going to slip back into my old ways now and again, it's inevitable, but you'll need to forgive me when I do. Do you think that's possible?"

"There's a hell of a lot to forgive," I said, my arms firmly crossed.

"I know, I'm sorry."

"And the Portcullis?"

"Haven't seen it since it blew off its hinges, ooh what, about a week ago now? AND – I've thought of something. How about I come up with a codeword for when something triggers you off? Something that'll break your thoughts, and calm you down. 'Nell, relax and breathe', perhaps."

"Sure, why not," I said.

"Brilliant, I'll try it."

And then, in front of my eyes, Cyd held out her arms. *"Come on, let's have a hug."*

I uncrossed my arms, and we held one another like long lost friends – which, I suppose, in essence, is what we are.

"Twenty-four years," she said. *"We've had a bit of shaky start, I'll admit, but I think we're going to be great friends."* She hugged me tight to her.

"Shaky start? That's a bit of an understatement." And then we started laughing.

The screen cleared. Cyd and I are, officially, friends.

It's the best feeling ever.

Elation swept up through me. I struggled up out of my beanbag and jogged a celebration lap of the room, weaving in and out of the other beanbags, my arms flailing out to the sides.

Alice's ears shot back, flat against her head.

"Don't be embarrassed, Alice, this is what we've always dreamed of."

"It's the dance I'm concerned about, not the achievement – you look demented."

I collapsed into my beanbag and picked up Greenie: 'I have my best friend who I trust, right here inside me, and together we can conquer the World'.

Fantastic. When do we start?

JED

"Waste of time this is," Mara said. "I know I'm going to be an election monitor, Ty and I have sorted things out, so why the hell I need to continue with all of this I don't know."

"Well you've come this far, you may as well finish," Jupe said.

The screen showed a massive expanse of concrete – just like in her first projection – but without the woman dressed in blue. The image stayed on screen for a long time, before fading out.

"Cured, Sally," she said.

"I must say, it looks that way. Well done, Mara."

"It was nothing."

"And so, Ty, please."

He relaxed back and for the longest time we sat there, staring at a clear screen.

"Try and focus, Ty."

And then I found myself staring into the dark eyes of a curly-haired, probably two-year-old, boy. His mischievous grin beamed out from behind a layer of ice cream and chocolate, and his grass-stained fingers stuck to the spoon. He clung manically to it, waving it in the air, specks of ice-cream flying in all directions. His polo neck sweater was covered in large creamy blobs.

He was standing with his back to a huge lake. His sky blue baggy hemps were way too long for him, and the sun shone onto a table, melting the enormous heap of ice cream and chocolate.

"Jed?" a woman's voice called, off to the right.

Jed promptly ran in the opposite direction, tripping over the bottom of his trousers. He giggled on the floor before getting up and running out of the image.

The woman's voice continued calling, "Jed?" We could hear giggling from the little boy, but couldn't see him.

That image remained until the screen cleared.

Sally hit replay.

"Who on earth is that?"

"Is he not one of your children?" Sally asked.

"Nope I've never heard of a Jed. My two are Sharun and Ludo."

"Fuckin heck man, who chose those names?" said Jupiter.

"I don't get it," Ty said. "There were two spoons before, and I was sure it was about the two boys. Now there's one and it's held by a child I've never seen before in my life."

"Maybe it's a child you'll have in the future," Jupe said.

"I doubt that," Ty replied, avoiding his eyes.

"You never know."

"Oh, I think I know."

Mara squeezed his knee.

Why's she being this nice to him all of a sudden? I should be touching him, not her.

It's purely a geographical issue. She's the closest to him – it's no more complicated than that.

"Okay everyone," Sally added, quickly. "Those are all very positive projections – you've all done really well. We'll meet back here in three days as a group, in between I'll see you all individually," Sally said.

"This is all a waste of time," Ty said, getting up, looking at me for a nano-second, and walking out of the room.

It's okay. He's distracted.

My ribcage tightened, and my head felt really hot.

It's okay, Nell. All is as it should be. Breathe.

"Is he okay, Mara?" Sally asked.

Why's she asking Mara? I'm the one he loves.

Listen to yourself! You sound like a spoilt teenager.

"I was with him last night, and he seemed fine," Mara said.

There you go. I was stupid to think he wouldn't turn back to his wife when things got tough. My ears started ringing and the room was too small for me to breathe.

Okay. Nell Greene, what evidence can you provide that Ty Martins spent all of last night with Mara, or that he was unfaithful to you?

None. But…

None. Correct.

COINCIDENCE

Go round and see him, that'll make you feel better.

Ty flung his door open and gave me a long, passionate kiss.

All your anxiety was unfounded, see? It is safe to trust.

Well I can see that now!

"You'll never guess what!" he said

I bet you can!

"I had a visual with a communication panel yesterday, and they informed me that I'm sterile."

"What?" I said.

Nice fake shock.

He ran me through the whole series of yesterday's events.

"Can you fucking believe it? They're going to re-allocate me because I can't reproduce."

"Shit. What?"

"They've picked on the wrong person."

"Oh God, Ty. Really? I can't believe this is happening."

He held my hands. "And you know what this means for us…"

"…that I can't accept…"

"…the Award. Exactly. Don't you think that's just a bit suspicious? The only way you could accept it is if you trash me and go with Derek."

"Well there's no chance of that. I'll take reallocation any day over Derek."

"I don't even believe I'm sterile anyway. Why have they all of a sudden researched my medical records? I've asked them for a re-test – I want proof. I think this has got something to do with forcing you with Derek."

"It can't have, Ty. Why would the System do anything so complicated just to force me to couple with Derek? That's mad."

"I'm also going to ask for a DNA test for my children and myself. That'll stall. I've got to play for time. And I've contacted the Foundation to see if they can help find out the truth. Do you think it was just coincidence, my getting that letter when I did?"

"And what did TOHF say?"

"They're going to investigate. They said it could take up to a week. I mean, this is our lives, we're talking about. We don't have a week to waste! I know this may sound extreme, but I think all of this revolves around you, Nell. I get the feeling you've been set up, and everyone around you is part of it."

"That's mad."

"I'm serious. Look at the evidence: there's your relationship with Youssan not working which forced you to come on therapy: you get here and Sally's a member of TOHF: Derek is sent: I'm reallocated."

"I'd hardly call that evidence for some mego-plot involving me."

"But what about Derek and the Windfall Committee boat, and the committee bulletin Derek said he'd read on his roamer the day you picked him up. And what about what Granma said after she'd watched Accountability Matters about the fake programme in Scandi," Alice said.

"There you go – there's more evidence!" Ty said.

"Why on earth would anything revolve around me, Ty?"

"Well that's what we need to find out. Do the System know your Mum and Dad are members of TOHF?"

"I would imagine so."

"Maybe they think you're here discussing the Foundation's election strategy with Sally."

"That's ridiculous," I said, looking out the window. "All they have to do is talk to the Earth Matters editor, and she'll verify I've never shown an interest in the Foundation's activities."

"You could have been faking – the System wouldn't know, would they?"

"That's ridiculous."

"Well, something strange is going on, Nell, you've got to admit."

"When's your reallocation date?"

"One month after we're done here," he said, squeezing my hands.

"God. So what's the point in you continuing with the therapy?"

"Exactly," he said, "there isn't one. I was informed I'm being reallocated after you told the Dating Committee about our relationship. So, have the Windfall Committee set all this up to avoid paying you Award money? Have the Dating Committee set it up so that Derek doesn't fail? Ems came around last night to sign all the paperwork to dissolve our marriage, and she thinks there's something strange too."

See, his evening with Mara was totally innocent all along.

"Yes, but, Ty, you were also informed about your reallocation after you got the letter from the Foundation inviting you to join – so maybe the System know about that. I can't believe it's all to do with me, Ty, I'm sorry, you must admit it all sounds a bit out-there. I'm just one person, there are lots of people the Committees have to deal with – why would there be any plot involving me? It doesn't make sense."

"It does seem out there, but that doesn't escape from the fact it's all really happening."

A REPLY FROM TOHF

The following morning, just as Alice and I were leaving Ty's, his roamer bleeped:

Dear Ty Martins

Thank you for your message.

We are sorry to hear of your impending re-allocation. We have been expecting this news, as we suggested in our first letter to you. It is of great curiosity to us as to why you are on the therapy course in Scandinavia, if indeed, you are earmarked for reallocation.

Nell Greene is a name familiar to us because of her parents, Jenny and Rufus. Nell has been a member since birth, but is another who has chosen not to be actively involved.

We cannot think why there would be a link between the recent events and Nell, but we are carrying on with our research, and if we uncover anything, we will of course let you know. Sally, your course leader, is an active member of TOHF.

We have messaged Sally, and may I suggest you arrange a time to see her in strictest privacy to discuss how you may proceed with fighting your reallocation. As you have a limited time left at the centre, I would contact Sally as soon as possible, as it will be difficult to have any contact after your departure.

We are prepared to engage in some civilian awareness programmes to highlight your case. You need to understand how much this will annoy the System, especially with the upcoming elections, but it is a risk you must be prepared to take. It may count against you, and they may downgrade your reallocation assignment to something more similar to Nell.

If you still want to campaign, please do arrange to see Sally as soon as possible.

The Original Human Foundation

"Good, that's positive," Ty said.

"Hang on a minute, how do they know what my reallocation assignment is?"

"Sally, I guess," Alice said.

"Well how does she know? I don't remember discussing it with her."

"I'm going to talk to her about my reallocation protest this evening, Nell, if you don't mind," Ty said.

"Not at all. I'll go and break the news to Derek about you and I."

TELL DEREK THE TRUTH

"Hi Derek," I said, tipping my head down to avoid him kissing me.

"Hi. How's therapy going?"

"It's exhausting."

"I came around to yours last night for a chat, but you weren't there. Were you with Sally?"

"How's your research going?"

"It's going well, but I was hoping you and I would be growing closer by now."

Urgh.

"Really?"

"Well you enjoyed my chilli the other night."

"And you think it's as easy as enjoying a chilli?"

"Why not?"

"Listen, I have no idea where I'm going to be after I'm finished here in a couple of weeks, so what's the point?"

That sounds like you don't want to start a relationship with him because you don't know what the future holds for you both. It's not that. It's because you're in love with someone else!

"You could stay here with me," he said, moving closer.

Gross. Get away from him!

"And do what?"

What are you playing at? Tell him the truth. NOW.

"Well, see less of Sally for a start. Why do you need to spend so much time with her?"

"She's the course therapist, Derek."

"And you could help me write my promotional information," he said. "You'd be great at it – you're an environmental journalist, aren't you? I'm a geologist – what could be a better match?"

He's got it all figured out. TELL HIM THE TRUTH.

He took his roamer out of his pocket and selected 'Scandi'. He showed me images of a beautiful pine forest with small log cabins dotted around at uniformed intervals, each set in its own little clearing.

"That's as far as I've got. It's Pine Needles Park. I need to add text – that's where you could help out."

"It looks lovely, but I'm not going to be staying here, Derek." I said.

"Right, there's something I should tell you, Nell. You deserve to know the truth about me. But you must promise not to mention it to the others."

"Go on."

"Alice," he said. "Promise?"

"Depends what you're about to tell us. If it is a threat to Nell's safety then I will be obliged to tell somebody."

Derek laughed. "Threat to Nell's safety? Where did you get that idea from!"

Alice's ears flattened.

"The geo-thermal project isn't real. I am here researching ways of getting information from therapy participants."

"What sort of information?"

"Stuff that usually forms part of the love-test."

"Really?"

"Really. It isn't relevant with your group, but there are other centres – Pine Needles being one of them – where new couples are on 'harmonious relationships' therapy. The love-test is so unpopular, and so obvious, that the Windfall Committee is looking at more subtle ways to gather the same information."

"Why didn't you tell me the truth from the beginning?"

"Would you have taken me seriously if I'd said I was up here to implement love-test techniques?"

No. But you don't take him seriously anyway, so it doesn't matter.

"Granma watched an Accountability Matters a few nights ago and they said there were bogus projects in Scandinavia looking at exactly what you've just described. But in reality, people are taking information from the centres to feed into the Programming Team's secret trials on artificial consciousness."

"I saw that emission. That's why I couldn't tell you what I was really doing here – I mean, what conclusion would you have come to?"

"That you're here stealing information for the Programming Team?" Alice said.

"Yes, exactly, Alice. Well I'm not."

"How did you see that emission before you arrived here? It was only broadcast live a few nights ago."

"Pre-emission rights – for anyone coming to do research here. Look, I understand all you have is my word on this. You could ask the Dating Committee for verification."

"Are you even a geologist?"

"Yes, I am."

"So who's crediting you units?"

"Half Dating Committee, half Windfall Committee."

"Why, as a geologist, would the love-test interest you?"

"Change of scenery. More units. Meeting you." He held my hands.

"Listen, Derek. You've been honest with me, now I need to be honest with you – Ty and I are going to try and set up a life together once the course is over."

He dropped my hands. His eyes turned cold.

"But I thought you…"

"What?"

"I thought Ty…and Mara…aren't they married?"

"Their marriage is over – Ty's with Sally now, sorting it all out."

"I didn't know."

"Why would you?"

"Well that changes things quite drastically, Nell."

"I'm sorry, Derek. I did tell The Dating Committee and they said it was too late to cancel your trip."

"Right," he said, looking out into the darkness. "They should have told me."

"They should."

"Come on, let's go away for a couple of days, get to know one another."

Unbelievable.

"So you'd still like to see if we can work it out, even though I've told you about Ty?"

Why ask him that?

"Of course."

"Why?"

"I've been wanting to get the research appointment up here for a long time. I've hassled the Committees for the last two years, trying to persuade them to send me. What finally tipped it all in my favour was being single, because you were here and they needed to send you a perfect match."

"So it's not really that you want us to be together, it's because you wanted to get a promotion to research up here."

Why ask him that, for God's sake. As if you care!

"I do actually like you, Nell. As blind dates go, you're the best one so far."

He can't have had many then.

Oi!

"I've fallen in love with Ty. I'm sorry."

"I'm sorry too, Nell, because there's nothing I can do about the situation. I'm here specifically as your perfect match, and I'm not about to contact any of the Committees and tell them it isn't working," he said, standing taller than usual.

"Then can we agree they'll never know any different?" I said. "I won't tell anyone why you're really here, if you don't mention anything about me and Ty."

"If they don't ask, I won't tell," he said, walking me to the door.

PASSWORD

The following day I had a session with Sally before I'd had a chance to see Ty and tell him about my chat with Derek.

"Ready for Little Nell?" Sally asked, putting the leopard print hat in place, "it's a strand of your spaghetti we still haven't visited."

"Before we start, Sally, Ty's surveillance device is still live – I watched another recording."

"Was it helpful?"

"No."

"Maybe it was, but you don't yet understand why."

"Look, Sally, I don't care. I want it deactivated, okay? You said you would."

"I'll code it in – sorry it's not been as effective as I'd hoped."

"So, Little Nell?"

"Yes, for starters we need to find out how old she is, so get comfy, close your eyes, and take some deep breaths. I want you to imagine you are standing at the top of five steps. You walk down the steps, one by one, taking a deep breath, and breathing out with each step down. Take your time, breathing deeply. When you arrive at the bottom of the steps, you are totally relaxed and you find yourself surrounded by ten doors – numbered – from one to ten."

Obviously!

I closed my eyes and pictured myself walking down five stone steps. At the bottom *Lily the Pink* was waiting for me, door open. Lily! I patted her shell, jumped in, and kissed her handrail. A monorail appeared underneath us, and Lily started moving forwards. We meandered our way along, through a network of bright, yellow tunnels. I let go of the handrail, as Lily drifted left and right. I looked at the brightly lit junction names as we ambled past them: Trust: K̶V̶ Cyd: Control: Rejection: Fear. I felt warm and buzzy, just as we stopped at a T-junction. Lily turned right, the lights went out, and we dropped vertically into pitch black. I grabbed out for the handrail as she jolted violently left and right.

"Get a good picture in your mind of how the doors look, where you're standing, what's around you, and let me know when you're ready for the next stage," Sally said.

Lily screeched to a halt in the middle of a light grey marble floor. A wide metal staircase led up to a landing where it split off to the right and left. Either side of the bottom of the stairs, five wooden, arched doors curved around me, forming the shape of a horseshoe. Each door was intricately carved with different flowers and birds, and they stood alone, without ceilings or walls either around them or in between them. The doors were numbered, running anti-clockwise around me, with Number One starting to the far-right of the stairs. I stepped out of Lily, and although the floor was marble, it felt warm against my bare feet.

"Ready, Sally," I said.

"I'd like you to pick a door, and tell me the number."

"Nine." It was diagonally opposite my left shoulder.

"I'd like you to walk over to door number nine, Nell, open it and step inside."

I walked across the marble towards door number nine – enormous carvings of dahlias and robins covered the frame. The deliciously thick dark wood looked good enough to eat. I knocked.

Why the hell did you knock?

Footsteps came rushing towards me from the other side. The door flew open and there, standing in front of me was Shoo, my little sister.

I burst into tears. I opened my eyes and Sally handed me a tissue. "I haven't seen Shoo for so long, Sally," I said, snivelling. "She's in a meltdown centre after two miscarriages. The Silvers couldn't save the foetuses. They diagnosed meltdown when she shaved her head and walked naked through Sissoko market."

"I'm sorry, Nell."

I took some deep breaths and blew my nose.

"Okay. I'll have another go." I closed my eyes and pictured myself standing outside door number nine. Again I knocked. Again Shoo opened it.

Her big blue eyes stared up at me. Her blonde hair hung in a fringe, over the top of which she had a bright purple elasticated hair band. She had a matching bright purple pair of tights on, and covering those a turquoise and purple dress.

She started at my head and worked her eyes downwards.

"Hello," I said, wiping my eyes.

"What do you want?"

"Can I come in?"

"What for!"

"I'd like to see Nell."

"Why do you want to see Nell?"

"I need to talk to her."

"What's the password?"

"Tomato."

"Nope."

"ShooShoo."

She giggled. "Nope."

"Look, just let me past, please?"

"Nope. Not without the password."

"Riddledumdee."

"Nope."

"Look, I'm here to see Nell, not you." I pushed past Shoo, and she disappeared into thin air.

She's still just as annoying as an adult!

LITTLE NELL

I stepped onto sand and waited for the soles of my feet to adjust to the heat. I was standing at the edge of a sandy expanse of young cassava, planted in uniformed rows, with wilting leaves. Directly to my right was a huge old Baobab – "The tree God planted upside down," Granma says. A shimmering line of vetiver grass grew away from the Baobab, stopping at an over-ground irrigation channel. I looked to my left.

WOW. Freaky.

Little Nell: Me: Little me, was sitting, maybe 15 metres ahead of me, on the far bank of the field's storm gully.

A poem I'd written years ago burst into my head.

Meeting you brings my tears.
Not for childhood I grieve,
but for all my lonely years.

I walked slowly towards her. She was sitting side-on to me, and with her legs bent up tight under her chin, she gently rocked backwards and forwards. She had on my – her? – favourite dungarees and light blue shirt, and her hair looked like flames dancing around in the sunlight. "78, 79, 80," she shouted as she rocked.

"99, 100. Coming to get you!"

She opened her eyes and jerked backwards when she saw me. She looked around and then eyed me slowly from head to toe and back up again.

God, I was so beautiful. Why had I spent most of my childhood believing I wasn't?

"Hello," I said, stifling my tears. What else do you say when you meet yourself, aged nine?

She didn't answer.

"Are you playing hide and seek?"

Silence.

I sat down on the opposite side of the gully and we just looked at one another. Her big green eyes stared out at me from under dark bushy eyebrows and the red madness, posing as hair.

"How long does Shoo wait until she gives up?"

"We never play like that. We never give ourselves up – giving up is stupid. If one of us doesn't find the other after half an hour, then we go home. Simple."

"I remember that rule," I said, smiling. "Do you know who I am?"

"I think so," she said.

"Who am I?"

"I think you're me when I'm older and wear boring clothes."

"You'll be pleased to hear I'm actually considered quite fashionable."

She hunched her knees closer to her chest and looked down at the baked, orange earth.

"Are you okay?"

Stupid question. What nine-year-old is going to turn around and pour their troubles out to an adult, let alone one they've only known for two minutes?

"There's a reason why I'm here today, and I think it's because you wanted me to come, even if you don't know it."

"Are you here because I'm dead when I get to your age?"

"No! No – I'm very much alive, Nell. I'm at a therapy centre, doing an exercise to meet you. It's all a bit complicated, but I've been going for rides in a coconut shell, and it's fun – you'd love it," I said, sounding mad. "Do you know why I'm here today?"

She shrugged her shoulders.

We sat in silence, the midday heat rising out of the gully.

"Would you like to come over to this side and sit with me?"

"No."

"Well then, can I come over there and sit with you?"

"No."

"Okay, how about we go and play on the swing?"

"Don't want to."

"Shall we go home then? I'd like to see Mum and Dad looking young."

"Dad's not there," she said.

"Where is he?"

She shrugged her shoulders.

"They had a row."

"Really?"

"Yep." She started up at me. "He's gone. Three days ago."

"*Dad, gone?*" I said. I searched her face with my eyes. "Are you sure?"

"Of course I'm sure. They had a big row and he left."

"What did they row about?"

Shrug.

"Were they arguing during the day?"

"Night."

"Were you in bed?"

She nodded, her bottom lip starting to quiver.

"Did you hear anything?"

"I heard Dad saying he was leaving. Then I heard the front door open and close."

This is the moment, Nell, right now. Rejection. Fear. Keep her talking, you need to change the energy of this memory.

"What did you do?"

"Nothing."

"Did you go and see Mum?"

She burst into tears.

Great, now you've made her feel guilty.

"It's okay, Nell. Did you cry when you heard Dad leave?"

Slowly she nodded.

"Did you cuddle Patch?"

"He was in the washing machine," she said. "They were arguing about me," she mumbled, wiping her nose on her arm.

"About you?"

She nodded.

"How do you know that?"

"I just do."

"Did you hear them mention you?"

She shrugged.

"Is that what you think? That he left because of you?"

She nodded.

Change the relationship with the memory of him leaving. NOW. She needs to feel safe, not abandoned, or scared.

"It's not true, Nell."

"How *would you* know?" she said, snapping at me.

"Because I know Mum and Dad. He would never have left you, or Shoo – he loves you both too much for that. I promise."

"How can you be so sure?"

"I've had twenty-seven years longer than you getting to know them, Nell. Trust me. It wouldn't have been because of you, or Shoo. And they've just celebrated forty-four years together, so he didn't stay away for long."

Her dusty, tear-stained face looked up into mine, and she was the most beautiful little girl I'd ever seen.

"*Forty-four years married*?" she said. "Wow. That's long. You must be *really* old."

"You may have felt alone that night, Nell, what with Patch in the washing machine, but you weren't. Mum and Dad still loved you, they just had things of their own to sort. Can you imagine living together day in day out without getting on one another's nerves?"

Just because you've never managed it!

"No, sounds awful!"

"Plus, Granma gives you a cowbot, Alice, when you're ten, and you're best friends for life."

"My best friend is going to be a robot?" she said, making a face.

"Not any robot," I said. "Alice."

"No wonder I'm in therapy when I'm old, if my best friend's a robot."

That's exactly what I said!

"Don't be cheeky!"

She forced a smile.

"Come over to this side of the gully, and we can chat properly."

Her head dropped.

"Come on, you won't fall in, I'll catch you. We can go and play on the swing, or we can run around the field and play for ever and ever more."

Her face lit up.

"Come on, let's do a gully-jump warm up."

We stood up.

"Okay, three jumps to the right." We jumped right. "Three jumps to the left." We jumped back. "And run around in a circle." We ran around laughing.

"Ready to jump the gully, Little Nell?"

She ran full pelt, leapt into the air and came crashing down about half a metre in front of me, clear of the gully's edge.

"Nice jumping!"

I dusted her down and tried to give her a hug, but she pulled away.

Don't force it.

"It's okay, Nell. Dad comes back, Patch dries out, and you don't ever have to be alone again."

She ran into me and threw her arms around my waist. I lifted her up onto my hip and she draped her arms around my shoulders, nestling into my neck.

"Can I be called Nelly, please?" she said.

"Sure. So, Nelly, how would you like a new forever-playmate?" I asked her.

"More than anything," she said, straightening up.

"Brilliant, I've got just the person."

ME?! Yes please. I can teach her to knit, and make rag-rugs. Oh yes please!

"Cyd, meet Nelly. Nelly, meet Cyd."

DATING COMMITTEE

Ty was waiting at my space when I got back from meeting Nelly.

"You're a Sally-hog," he said, eyes sparkling.

He kissed my eyelids, and held me tight.

Ouch! Yuk. Me kissing a grown up! Gross! Let me down!

"Hang on a minute Ty. I met me, aged nine, today, and I've been carrying her around with me. Sounds mad, I know."

"No madder than everything else that's going on," he said, taking a step back so as not to crush her.

Come and hang out with me, Nelly. Leave those two grownups to it – we could do some baking, and knitting.

Yes please!

"That's better – she's gone off to be with Cyd. Right, where were we?" I said, reaching out for his hands.

"Thank God we met on therapy, Nell, otherwise I'd definitely be thinking you're a meltdown case!"

He held me tight to him.

"The clock's ticking, Ty. One week left, I can't bear the thought of it."

Relax and breathe, Nell. Breathe.

"It'll all be okay, Nell, I promise," he said, wiping my tears with his index finger.

"It seems like only five minutes ago Granma was remarking on my 'garish pink' chairs."

"I know. When I first arrived, I wondered how Ems and I were going to survive it, and now I don't want it ever to end."

"Me neither," Alice said.

"Nor me," Shilly added.

"Sally's not helping me," Ty said quietly.

I pulled back, wiping my nose.

"Why the hell not? Effing hell. What *is* the point of all of this?"

"What, *us*?" he asked.

"No, not *us*. All this therapy shit, and all the other shit."

"Steady, Nell, that's fighting talk."

"Well, what do they expect? Why isn't Sally helping?" I snivelled.

"She says she will, but never gets to it."

"And have you had any more written comms from TOHF?"

"I got a message yesterday saying they have some volunteers willing to anonymously contact the Livelihood Committee about our case."

"That's great news!" I said.

"It is – apart from the fact that due to all the election business, the Committees are taking three weeks to process any requests."

"So what are you going to do?"

"If I haven't heard anything positive in the week, then I'm going public."

"Don't. Please. That's dangerous. The Silvers are looking for reasons to prove humans aren't worthy of governing again, you'd be playing right into their hands. Please, Ty, don't."

"I have to Nell, I'm sorry. I can't accept being reallocated. I can't believe you can accept everything that's happening to you, either. I want to stay on my farm, I want you with me, writing your articles. The System has no right to decide how I will live my life."

My roamer bleeped, and we both looked at my screen.

To Nell Greene

It has come to our attention your relationship with Derek has not got off to the best of starts. Be sure there is no future for yourself and Ty Martins, as we believe he has already been given a reallocation date. We strongly urge you to think of your future, Nell, and start to spend more time with Derek.

We will also be held accountable if your relationship with Derek fails.

The Dating Committee

"I thought we'd sorted things out, Derek," I shouted the second he answered my call. "Why the hell did you tell the Dating Committee we aren't getting on?"

"What? I haven't said a word. What's going on?"

"I've just had a threatening message from them saying I need to see more of you."

"Do you want me to come over?"

"No."

"Do you want me to call the Dating Committee?"

"No. I'll do it." I cut the call.

"Calm down a bit before you do that," Ty said.

"Calm down? How the hell do they know I spend more time with you than I do with Derek? Have they got cameras everywhere?"

Alice started whizzing up and down, ears back flat. Shilly was whizzing side to side under the table.

There was a knock at the door. I opened it to Derek. He shoved past me.

"Honestly, Nell, I haven't said a word. I don't know what they're up to."

"Hi Derek, I'm Ty," Ty said, holding out his hand.

"Oh. Hi," Derek said. "Look, I suggest you contact the Dating Committee and ask them where they're getting their information."

"Drink?" Ty asked him.

"Better not. I'm busy writing up a report. Contact the Dating Committee and let me know what they say, Nell."

S x and P

I picked up my roamer to message the Dating Committee. My wall-screen flashed on, and Ty and I were looking at Sally, who was sitting on a giant beanbag, writing a message.

"Hang on," Ty said, looking straight into my eyes, "why isn't Sally talking to you?"

He mustn't know it's happened before.

I stared, dumbfounded at the screen, before looking at Ty.

"Is this a recording?"

"I have no idea."

"How can your screen be showing Sally's space?"

"I don't know. Alice? Do you know what's happening?"

Oh nice! Dump it on Alice!

"No idea, no clue, not the faintest. Weird," she said, whizzing.

Ty searched my face and my eyes. Any flicker would give me away.

"Shilly, any ideas?"

She dashed over to join Alice. "None," she said.

He kept on looking at me.

"What!" I said, "you think I'm some kind of spy?"

We were distracted by the screen showing the message Sally had written.

P,

Things here are getting difficult. I'm supposed to be helping Ty with a protest to the Livelihood Committee about his re-allocation.

How can I do that? And if I don't help – how can I keep putting him off? I know it will be alright, but Nell and Ty don't, do they.

I need your help, please tell me how I should proceed.

S x

"Oh my God! S kiss, and P!" I screamed, at Alice.

Alice and Shilly took cover under the table, making tiny little bumps into one another's sides.

"Right!" Ty yelled. "I'm going round to Sal's right now. This is my effing life we're talking about. What does she mean, 'keep putting him off?'"

"Ty, wait! S and P – those two initials were most of the reason my relationship with Youssan failed – which pushed me to come on this course. They came up in my first thought-projection – do you remember?"

"What does she mean 'supposed' to be helping Ty? I'm off over there, NOW."

"Ty, wait!" He jumped, I shouted so loud.

Alice started whizzing up and down in straight lines, with Shilly in hot pursuit.

"Are you listening? S and P. Those were the initials of whoever was sending messages to Youssan!"

"And?"

"Well isn't that yet *another* rather bizarre, coincidence?"

Ty shut up and stared at me.

"So, what, you think Youssan is in on all of this too?" he said. "Why would he be?"

"Beats me."

"Well there's only one way to find out, let's go round and see Sally."

"We can't, Ty. If we go and confront her she'll wonder how we know, won't she. Let's wait and see if she receives a reply."

Why the hell would Sally have activated her own surveillance device?

"She won't know anything of the sort. We can go round and ask if there's any news about her helping me. It doesn't have to be connected."

"This is too weird," Alice said. "I'm not enjoying this, at all."

I'm finding it all very exciting!

"Let me just message the Dating Committee a moment." I tapped into my roamer.

To the Dating Committee

Where are you getting your information? Because it is wrong. Derek and I are getting on very well, as are Ty and myself. I am sure I will stay in touch

with both of them when I have left the course in a
week's time. Who knows which one I will choose.
Nell Greene

"Why would you say that?" Ty asked.

"You can't send it," Alice said. "They'll flip."

"I'm just playing for time, Ty," I said, pressing send.

"Incoming!" Alice said, as my screen bleeped.

S,

Help Ty with the protest. Make sure he is the one who sends
it though – remember who you work for.

Good luck, see you soon

P x

"Result! Let's go over to Sally and get things in motion," Ty
said, getting up.

"Too suspicious," Alice said.

"She's right."

Ty studied us both, and let out a massive sigh. He grabbed my
hand and we scrambled up to the sleeping platform.

"Whatever this is all about, Nell, and whatever happens to
both of us, I will always love you. I will never forget the weeks
we've shared, I'm just sorry it took until now to meet you."

Melt!

I cuddled into his chest.

"I'll cherish every moment we have, Ty," I said. "For as long
as I live."

All is as it should be.

SALLY HELPS

Sally helped Ty with his protest the next day:

To the Livelihood Committee
As you will remember, you have given me a reallocation date one month after the last day of my therapy course. The reason given is I am sterile, and can therefore not contribute to the repopulation of the planet. However, I would like to remind you I am the father of two healthy boys, who will lose me if I am reallocated. I am sure you would not like headlines such as 'Two little boys robbed of their father' to appear in any Human Voice bulletins at this a crucial time leading up to the elections. I am therefore sending this message to ask you to reverse your decision about my reallocation. If you do not I will be forced to enlist public support in challenge.
Ty Martins

The reply came back:

To Ty Martins
We understand you feel strongly about this matter. However, may we remind you the children are in fact, not yours, and could be satisfactorily raised by your brother and his wife, if they agree. Enlisting public support will not lead to us changing our decision. It may, however, lead us to reviewing the reallocation assignment we have worked so hard to acquire for you.
The Livelihood Committee

Ty returned:
May I remind you the System has no power over my right to live the life I choose. You will be reading an article in Human Voices shortly, following which I will expect a reversal in your decision.

He put down his roamer. "I haven't heard anything since that," he said.

"Why did you need Sally's help to write that?"

"Believe me, the Committee would have liked my version a lot less."

"Seems to me all Sally has helped you do is waste time."

BELIEVING DEREK

"Nell, darling. I've found out there is no-one employed on the love-test exercise thing for the therapy centres in Scandinavia. Remember me telling you about it? Accountability Matters reported it as being one of the cover-ups for the Windfall Committee's embezzlement. Well, it appears claims that the Programming Team were gathering information from the therapy centres to feed into their artificial consciousness research were false. So that means Derek is probably nothing to do with the Windfall Committee."

"But he is, G. He told me the other night he's here working on the love-test program. He's being paid part by the Dating Committee part by Windfall."

"And you believe him?"

"I don't know what to believe anymore, G. I'm not worried about Derek. Apart from the fact he wants to see more of me, I think he's harmless. He's met Ty."

"How did he take that?"

"He seemed okay with it. Anyway, there's not long to go and then I'll be free of him."

"You hope!"

TOOLKIT

Affirmation for today: I am committed to change.

We sat on our usual beanbags, only mine was now resting up against Ty's, and Mara's was next to Jupiter. Alice and Shilly stood together near Sally.

"This morning we're going to work on developing a self-help toolkit," Sally said.

You've already got Greenie.

"For example," she said, "if I'm feeling anxious about something, one of the techniques I might use from my toolkit is to concentrate on my breathing. Counting my breaths in and out breaks my previous thought pattern, which in turn breaks the energy of the anxiety."

Ty held my hand, as if I were one of the tools in his.

"It's remembering to open the toolbox, though, isn't is, Sally!" Jupiter said.

"With time, it'll become second nature," Sally replied. "Having been inspired by Nell, thank you, Nell, I've bought you all one of these," she said, reaching into her bag and taking out four dark-blue pocket-sized notebooks. Mara put hers down by her shoes. "Nell, hang onto yours for when you've no more space in Greenie." She handed each of us a bronze ink-pen. "The object is to enter into the notebook whatever you'd like to have in your toolkit."

"I'll create a notebook on my roamer thanks, Sally," Mara said.

Ty flicked through the empty pages.

"What I'd like is for each one of you to say one technique, or one part of the therapy that has been most helpful to you. It needs to be one you would suggest everyone adds into their toolkit."

"Easy," Jupiter said, "mine is forgiveness."

Mara cut Jupiter's hair a couple of days ago, and with the amount of time he'd been spending on his favourite rock he'd developed a healthy glow.

"All I knew when we first started working on forgiveness was that I needed space around me, so Sally and I clambered up GreenWaters Rock. She helped me to say out loud things I wanted to forgive, but after two sessions I realised I didn't really mean any of them – I was just spouting words. The third session I went up alone, and I started to feel angry and disgusted with myself at all the stupid things I've done. I cried solidly for two days. I thought I'd never stop – Mara nearly exhausted her stock of facewipes! Then, Sally suggested that firstly, I needed to forgive myself. I clambered back up the rock, and I repeated out loud, 'I forgive you, Jupiter', 'I forgive myself'. Each day I sat up there, repeating those two phrases and being kind to myself. Then one afternoon I caught myself laughing at a memory of Fran, and I knew feelings inside me were shifting. I carried on, every day, sitting on my rock, being kind to myself, and eventually, about 10 days ago, I stood up to leave and I felt joyful. I felt free: unburdened, I suppose. It was at that moment I knew I was clean, and would stay that way. So, my entry into the toolkit? Forgiveness. Forgive yourself. Be kind to yourself."

Mara wiped the corner of her eye.

"Thanks, Jupiter," Sally said, "that's a great addition."

I turned the page in Greenie and wrote: 'Forgiveness', and on the following page: 'Be kind to yourself'.

"I've got something to add," Mara said, "though it's not really a tool, because since Ty and I sorted out what we needed to, all I've really done is hassle Jupe..."

"Help me, Em. Not hassle," said Jupiter, squeezing her hand.

"But if there's one thing I'd say after my time here, it's to always tell the truth. People lie because they're scared of the effect the truth will have. So to avoid all this inner searchy shit, and having to look at the feelings surrounding why you're scared of telling the truth, just be brave, and tell the fucking truth. I'm so sorry, Ty, that I couldn't, I really am."

"It's okay, Ems," Ty said.

"So, how does avoiding all the 'inner searchy shit' fit into a toolkit, Mara?" Sally asked. "If I'm feeling scared about telling someone the truth, what can I use from my toolkit to stop that feeling?"

Mara straightened up: "Put your hand on your ribcage, take a deep breath and say to yourself 'be brave'," Mara said, doing the actions, and looking very pleased with herself. "Telling the truth may feel horrendous at the time, but it'll be worth it in the long run. I mean, how bad can it be?"

Pretty bad.

"Be Brave – ribcage – breathe, is my contribution to the toolkit."

"Okay, Mara, thank-you."

We all wrote in our notebooks.

"Ty? Anything?"

I've got one!

"Two, I can think of, Sally, if that's okay?"

"Absolutely!"

"My obvious first choice, is corn-flakes. If something's bothering you, get hold of some flakes, go and sit somewhere peaceful, and talk your problem into a flake. Then destroy it. I can promise you, it works," he said, squeezing my hand.

"And if you want, do it with someone else," he said, "that makes it really special, because the other person will give you a different perspective."

Entry into Greenie: 'Corn-flakes with friends'.

"My second one I'd like to call 'Planet'," Ty said.

"Here we go," Mara said. "I knew he'd have to mention it somewhere or other."

"Well, Mara," he replied, laughing, "I wouldn't be me if I didn't, would I! Anyway, my suggestion is, whenever something is frustrating you, hurting you, confusing you, etc., go outside, stand firm and strong on the ground, look up to the sky and breathe in and out with your mouth open. Imagine breathing in the sky, and it travelling down into your feet, and then back up and out with your breath. And say, 'thank-you', to our planet, for being here."

"That's a lovely addition, Ty," Sally said, "thank you."

"It's what's saved me over the last few years. Whenever I look up and breathe in the sky, I believe everything will be alright."

Greenie: Planet – thank-you. Breathe the sky in and out.

My turn! 'Practice'. Believe change is possible – and then practice.

"The affirmation I picked for today, is, 'I am committed to change', which is spooky, considering what we're talking about," I said. "I was pretty cynical when I started here – I doubted dredging up old feelings and memories would help me in any way at all. But more than that, I doubted I'd be able to stick to it."

You have, though. Which is brilliant.

"I don't feel unconditional love for everyone and everything, and I still haven't experienced anything close to enlightenment," I added, "but that's okay. I used to expect a miracle, but what I'm expecting now is it's not going to be easy. But I have made a commitment to myself to change, and I am going to stick with that commitment. That muddle of spaghetti in my head, my issues with Cyd, stem from very 'ordinary' experiences, and at the beginning I felt childish admitting them. But we're all unique, and we all process things in different ways. I have internalized things that might not even affect other people. So be it. That's who I am."

"I'm glad you mentioned this," Sally said. "Your experiences may be very ordinary, Nell, and many people may have shared similar, especially when it comes to rejection and young love, but how ordinary, or common the experience is, is irrelevant. During my time as a therapist, I have learnt the vast majority of people share similar issues, but it's how each individual reacts, that is important. I can say, without fail, that everybody, reacts to an experience differently, and if it's an unhelpful reaction – then it needs looking at – no matter how insignificant the cause may seem."

"Thanks, Sally. Plus – and I never thought I'd hear myself say this – now I'm friends with Cyd, we can keep one another on-track –"

Definitely.

"– I'm just sorry it's taken this long."

Better late than never.

"And no matter how rough it gets – and I've got a horrible feeling it's going to get pretty rough – I promise myself to stick with it. And so, for the toolkit? I guess I'd like to add

Affirmations – write them and repeat them, over and over, until you believe them. I'd like my entry in the toolkit to be 'All is as it should be'."

That's a fantastic one. Now, what about mine?

"And Cyd would like to add one," I said. "Practice. Believe change is possible – and then practice."

"Thank-you, Cyd," Sally said.

Brilliant! Thank-you, Nell.

THE FINAL SESSION

"I shall miss this beanbag," Jupe said, the following day.

"Take it with you," Sally said.

"I'll miss all of you," Mara added.

We looked at one another in silence, waiting for her to add a sarcastic comment.

"You've worked miracles, Sally," Ty said, smiling.

"Ty, I'd like you to begin. I'd like you to think about your two boys, and we'll see what images you now project."

"That's cruel," Jupiter said. "We all know about his reallocation."

"I'm okay with it."

"Same method as before," Sally said, "I'll place the pad, and your thoughts will be projected onto the screen."

He closed his eyes and his two boys appeared on-screen, and then were engulfed by a huge crowd. Ty rose, out of the crowd, on somebody else's shoulders, with the little boy, Jed, in his arms.

The screen cleared, and Ty opened his eyes and watched the replay.

"The meaning of it is totally irrelevant," Ty said.

"You're being held in the air, Ty, like you're victorious," Sally said, looking him in the eye for what seemed like forever.

Was she passing Ty a message? My heart started racing.

I absolutely refuse. I am not going to lower myself. I agreed to stay calm if your insides started flipping out, so I am staying calm. Sally! Passing Ty a message? Get a grip, Nell. Those days are over, gone, well and truly behind us. I categorically refuse to take the bait when you feel insecure and threatened.

No, Cyd! My heart's speeding up because maybe there's hope. Maybe his reallocation isn't inevitable.

"Well, thank you, Sally. With the course about to finish, you thinking I have any hope of being victorious is of great comfort to me."

I kicked his beanbag.

"Mara," Sally said, shifting her gaze from Ty. "I know you don't really care about the outcome of this, but please, put a little bit of effort in. I'd like you to think about how you'd feel if somebody offered you a whiskey."

"That's easy. I'd feel fucking elated."

"Right, well, let's see how that looks on-screen shall we?" Sally replied.

The woman in blue leapt onto the concrete, dancing around with a glass in her hand. Lots of people of similar age flooded into the picture, and they danced and laughed, and cheered. Then the woman in blue led them, dancing, off the edge of the concrete and out of sight.

"Do you think they'll have whiskey for monitors?" Mara said, after she'd watched the play-back.

"I think you'll be lucky if they have a glass of Malbec a year," Ty said.

"Nell, over to you. I'd like you to think about how you'd feel introducing Ty to Ruby."

Nasty!

Sally hit replay, and Cyd instantly flashed onto the screen. She was smaller in height and width than before, and had mad curls of chestnut hair. Her googly, piercing blue eyes had softened, and she smiled and waved from the veranda of her cabin. She was wearing a long emerald green skirt with a baggy black jumper over the top. Above her head a 'welcome' sign swung back and forth. There were two rocking chairs on the veranda and in one, also waving manically, was Nelly. Sharing her chair was a carefully knitted, Patch, who she picked up and wiggled at me.

"Nell, it's working!" Cyd shouted. "Look!"

She pointed off to her left. The image zoomed out, and there, lying to the right of her cabin was a stack of perfectly straight, not-a-kink-in-sight, spaghetti.

"We've done it!" Cyd shouted, as she leapt up and down. Nelly joined in.

Then one of the strands burst out of the stack and wrapped itself around all of the others, with its ends twirling and flicking in the air.

"No! Stop it!" shouted Nelly.

The strand twisted tightly around the others, and a word appeared along its length: LOVE.

Cyd and Nelly stopped dancing.

"Relax and breathe," Cyd was saying, "love yourself, no matter what. Believe in yourself and Ruby can never be a threat to you. LOVE is the answer. Quick! Calm down! Breathe! Think of love!"

The screen cleared as the love strand strangled the others. I sat staring.

"What a moron. How did I manage to forget my 'love' strand?"

Ty came and sank into the beans next to me.

It's okay. You thought it would be dealt with automatically once all the other crap was out of the way.

"Cyd looked great, if it's any consolation," Jupe said.

"I'm sorry, Nell, it's partly my fault too, I should have returned to Love in one of our final sessions."

"Ashing shit. I can't believe it."

"What does it mean, exactly?" asked Alice.

"It means there's something left to look at, Alice. But Nell, you know enough techniques to help yourself through whatever it is LOVE needs to show you, so make sure you address it in your own time. Alice, Cyd and your notebook are all there to help, yes?"

Yes.

"Yes. Just make it quick and no shouting out ridiculous statements."

I felt gutted.

"Jupiter, I'd like you to close your eyes and think about how you'd feel if somebody were to offer you an injection."

"Well, you're really going for the jugular today, Sally!" Ty said.

"It's the only way we can tell if Jupiter's really over his addiction," said Sally

"No sweat man – I'd kill them, plain and simple."

"Okay, let's find out."

Jupiter laid back and closed his eyes.

The warriors returned, but now they had kind, tanned faces, rather than worm-heads. They stood in-front of the glass-fronted tree house, where Jupiter was sitting, atop of a giant heap of cushions. He sat with his back straight, listening to rock music, looking out of the window over the pond. He waved to the warriors and beckoned them to climb up into the tree house. They sat around him in a circle.

One of the warriors leant on the shoulder of another, and rose to his bare feet. "We would like you to know, Jupiter, we have voted for you to be our leader. You have shown you are a true Warrior, and we promise to protect you forever more. And could we please have some walking boots."

All the warriors cheered and laughed, and Jupiter joined in.

"That was brilliant, Jupiter," Sally said.

Jupiter picked up his notebook. "I am a Warrior," he said as he wrote it.

FINAL MESSAGES

The instant Jupiter put his notebook on the grass, the screen lit up with a written message:

Ty Martins
You have successfully completed your eight-week therapy course, and you will be provided with transport back to your farm the day after tomorrow at five in the afternoon.
Please be ready at Trelleborg Port.
The Personal Development Committee

A heavy-weight boxer punched me in the stomach.
Relax. Breathe. Focus on your breath.
Ty wrapped both his arms around me, but even so I felt something had hold of my ankles and was pulling me down into a deep tank of compost sludge.
Stay with it, Nell, you're all right, it's okay to feel sad. All is as it should be.
Mara pulled a tissue out of her pocket and handed it to Ty.
There's always hope, Nell. Don't be afraid to cry. You're losing someone you love – it's only natural. Touch your waist and remember the warm happy feeling of having Nelly wrapped around you.
I put my hand to my waist, and didn't feel either warm or happy. I felt destroyed.

Mara Radoon
You have successfully completed your eight-week therapy course and you will be provided with transport back to the farm to see your boys and say your farewells. You will travel with Ty, at five in the afternoon, the day after tomorrow.
The Personal Development Committee

Clamps tightened around my chest. Why the hell has she got to go back with Ty?
Breathe, Nell. Remember your commitment to change. Mara is no threat to you.

228

I took deep breaths in and out. Ty kissed my cheek.

"It'll be okay," he whispered.

"I don't want to go back to the farm!" Mara said.

"What about the boys, Ems? Surely you want to see them?" Ty said.

He wants her back there with him.

Shut up.

"And make the goodbyes even harder? I did all of that eight weeks ago."

"When's your reallocation date?" I asked.

"Two weeks."

Shit.

"All this faffing around. Maybe I'd like to spend some more time with Jupiter. Or Mum and Dad."

"Aren't your children more important than that!" Ty said.

"I've said my goodbyes, Ty. The boys know that. Can I challenge it, Sal?"

"Between now and the day after tomorrow at five? No chance," Sally said.

Shit.

Jupiter
You have successfully completed your eight-week therapy course and you will be provided with transport back to your home tomorrow at two o'clock in the afternoon.

Please be ready at Trelleborg Port.
The Personal Development Committee

"At last, I'm on my way!" Jupiter said cheerily.

It was Mara's turn to look sad.

Nell Greene
We have assessed you have yet to complete the course satisfactorily, and have secured another week for you having one to one sessions with Sally.

You will keep the same livingspace. Please try to see more of Derek.
The Personal Development Committee

I was nearly sick.

Breathe.

Oh sod off.

Ty squeezed me tight to him, "Did you know anything about this, Sal?" he asked.

"No."

"Are you free for the next week?" I asked her.

"Afraid so," she said.

"It can't get any worse," Ty said.

"Shall we say the Words to close out our time here," Sally said. We all joined hands:

'We shall never forget those who perished. Our gratitude to them for who they were. Our gratitude to Yellowstone for who we have become.'

Sally said a lot about carrying out some sort of evaluation, bade her farewells and left the four of us in the lounge. Even Alice and Shilly looked miserable, huddling together by the door.

"This is it then," Mara said.

"Looks like it," Jupe said.

"I probably won't see Jupiter or you ever again, Nell," Mara said. "You're both wonderful people, and Jupiter, I'm really sorry we're splitting."

"Remember the good times," he said, moving to hold her.

"And don't be afraid to feel," Alice said, not even bothering to look up.

Everyone drew breath and turned to look at her, then we all burst out laughing.

"Shit, I feel I could become a fucking therapy leader with all the jargon I've swallowed over the past eight weeks," Mara said.

She and I hugged and cried and kissed one another.

"Try being a little softer with people, Mara, and you'll make lots of friends," I whispered in her ear.

She drew back from me and laughed. "Am I really that bad?"

"You really are," I said.

Ty and Jupe hugged. "Thanks man, for everything. For your patience, your understanding, the space you gave Mara and me. You're a good man. I'll miss seeing you around."

"Thank you for looking after Ems for me, Jupe."

"See you, Spag Head," Jupiter said.

"Good luck, Jupes."

We left Jupiter and Mara hugging, kissing, crying, apologising, and thanking one another.

We walked back to Ty's livingspace, holding on to one another as if even the faintest breeze could blow us apart. Alice and Shilly rolled silently along behind.

"I love you, Nell, don't ever forget it," he whispered into my ear.

May I repeat. Don't EVER FORGET IT.

"I love you too, Ty Martins."

Hoorah. You've said it. It's official!

"Well, whoopdydoo for you two," Alice said.

CLOUDS

Affirmation for today: I am welcoming miracles into my life.

We packed some food into a thermal bag and headed up into the meadow. Alice and Shilly found a patch of wild geraniums, and Ty and I laid down in the sun. I rested my head on his stomach, he put his arm across my chest, and we breathed the sky in, down to our toes, and then up and out.

We listened to the birds, and watched the clouds floating past.

"See that cloud, Nell?" Ty said, pointing.

"Yes."

"Let's imagine ourselves on it, with my two boys, heading off into the future."

We spent the warm afternoon cuddling, chatting, laughing and putting ourselves, Alice and Shilly, and his boys, on every cloud that passed, and wished ourselves into the future.

"We are welcoming miracles," we said out loud, over and over.

"Let's write some things in our notebooks," Ty said. He passed me a pencil.

I took Greenie out, opened to a clear page and wrote: Clouds.

Ty wrote the same in his.

"How about 'All there is, is here and now," Ty said. We wrote it down.

"And 'Thank you'," I added.

"Pass me Greenie a minute." Ty took the pencil and wrote something on the back page. He handed the book back to me. 'Nell Greene, you are the woman I've always wanted to meet. You are the light of my life, and the love of my life – never forget that'.

"You need to look at that page often, Nell," he said, kissing the palm of my hand. "It's all happened so fast between us, but I really do mean what I've written."

"Hand me your book," I said, and wrote, 'I loved you from the moment you whispered into your first corn-flake. I am so happy that you love me back. I am, forever yours'.

"Anybody would think we're never going to see one another again!" Ty said.

We ate and chatted and laughed and cried our way through the day, trying to hang on to every moment.

But time passes anyway, no matter how much you make of every second.

TY LEAVES

Ty left the next day.

I don't know what else to say about it really. How do I describe watching the only man I've ever truly loved walk away from me?

Say it was shit?

We promised to love one another forever, to message daily, to wish for one another, and to carry on questioning the System until our reallocations were cancelled. Alice was almost worse than me when she had to nudge Shilly's shoulder for the last time.

Mara arrived at the last minute, we said a second goodbye, and with that, they walked through the departure door and out of my life.

My insides flipped the moment he was out of sight. Maybe they would reconcile?

Don't be ridiculous, they're over. He loves you Nell, not Mara. Relax. Breathe. Touch your waist.

You're right, Cyd. He loves me, I have to believe that. I put my hand to my waist. I felt warm, but not remotely happy.

One out of two is good. Stick with it.

LOVE

Affirmations for today:
I am welcoming miracles
All is as it should be
Love is all around
You are never alone

The next morning I walked to the burgundy treatment room.

"Dinner tonight?" Derek shouted across the clearing between the cabins.

"No thanks."

"Great. Come over at 8," he said, and hurried off.

"Not going," Alice said.

I walked into the treatment room with Alice following closely behind.

"Hi, Nell. How are you?" Sally said.

"I've been better, Sally."

"It'll turn out okay, Nell. Let's see if we can sort that rogue spaghetti strand out. Same method as when you visited your memory pods – except I'm going to add a heart sensor pad as well."

I put on the leopard-skin cap, and Sally stuck a pad to my chest. I sat up on the bed, leaning against the cabin wall.

"Ask your Love strand of spaghetti to show you what you need. I'll be watching the images and will talk to you throughout. You don't need to reply, just stay focussed on what you're looking at."

I closed my eyes.

Lily the Pink chugged towards me through a pale-yellow tunnel. She stopped in front of me, opened her door, and I climbed in.

Hello, Lily.

The handrail started flashing red which was a new feature – I gathered it meant I needed to hang on. We plummeted vertically downwards and started spiralling like we were travelling around the wires of a coil spring. We picked up speed, before dropping out of the spin, onto a platform, decorated in green and white swirls. I recognised it immediately.

Nice to know you haven't lost your sense of adventure, Lily!

'LOVE', read the massive oval sign hanging above us.

"Welcome back... at long last... I'd almost given up waiting... follow me," the Pomeranian Goose said.

We slid along behind him and stopped in front of a massive, vertical square panel.

"Enjoy yourselves," the goose said, and disappeared.

I looked up at the panel and moved my eyes over it from left to right. It was a giant grid of squares. Some squares were yellow, some green, a few purple.

Lily the Pink moved forwards and into the first yellow square, bottom right of the panel. She turned through 90° so the row of squares lined up in front of me. An image of Shoo and I having an argument over who could eat the most mangoes flashed up. I laughed at the memory, and the square changed from yellow to green. Lily moved forwards into the next square.

"Right," Sally said. "What you have here is a symbolic representation of your heart. The yellow squares represent a memory or emotion that is either useful or not in your life. You will only know once you enter the square. Once you have dealt with the memory satisfactorily the square will turn to green. The purple squares, are, I believe, a memory that you definitely have an unhelpful attachment to – and will need to be dealt with before you can move on – once again, needing to convert the square to green. Once all of the squares are green, I am hoping your Love spaghetti strand will stay straight. Green is the colour for the heart chakra, so that makes sense."

"And exactly *how* long do we have?" I heard Alice say.

"Be patient, Alice," Sally said.

The next 2 rows of yellow voluntarily changed to green as Lily and I passed through them. Then I was surrounded by purple, and an image of Rupe appeared

"Forgiveness is the only way you can move forward," Sally said.

I felt sick.

"You can keep the memory of Rupe, just forgive yourself for behaving the way you did."

I forgive you, Cyd.

I had an image of her creeping into the square from behind the cabin.

I couldn't have done it alone!

That's true. I forgive myself. We didn't know any better back then, did we?

She blew me a kiss. The purple faded into green.

As Lily and I moved along the rows, climbing up through the grid, I felt overwhelmed by the enormity of the crime I'd committed against myself throughout my life. All the destruction and negativity I'd carried inside me, and taken no responsibility for it at all. For what?

Yellow and purple turned to green, as I sobbed, forgiving myself, and forgiving Cyd. Sally handed me tissue after tissue.

Eventually Lily and I arrived in the top right-hand square of the panel. Green. For a second. Then it turned to a bright purple, and Ty appeared in my mind. His short dark hair and beautiful dark eyes looked into mine.

My throat shrunk.

Relax. Breathe.

My solar plexus tightened. I wiped my hands against my trousers.

"Shit, I miss him."

"Stick with it, Nell, you'll be fine."

I appeared in the image, next to Ty, and we held one another as tightly as we could. I stroked the back of his neck. He held my face and kissed my closed eyelids.

Ty, I'm so sorry I haven't believed in you at times – it's habit – you know what I'm like – *was* like – with trust. I'm trying to change, and I promise from now on to believe in, and trust you. And, Cyd – I'm sorry I've had wobbles back to how we were before therapy – I promise I'll try harder.

It's early days, Nell – you're doing fine.

Ty smiled and kissed my forehead. Purple changed to green.

Lily slid down the outside of the panel and stopped once again in front of it. I looked up, and there in front of me was a giant grid of pure green.

We've done it, Lily – I've got a heart of green. Thank-you so much!

"Great. Can we go now?" Alice said.

I opened my eyes.

MY LOVE YURT

"Well done, Nell, that was brilliant," Sally said, removing the cap and the heart pad. "Now, whilst we're here, why don't we reinforce your heart-full of green by tuning into it and seeing how you feel."

"Really?" Alice said.

I closed my eyes and found myself standing in a huge patch of groundnut flowers. Out in the middle was a raised mound, and on it stood a canvas yurt. I walked across the meadow, up onto the mound and into the yurt.

"Hi, Nelly G!" Granpa said, limping towards me.

I didn't move. The yurt walls had shimmering strips of white material floating down to a coconut-matting floor. China, my Siamese cat who died just after my tenth birthday, sauntered out from behind Granpa and rubbed along my calf. I scooped him up into my arms, and brushed my cheek against his.

"Don't cry, Nelly G," Granpa said. "Remember when we visited you at the FEAR platform, and you breathed us all into your heart? Well now we've set up home here, and you can come and visit anytime you like."

I looked around as the yurt filled with everyone and everything I'd seen on the platform, and more. *Lily the Pink* was over in the corner, and Apollo, my childhood pony, was scratching up against her. I ran over and flung my arms around Apollo's neck. I patted Lily's shell. Shoo waved at me from over by our old sunbikes. In the middle of the yurt was an enormous piece of rose-quartz, rising up and out of the canvas, and standing next to it, was Ty. Mum and Dad stood to the side of him, smiling. I ran over and the four of us hugged.

Cyd and Nelly were skipping around the circumference of the yurt, and Alice and Shilly span in circles in the middle.

The yurt grew warmer, lighter, and more crowded the longer I spent in it.

"Have you found anywhere?" Sally asked.

"Oh yes."

"Good. Now move it out of your imagination and into the centre of your chest. Just move it down, physically. When you've done that spend as long as you like there making it part of you."

I announced that I was moving the yurt out of my head – Granpa looked worried, and asked everyone to either lie on the flooring or sit on the old sofas dotted around. It took seconds to move the yurt downwards, into my heart.

"Well done, Nell, I'm amazed at how smoothly that went," Granpa said.

I spent what seemed like hours cuddling everybody and everything, feeling my heart growing lighter and freer by the second.

"Visit anytime you like," Granpa said, "we'll always be here for you."

I opened my eyes, smiling.

"That was beautiful, Sally. Thank-you."

I picked up Greenie, and wrote, 'Visit my love yurt'.

COMMEMORATIVE ARTICLE

I was exhausted and happy to get back to my livingspace.

"So, Alice – that went well, don't you think? We're done here."

"At last."

"I've got a heart full of green, with a love yurt in the middle. How good is that!"

"Well, bully for you," she said.

I sat on the sofa, picked Alice and up, and gave her a cuddle.

"I'm sorry about Shilly, Alice. But you'll see her again, I know you will."

"I very much doubt it."

There was a knock at the door. "Fancy making me a coffee, Nell?" Derek said, inviting himself in.

"Not really," I replied.

"Oh go on. I was just wondering how it went with Sally?"

Why bother!

"Brilliant. I can finally get out of here."

"What do you talk about all the time? Surely there's a limit to how much of your head needs sorting out."

He doesn't know you very well!

"Well, if you're interested, today I was travelling around my heart in the hollowed-out half of a pink coconut shell, turning blobs of yellow and purple, to blobs of green."

He raised his eyebrows. "Right."

"You asked," Alice said.

There was a bleep. I turned and looked at my screen.

To Nell Greene

We are pleased to announce that Earth Matters will be running a series of articles commemorating the 73rd anniversary of the Disaster. We would be honoured if you would conduct an interview with Professor Hisk, the last surviving scientist who was based at Yellowstone before the eruption. This will be a two-week assignment, and you will be given sixty

units per day, in advance. Transport will take you to
Trelleborg Port and you will sail to Rostock. You
will be met at Rostock Port by Patsy Shen, who will
take you to your accommodation in Berlin. You will be
able to fly home directly from Berlin once you are
finished.

The Editor of Earth Matters will contact you with
further information about the interview.

The Livelihood Committee

"Why don't they ask a journalist in Australia to interview the professor?"

"Because Earth Matters likes your work I would imagine," Derek said.

"Because it's a two-week assignment," Alice said. "So by the time you're finished, there'll be one week left before Ty and Shilly are reallocated."

"Fuck."

"And what the shit am I supposed to do here without you?" Derek said. "I can't believe the Dating Committee haven't told me the plan."

"But you haven't finished your love-test research yet, have you?" I asked.

"Maybe they're going to tell me I'm going with you!" he said.

"Is that supposed to be a joke?"

"Well, why not?"

"Listen, Derek, I need to message the Committees, can we have a coffee tomorrow?"

"Let's go out walking tomorrow, Nell. It'll do you good."

"I've a meeting with Sally."

"Another one! What will you be talking about this time?"

"Therapy techniques."

"Must get boring after a while. No?"

"That's why Nell's here, Derek," Alice said. "She might as well make the most of it."

"Anyone would think you and Sally were plotting TOHF's election campaign."

"Anyone who didn't know I'm not an active member."

"Well, when you can afford a few moments of your precious time, do come and see me," Derek said, slamming the door behind him.

"Moron," Alice said.

"I want to go and see Ty, Alice. I need to figure out a way to do it."

I replied to the Livelihood Committee, thanking them for the assignment, and saying I'd like to have some time off before interviewing Professor Hisk. I asked for a break of eight days, so I could get the weekly flight from Berlin to Buenos Aires, then with transport to Ty's farm it would give us three days together.

"Great idea. Never going to work though," Alice said.

"They've agreed, Alice! Can you believe it? We're off to see Ty and Shilly."

"Highly suspicious," she said.

I agree with Alice.

TY'S PROTEST

Affirmations for today:
I am welcoming miracles
Love is all around
I am never alone

The following day Mum called. "How are you, darling? Thanks for your message last night."

"Great, Mum. My spaghetti is straight – I'm done here."

"That's brilliant news. Listen, have you seen the Self-Sufficiency bulletin on Human Voices?"

"No."

I tapped it into my roamer.

It read:

A RIGHT ENVIRONMENTAL PROTEST

It has been confirmed that yesterday, the headquarters of the Livelihood Committee received a parcel containing an artificial insemination kit, which included sperm from a rare breed of sheep, the Hampshire Down. The parcel is believed to have been sent by Ty Martins, one of the planet's leading self-sufficient farmers.

A little over two weeks ago, Ty received a communication from the Livelihood Committee informing him that medical records show him to be sterile. As he is unable to contribute to the repopulation of the planet, it has been decided by the System he will be reallocated, to a job he does not want, in three weeks' time.

"It is all complete nonsense," Ty said, in an interview with our reporter, late last night. "My wife gave birth to two boys, who I've raised as my own. Due to the breakdown of our marriage, she too, is to be reallocated. What will happen to our two boys? To reallocate both their mother and father is wrong. Who has made this decision, the Programming Team? The Silvers? I will fight against the decision until it is reversed."

By highlighting his situation on the Human Voices stream, Ty Martins is hoping to raise awareness around the introduction of new re-allocation rules. He is hoping his followers will realise the importance of voting in the up-coming elections.

As this article went mass, in the early hours of this morning, the Livelihood Committee were unavailable for comment.

Has he gone mad? What a stupid thing to do.

"Fuck. An artificial insemination parcel is a stroke of genius though, Mum. What do you think?"

"I think the System won't see it that way. But that aside – your message – about the Hisk interview. Well done, you! Your Dad and I are so proud of you – it's fantastic news – you deserve it."

"Thanks. But what's better is the Livelihood Committee have approved my travel plans to see Ty before I start working on the interview. Can you believe it? I'm so excited."

"It's all brilliant, Nell. Enjoy it, and try to be in touch more than you have been from GreenWaters!"

"Will do. Love to Dad."

I cleared my roamer. "Right, Alice, let's send Ty a message."

Ty, I've just read the Human Voices stream. Brilliant idea sending sheep sperm. The Livelihood Committee have approved me coming down to see you next week. Amazing, eh? I cannot wait to see you, I miss you so much. Let's talk later. I love you forever and beyond, Nell x x x x x x x

"The only hurdle in front of us now, Alice, is my final session."

"Don't muck it up then!"

SPAGHETTI HEAD

Sally placed the sensor pad behind my head.

"I'd like you to think of Ty back on the farm with Mara."

"Nasty," Alice said.

"But necessary," Sally added.

Doesn't matter what she asks you to think of – we're cured.

I closed my eyes and after a first little feeling of insecurity, I imagined only nice things.

Sally eventually brought my attention back to the room, I opened my eyes, and she hit the re-play button.

Long, straight strands of spaghetti appeared on-screen. They lay peacefully side by side on a wooden board. I was standing in the image, looking nervously at the strands. They didn't move.

I looked up to see *Lily the Pink* chugging towards me, with Cyd and Nelly sitting inside. Lily stopped in front of the spaghetti, and Cyd and Nelly waved manically, "We did it!"

I walked over to them. "Thank you, Lily. Thank you so much. Thank you, Cyd, Thank you Nelly. I'll see you all in my yurt."

"Oh come on, one last group hug," Cyd said.

I climbed into Lily and the three of us stood hugging, with Lily flapping her door open and closed. The spaghetti didn't budge.

The screen cleared.

"Thank you so much, Sally. I wish the others were here to celebrate with."

"Just remember to use everything you've learnt here, Nell. Keep practicing techniques. Have something by your bed that'll remind you when you wake up, and before you go to sleep, to say some kind words to yourself, or just remember to say 'thank you' every day."

Oooh, I could knit you something – a heart. Or a dahlia. Nelly and I will knit you an orange dahlia.

"I'll remind her, Sally," Alice said.

"That's a good idea having something by my bed, Sally. Maybe I should set your alarm, Alice, to go off twice a day as my prompt to practice?"

"I like that – prompt to practice," Alice said. "I could say 'Hey, Nell, this is your PTP alert!'."

Sally and I raised our eyebrows, before standing up for a hug. "Thank-you so much for everything, Sally. What does life have in store for you next then?"

"Me? I have two weeks' leisure time and then I'm back here for my next group."

"Well enjoy your break, and good luck with the next lot."

"Thanks, Nell, I really enjoyed my time with the four of you. Stay strong, and have faith in yourself."

I arrived at my livingspace with my head and heart feeling peaceful and happy.

"We did it, Alice! Ty and Shilly, here we come! Ex-spaghetti-head-Nell is ready for action!"

And then everything shattered into a trillion tiny shards.

TY

Congratulations on passing the course.

As you may or may not already know, Ty Martins has, unfortunately, been taken into holding, due to anti-System behaviour. He has been carrying out public protests which the System fear will spark an anti-System sentiment in the run-up to the elections. He will remain in holding until his re-allocation date.

You will now travel directly to Berlin to start work on your article. We have agreed for you to have the first week as leisure time so you may recover from the challenging last eight weeks.

Please be at the Port at 2pm tomorrow.

The Livelihood Committee

Frantically, I sent message after message. Each one returned an automated reply – 'All communication with Ty Martins is blocked'.

I threw my roamer at the screen.

All is as it should be.

"Told you they wouldn't like his little sheep-sperm protest. I bet Shilly's furious," Alice said, sweeping up the casing. "You're going to need this," she said, pushing the pieces over to me for reassembly.

To the Livelihood, Dating, Health, Windfall and Population Committees

I cannot believe you have taken Ty Martins into holding. I would have thought that leading up to the elections you would wish to show how caring the System is towards humans, rather than the complete opposite.

Please can I talk to Ty? Maybe I can persuade him to offer a public apology.

Please, I ask for your understanding. At least let me talk to him.

Nell Greene

The next morning, I was woken up by Ty's voice.

"Nell? You there?"

I grabbed my roamer.

"Oh, thank God," he said. "How are you?"

He was leaning towards the screen, his elbows resting on a table. His dark fringe sat just above his eyebrows and he had a khaki-green sweater on. I smiled as I studied his face. How had I convinced such a gorgeous man to love me?

By being totally amazing?

"I miss you, Ty, like you would not believe," I said, putting on a t-shirt and walking downstairs to transfer his image onto the big wall-screen.

"I miss you too, my love. How's your spaghetti?" he asked, his eyes twinkling.

"Straight. I'm done here, thank God. How are you?"

"Apart from not being with you? I've been better, but I'm sure being put in holding will help my case, Nell. Everyone supporting me must be able to see how ridiculous this all is. I'm convinced they'll overturn their decision."

"What happened to the DNA test you were going to have done with the boys?"

"It was scheduled for the day after tomorrow. I've just been told it's been cancelled."

"That's outrageous! If the test shows you're their father then it proves all of this is one big mistake."

"Well exactly – and the Silvers wouldn't want a mistake like that being streamed in the election run-up, would they?"

"Can't your Mum have the boys tested?"

"Yes. But that still leaves testing me, and I doubt there's much chance of anyone finding one of my hairs with the root still attached lying around at my place."

We laughed.

"Oh shit. I miss you so much, I can't bear it."

"I miss you, my love. We've got to stay strong. It'll all work out, I promise."

"I'm not so sure, Ty. They're only letting me speak to you because I said I'd try and make you give a public apology."

"Well done you. That was quick thinking."

"Will you?"

"Will I what?"

"Make a public apology."

"I can't, Nell."

"Is there any way you could send something to Human Voices – apologising for your behaviour? Maybe they'll be more likely to look again at their decision. Surely it's worth a try."

"That's never going to happen, Nell."

"Why not?"

Alice rubbed up against my shin.

"Because I don't have anything to apologise for. They can't get away with this – and the approach to the elections is the perfect time for everyone to realise how things have become."

"But how will anyone hear about it? Human Voices is the only 'free speaking' stream – and they won't want to fall out with the System, so I imagine they will drop your story. No-one will write any more about it. That's the problem." My eyes started watering.

Breathe. All is as it should be.

Ty put his palm against his screen, and I put mine to touch it.

"Maybe *I* could write something about it for Human Voices," I said.

"No, Nell. There's no point if both of us are in holding. They can't keep me in here for much longer – Mum is harassing them too. My brother has also told them he has no intention of bringing up my boys if I am reallocated. Mum got a message to me saying I should be back on the farm in a couple of days. Then once you've finished the article with Professor Hisk – well done being offered that opportunity by the way – you can fly down here, as planned. Then after we've caught up on lost time, we'll figure it all out. When are you leaving the centre?"

"In an hour. Derek's taking me to Trelleborg."

"That'll be a fun journey!"

"I'm dreading it – no doubt Derek will carry on trying to persuade me to stay with him. It's all too grim."

"Put your earphones in – that'll stop him," Alice said.

"Listen, my darling ex-spaghetti-head – I'll message the next chance I get."

"I just hope you're right about them releasing you. I miss you so much."

"I miss you too – and never forget I love you, Nell," he said. "I'm doing this for us, focus on that. And good luck with the Hisk interview."

"Thanks. I love you too, Ty."

"Is Shilly with you?" Alice asked, quickly.

"Yes, she's here with me, Alice. She asked me to send you her love."

"Send mine back," Alice said, tipping her head down to stare at the carpet.

***

"Shame it didn't go quite as planned with us," Derek said on the drive to Trelleborg port.

"How much longer are you staying up here?"

"One more week, then they're stopping my units. I'll be flying home from Berlin to wait for my next assignment – maybe we could meet up?"

"Call me when you get there then,"

"I will," Derek said. "Good luck with everything."

"Thanks, Derek. And you."

"Bye, Alice."

"Bye," she said, her ears flattened back.

REALITY

Affirmations for today: I am welcoming miracles

I arrived in Berlin late and tried contacting, Ty. No luck. My stomach churned.

Relax and breathe.

"It's late, Nell. Try again in the morning," Alice said.

Somehow, I managed to sleep.

I tried again the following morning, again, communication was blocked, so I distracted myself with research for the Hisk interview.

Late afternoon a Human Voices bulletin alert appeared on my roamer:

NO BACKING DOWN

At around five o'clock yesterday afternoon, Ty Martins, the first farmer ever to lead a public protest against the System, was reallocated.

Due to his unorthodox anti-System behaviour, the Director felt Martins posed a threat to global peace leading up to the elections. Martins' assignment is as part of the team monitoring the planet's geological stability. Given events of all those years ago at Yellowstone, this is still regarded as an assignment of great responsibility and respect, reflecting, the Director feels, the contribution Ty has already made towards the planet.

Martins was not available for comment on the day of his reallocation. There will be a peace-loving gathering on Human Voices live stream at fifteen hundred hours GMT, on Sunday, to give our respects to the ideals Ty lived by on his farm in Argentina.

I rushed to the toilet and threw up. I knelt on the floor retching and crying with my head hanging over the rim.

It's okay. His love is still with you, remember that. Relax. Breathe.

It's not bloody okay. It's a bloody disaster – so, shut up!

Stop it.

Eff off. I don't care.

You still have his love. Just because Ty's gone, it doesn't mean his love has gone too. Come on – kneel up, and breathe.

I don't want to.

Come on, Nell. Visualise yourself in your yurt – go for a ride in Lily – go and get a corn-flake – take up the fight where Ty left off. Go and read something from Greenie.

Why? Ty's gone. What's the point? I want to spend the rest of my life puking in this toilet, because I don't care.

Get up, Nell! Look at yourself! Go and visit your love yurt.

Go away. I don't care about my love yurt.

My roamer bleeped. I slowly raised my head, and looked at the screen.

Nell, Are you there, darling? I assume you've seen the bulletin. I'm so sorry. If you need Dad or I to come over, we'll be there as soon as we can get a flight. Reply straight away so I know you're alright. All my love, Mum

I didn't reply.

"So much for effing heart-green panel shite," I said to Alice.

Don't be daft. It'll all look different tomorrow, and the day after, and the day after that.

Alice sat by my right leg, her head drooping down to the floor.

My wall-screen bleeped, and I could hear Mum's voice. "Nell, are you there? How are you darling?" she asked.

"Great," I shouted.

"Where are you? Come and sit in front of the screen so we can have a chat."

I pushed away from the edge of the toilet.

"You've got sick on your hands," Alice said, bringing me a towel.

"I don't care."

Get a grip, Nell, for ash's sake! Look at the state of you! What the bloody hell was the point of therapy if you're just going to crumble into a mess at the first blip.

"Right. I have a good friend in Berlin. I'm going to send her round," Mum said.

"Mum, I'll be fine. Give me a day or two."

"Nonsense. You look awful my darling."

"I have to get on with research for the assignment – I'm talking to Professor Hisk in a few days, I don't have time for your friend. Really, I'll be fine."

"Listen, Nell. It may not feel like it right now, but everything is going to be alright, I promise you that."

How could I reply to such a blatant lie?

"Do you hear me, Nell? Look at me."

I raised my head and looked into her tired eyes.

"This will all be alright, I promise. Things are not always what you think they are."

"What does that mean!"

"Just trust me."

Trust her. It is safe to trust.

"You look tired, Mum, are you okay?"

"Yes, just busy, that's all – the cassava plants are doing so well there's not enough hours in the day to keep up with them. Think about looking after yourself, and writing your article. Then come home, Nell. Promise me you'll come home."

"It's not like I've got anywhere else to go."

TOTAL RELAPSE

"I'm never going to see him again, Alice," I said, rushing back to the toilet. I stayed there for hours – the vomiting and sobbing exhausted me, but I didn't care. Alice rested up against my feet.

What about the therapy? What about your affirmations? Go and visit your yurt. Ty's in there – everyone's in there. Maybe Lily could take you for a ride? What about promising to believe in yourself? Honestly! Pull yourself together. Go and look in Greenie!

What's the point? I haven't got anyone to make an effort for anymore, have I?

Apart from yourself, that is! Who else is going to look after you, if you aren't? Get up, now. Have a shower. Put on your favourite clothes and eat as much chocolate as you want. Followed by some fruit would be a good idea. Do nice things for yourself. Go on. NOW.

Go Away!

Right that's it. What is the bloody point! You give up at the first hurdle – well I'm not sticking around if you're not going to even try.

An image of Cyd disappearing inside her cabin popped into my mind. She came back out with a container of petrol and some matches, and promptly started to pour the fuel all over the veranda.

"What the hell are you *doing*?"

What does it look like? Going back to my pile of sleepers. I've tried being nice. I've tried to change. What's the fucking point?

"The sleepers have gone."

I'll live in the open then, like I used to before the sleepers. You always give me false hope!

"ME give YOU false hope?" I screamed.

Alice started whizzing backwards and forwards in a straight line, her ears back. "Who are you shouting at, Nell! Shut up. You're sounding like a meltdown case!"

There's no bloody miracle switch, you know. You don't get to flick anything up for an emotion free state, and down for complete inner turmoil. It doesn't work like that. It's a question of sticking to what you've learned. No one gets to be a concert pianist without practice.

"What the hell has a concert pianist got to do with anything?"

Nelly's terrified. She won't come out from under her bed. Breathe. NOW! Or I swear to Patch I'm going to burn this cabin down and leave you all alone.

"Drop the petrol can, Cyd!"

It's the matches you need to worry about.

"Very funny." I took some deep breaths in and out.

"Shut up, Nell," Alice said, bumping into the wall.

There you go, keep at it. We are both bound to have relapses, it's just that for the minute, I seem to be doing okay. It's only natural we're going to slip back to our old ways now and again – but you must keep practicing, Nell. We both must. Breathe. You'll be okay.

I put my hand on my waist and took another breath in and out.

Remember to be kind to yourself, Nell. You are all you have. Be gentle.

Cyd's words calmed me, and I knew exactly what I needed to do. I picked up my roamer.

Mum and Dad, I know you're never going to understand what I'm about to say, but please, for my sake, accept my decision. I have changed my mind about the Award, and am choosing reallocation. Please don't try to talk me out of it. There is no point in trying to find a partner with whom I will be miserable. And there is no point in having children if I cannot offer them a loving home. All my love, Nell

"Oh great. You're so selfish – now there's no hope of me ever seeing Shilly again," Alice said.

The moment I sent the message I unplugged my communicator, switched Alice off, trudged upstairs, and collapsed in a heap under my quilt.

MIRACLES

Somewhere in some distant tunnel, a long way away, I heard knocking. I put the pillow over my head, but still, at the end of an endless tube of nothingness the knocking persisted. I blocked it out and went back to sleep.

The knocks became frenzied thumps, waking me up. I listened – someone was banging at my livingspace. I hauled myself out of bed, and switched Alice back on.

"Oh shit, I hope it's not ashing Derek."

"So do I, Alice." We went to the door.

Sixteen hours I'd been asleep.

"Good God, what on *earth* do you look like?"

Not a 'hello,' not a 'surprise, surprise,' no advance warning whatsoever. But there, in front of me, in the middle of Berlin, after not seeing her for twenty-one years, stood Granma. *My* Granma.

"No need to stare, child," she said.

I threw my arms around her tiny frame and wailed and sobbed and cried and laughed, all feelings mixed in together. She gently pushed me to arms' length.

"May I come in, Nell?"

Through the tears we laughed. She hadn't even made it past the front step before she was covered in salt water and saliva.

At least she was spared the vomit.

Granma, my Granma, at one hundred and six years of age, was here, standing in my livingspace. I hadn't seen her in the flesh since I was fourteen.

I held her hands and looked at every line, every freckle, every eyebrow hair.

"This is the first time I've ever known you lost for words, darling," she said, smiling.

"I just can't believe it. You look so beautiful. Is this for real? Are you really here?"

"Ow!" she said, as I pinched her cheek. "Yes, my darling little spaghetti head, I'm really here. I'm standing in front of you, holding your hands. You're looking at my face like you haven't ever seen me before."

"It's been so long, G," I said, bursting into tears again. "Too long. I thought seeing you on-screen every week was enough. It wasn't. It hasn't been. How could we have let that happen?"

"Don't be daft, Nell, darling. It's all fine."

"How did you get here? I didn't think you could travel?"

"You're not the only one who's been in therapy, darling. Two day intensive 'claustrophobia coping mechanisms' course, plus 70mg of kava for the flight! Jenny contacted me after Ty sent the sheep sperm to the Livelihood Committee. She knew it wouldn't end well and thought you may need a friendly face. Thankfully the monthly flight left yesterday morning, with me on it. I'm a little tired, I must admit, but my claustrophobia therapy worked wonders – I kept my eyes closed and hummed O'Rafferty's Motor Car the entire way!"

"O'Rafferty's motor car?" I asked.

"One of Granpa's favourites from the survival park archives."

Thank goodness I wasn't the person sitting next to her!

"How long are you here for?"

"As long as it takes, Nell."

"How about all your insects?"

"They're all being taken care of. Don't you worry about any of them. Just worry about getting yourself back on track."

"Alice! Can you believe this? GRANMA'S HERE!"

"Hold on, Nell, I need to get the feeling back in my hands," G said, letting go and bending her fingers over one by one.

YELLOWSTONE

Granma slept for the first day, and then busied herself cooking, and fussing over me, whilst I researched Professor Hisk. It was good having something other to think about than, Ty.

Go and spend time with him in your love yurt.

I tried it. I visited my yurt twice a day for ten minutes. I also put a picture of an orange dahlia next to my bed, and I said 'thank you' every time I looked at it.

"Why does Alice keep shouting 'PTP alert'!" Granma asked.

"It's a therapy tool I've programmed in, G."

She laughed. "The world's gone mad."

Slowly, I felt sick less often when I thought of Ty in reallocation, and at the end of a difficult two weeks, I managed to submit the interview:

SEVENTY-THREE YEARS: An interview with Professor Hisk

The Professor is wearing a sky-blue trouser suit with a navy roll-neck jumper. His shaved head is tanned, and he looks younger than his one hundred and three years.

NG Thank-you so much, Professor, for talking to me today.

PH It's an honour, Nell, thank-you for this opportunity.

NG Professor, you were one of the scientists based at the Yellowstone Volcano Observatory in the years before the eruption. What exactly was your role?

PH Well, apart from trying to keep everyone calm, Nell, my professional role was seismic tomographist. Basically, I was using seismic waves generated by earthquake-swarms to create computer-generated images of the interior of the caldera. The swarms had started registering around, 2023, and so the Observatory thought it best to plan for additional staff. I arrived nine years later, in January 2032 – as an apprentice scientist, I must add. You cannot imagine how exciting it was for me, a nineteen-year-old, getting a position monitoring a super-volcano!

Yellowstone had erupted before, of course, blasting 1,000 cubic kilometres of rock, dust and volcanic ash into the sky. Vast ash clouds had travelled huge distances blocking out the sun, and combined with the release of toxic gasses, had altered the earth's climate. But that was half a million years ago!

We started to study the caldera's magma chamber, and found it was two and a half times bigger than originally thought. I mean, that's a massive difference in super-volcano terms. Despite concerns of a few of us based on-site, the vast majority of volcano experts believed the amount of molten rock contained within the chamber posed no threat at all.

Then in March 2032, two months after I arrived, there was an earthquake registering magnitude 5.0 on the Richter scale. God did the earth around us shake that day! I remember running out into the parking so I wouldn't be hurt if the building collapsed – which fortunately it didn't. It was the largest quake at Yellowstone since monitoring began, and shortly after, the floor of the caldera started to rise. Alarm bells started ringing.

We ignored the media, who were permanently camped outside the Observatory, desperate for a good story of doom and disaster, and stuck to our job of real-time monitoring. We knew the explosion would be massive, and we knew it would affect the entire planet, but we didn't want the media releasing the news – can you imagine the panic? I used my computer-generated images to reach conclusions with my colleagues, and we transmitted all of our data to the government

NG And your conclusions were?

PH That she was going to erupt. But when, and how big an eruption it would be were impossible conclusions to reach.

NG How long before the eruption did you leave the Observatory?

PH Most of the team left a year before. I left in March 2043 – four months before. You have to understand it was a very rare opportunity for a young geologist to be working on an actual real-time event. I didn't want to leave, but in the end, I had no choice: The Observatory was closed down. I stayed, camping, in the park for another month, in the sunshine. I knew the eruption was coming, and I knew it would eject enough sulphur aerosols into the atmosphere to change the earth's climate for at least ten years, so I didn't care about getting sunburn, or wrinkles, or skin cancer – I just wanted to spend every available moment loving the sun before it would inevitably disappear. A cloudy winter morning was going to be lasting for years. I also knew if I wanted to survive – which I did – I needed to get myself into a survival park. Artificial lighting for seven years! You can never imagine how the prospect of that felt, Nell.

My sister, mother and father were already in a park in Chile, and so I went to join them, three weeks before the eruption. But I never found them. They hadn't taken their places. I've no idea why, and I have no idea what happened to them – I've never found any trace. All my life I've imagined a niece or nephew knocking on my door one day, explaining what happened. Now I just think they'd better hurry up, because I'll be a hundred and four next month!

The eruption on the twenty-ninth of July was massive – two hundred million cubic metres of Yellowstone blasted twenty-five kilometres upwards. No doubt you've seen a recording – it was truly magnificent.

But what a horrendous tragedy. All those lives lost. It's terrible to think of it.

NG Do you need a few moments?

PH No, I'll be fine. But after all these years, it still upsets me.

NG Do you think more could have been done to save lives?

PH I don't think so, Nell. Apart from, I suppose, using military force to make people go into the survival parks. Back then people thought they were invincible, Nell, and nothing was going to persuade them to give up their life-styles based on a 'maybe'. The ironic thing is though, I think Yellowstone saved humanity. There was so much fighting before the eruption. Young people now can't believe how much we all hated one another, or how greedy people were. Nowadays you're all so nice to one another! People used to make millions from other people's suffering. Every region of the planet was engaged in a war, and the wars made millions. Thank God our planet stepped in and forced us to change.

NG And how did you change, Professor?

PH After I'd readjusted to natural daylight, and to the eerie silence, I put all my energy into the clean-up project. I haven't always been a thin, old man, Nell. I was thirty-eight when I came out of the park, and we worked day and night clearing away the dereliction, and creating new communities.

They were desperately sad times, as we realised how many had died. But they were also terrifically hopeful times, and I became more and more convinced if the planet could rip itself apart that violently, throw itself into darkness for years on end, and still survive, it was in very little need of me, as a scientist with all my fancy monitoring equipment. What the planet needed was healers, peacemakers, love-makers, community-builders. And so I collected all the sociology books I could find. I've always maintained an interest in geology, and I've given many talks over the years about my time at Yellowstone, but I call myself a sociologist these days.

NG I believe you travelled to Yellowstone for the 50th anniversary of the Disaster, Professor.

PH I did.

NG How did it feel to be back there?

PH Mixed emotions. It's an incredibly peaceful place now. Yellowstone Memorial Lake is huge – roughly sixty kilometres wide by eighty-five kilometres long. It was a windy day when we were there and I could see white-capped waves out on the lake. I was supposed to be going out in a small rowing boat with the film crew, but I hate rough water – so there was no way that was going to happen. I'm very happy this interview is taking place on-screen in the comfort of my livingspace.

It was hard when I was at the Memorial Lake to imagine it was the site of one of the most violent eruptions the planet has ever known. I think of myself as that young scientist, and how quickly the years have passed, and there's always the sadness at the thought of all the people who didn't survive.

NG And what do you think of Yellowstone's future?

PH It will sit quietly as a memorial lake for another few hundred thousand years, Nell, you can be sure of that.

NG Do you think there is a valid need today, Professor, for the human teams that are monitoring the geological stability of the planet? Could Silvers not play the same role?

PH I would question whether humans are needed for monitoring, Nell. Technology has advanced enough for machines to achieve the same.

NG Thank-you so much for talking to me today, Professor Hisk.

PH It has been a pleasure, Nell.

NG Shall we say the Memorial Words together?

PH That would be nice.

'We shall never forget those who perished. Our gratitude to them for who they were. Our gratitude to Yellowstone for who we have become.'

Article by Nell Greene.

GOING HOME

"Promise me you'll hold my hand the entire way," Granma said, as we boarded the weekly plane from Berlin to Timbuktu.

"As long as you promise not to hum O'Rafferty's Motor Car!"

"Agreed," she said.

Mum and Dad met us at the airstrip.

"Listen, you've got the next week to stand hugging one another, I'm starving. Can't we go and get something to eat?" I said. Mum and Granma had been locked in an embrace for over ten minutes.

Don't be selfish. How long were you crying all over Granma before you even let her into your livingspace?

"Can you believe we're all here, together?" G said.

"Not really," Dad said. "Shall we say the Words?"

We broke Mum and Granma apart so the four of us could form a circle-hug:

'We shall never forget those who perished. Our gratitude to them for who they were. Our gratitude to Yellowstone for who we have become.'

"Aren't you eating properly, Jenny?" Granma said, pinching Mum's arms.

"I'm eating fine, Mum – I'm running myself ragged between new plant nurseries. It's keeping me fit!" she said, trying to hurry Granma along, and failing miserably.

"Let's go on ahead, Nell" Dad said, "those two could be a while!" We started walking with our arms linked.

"No, wait up, we're coming now," Mum said. "How are you feeling, Nell?"

"Better. I just want to get busy with sorting out my reallocation assignment."

Good to get it out in the open right from the start.

Alice bumped into my shin.

We all stopped.

"I'm not changing my mind about refusing the Award, I'm sorry."

"Fight the bastards!" Granma said.

"There's no point, G. If there's no hope for Ty, then there's no hope for me."

"I find it hard to believe you're Jenny's daughter. What about your rights?"

The silence fell heavily in between us.

"Are you absolutely sure?" Dad asked.

"I am, Dad. I'm sorry."

"Whatever you decide, Nell, we'll support you," he said.

"Thanks, Dad."

"I wish Shoo was here with us," G said, "she'd love this little reunion."

"No she wouldn't," Alice said.

"She's almost off the meds," Dad said. "If you're here long enough, G, you might catch her when she comes back."

"I'm booked on the plane leaving Timbuktu in 10 days – so I hope she's out before that. I can't see one granddaughter and not the other, can I!"

"So you'll be here for our 70th birthday party. That's terrific," Mum said, grabbing Dad's hand. "That's probably why I'm looking tired – there aren't enough hours in the day to organise the party and keep up with the cassava fields."

"We're running around faster than the Silvers sprinting team!" Dad said.

"What are you doing for the party?"

"Oh, wait and see. Something quite special," he added.

BLACK-OUT

The four of us settled into the sofa that evening to watch the Human Voices bulletin: A new 'leisurely past-times' facility is under construction in Western Australia...

"You should see the size of it, Nell, it's bigger than your Mum's cassava plantation! They reckon it'll be finished in three years and have a separate 'pod' for every hobby or sport you could ever think of. Shame I won't live long enough to see it finished."

"Don't be daft, G," I said, "you're going to live forever!"

...Bot Kayta has been chosen as the election candidate for the Personal Development Committee. The System is eagerly awaiting the choice of election candidate for the Original Human Foundation...

"Let them carry on waiting," Mum said. "This is boring," she added, changing to the Self-Sufficiency stream. "There's a program about Dad's irrigation project coming on later."

"Fantastic," I said to Dad, who rolled his eyes.

...Ty Martins gave this interview with our self-sufficiency correspondent...

Ty burst onto the screen. His hair was long, with little curls poking out from behind his ears. He had his brown sweater on.

"Is this live?" I shouted.

I got up and stood in front of the screen as Ty talked about creating a paddy field with his heavy horses.

"Is this live!" I asked again.

"Ty's been reallocated, Nell, you know that," Dad said calmly, "It's just a recording. Come and sit down."

I started crying just as Ty said it had taken him four hours, walking the horses back and forth across the field to compact the soil. I looked into his eyes and felt sick, really, really sick.

"Come on Nell, come and sit down," Dad said.

And then everything turned black.

GRANMA

I woke up in a meadow. Was I awake? No. I was dead. Most definitely. Or was I? I wasn't in a meadow – there were walls, painted with flowers and grasses.

"Nell? Nell?" I could hear, coming from over my head. "It's Mum, Nell. Nell, can you hear me?"

My shoulders shook, and Mum came into focus, leaning over me.

"Nell, can you hear me?"

I nodded, "I'm so glad you're dead with me," I said.

"*Dead?* I'm not dead. I'm in an emergency clinic with you. You're okay, Nell. You're one hundred percent alive."

"What's going on?" I said, sounding feeble.

"Do you remember fainting yesterday?"

"No."

It was superbly dramatic.

"Well you did, and we called the emergency health service."

"I feel fine, Mum."

"Don't be daft – you just thought you were dead! You've had a full scan, and you've got an appointment tomorrow for your results."

"Did they scan me naked?"

"You know, Nell – that's the one thing I forgot to ask as I was pacing the corridors, worried sick about you."

"I'm starving," I said, unable to sit up.

Mum walked off and came back bearing fruit and cassava crisps. She moved me into a sitting position, and I ate and ate and ate.

"You'll explode if you carry on like that!"

There was an empty bed next to mine.

"Who am I sharing with?"

"Me. I'm staying until we go back home."

"What about G?"

"She's exchanged her booking for the plane a month later. She said she's not leaving until you're eating her spinach and beetroot stew."

"She may have to extend to two months!" I said, laughing.

A cozy, warm feeling, rose up from my feet, travelled up to my head and then down my arms, filling me with love.

Granma was staying, just for me.

IMPOSSIBLE NEWS

"Nell Greene?"

"That's me," I said, walking into a white room. A shiny black table covered in small computer screens separated me from Docbot Peters. His perfect face was framed in-between his cropped black hair, and pale lavender shirt.

Docbots and dentbots are always gorgeous. The theory is it takes your mind off any pain you may experience during treatment.

Docbot Peters smiled broadly.

"Good news, Nell, you're pregnant!"

"Brilliant," I said, "I thought my housebot, Alice, was the only bot with a sense of humour."

"I'm not being humorous. You are six weeks pregnant," he said, losing the smile.

Shitsville! I was NOT expecting that!

"I can't be!"

"Well you are."

Can you be?

"It's impossible."

"Not according to the scan."

I stared at his face.

"Look at the screen," he said, turning one of the computers. There, in front of me, was an image of a dark circle, containing what looked like a tiny groundnut-shell, over on the right-hand side.

"How do I know that's my scan?"

"Why would I be showing you anyone else's?"

"Because, I cannot be pregnant."

"It's obviously a shock, Nell, and I'm sorry you don't seem happy with the news," he said.

This is a weird one. Okay, breathe. Relax. Freak out. Relax. Freak out. Le Freak, said Chic.

I stared at my womb.

"This can't be true!"

"Take time to digest it. I didn't realise you had no idea."

"No idea! You don't understand. The only man I've been intimate with in the last seven months is sterile."

"Well, either you were intimate with another man around six weeks ago, and you don't remember, or your partner's Health Committee records are wrong."

"Does that happen?"

"Which?"

"The *Health* Committee!"

"I've never known it."

"So you're saying I'm lying about who the father is?"

"No, that's not what I'm saying." He shuffled three of the computer screens around. "All I know, Nell, is you are pregnant."

"So what do I do now?"

As if he's likely to help!

"I suggest you go home, rest, eat well, exercise well and think about which path to follow."

"What do you mean, which path to follow?"

"Just take some time to think. This is a lot to take in – especially if the father is sterile!"

"Ty Martins is the father. I don't know if you've heard anything about it, but he has been reallocated because of being sterile. He protested against the decision on Human Voices, and you Silvers didn't like it, so he's been reallocated ahead of schedule. I need to get him released. It's as simple as that."

"I don't know anything about Ty Martins. But I doubt getting him released will be simple."

I walked in a daze back to my room.

"*WHAT?!*" Mum held my shoulders and stared into my face. "Are you *serious*?"

"Totally. According to the scan I am six weeks pregnant!"

Alice started spinning round in circles, her ears forward.

"No way. Nell, that's fantastic news!" Mum said, smothering me in kisses and hugs and letting out squeals of excitement.

Soak up the love.

"Only one slight problem, Mum, the baby's father is currently underground monitoring the geological stability of the planet."

"But…"

"Don't say it, Mum. Docbot arse-wipe has already insinuated I'm lying about the father."

Her eyes stared into mine.

"Yippee," Alice screeched as she spun, "I'm going to see Shilly again. This is the BEST DAY EVER."

"I need to start trying to get Ty released," I said.

"Be careful, Nell – I doubt anything like this has been done before."

"Who cares – there's a first time for everything, right?" Alice said.

GREENIE

I stayed in bed for the rest of the day, and took the opportunity to read through all my entries in Greenie:

Sit quietly, breathe deeply and listen.
Have faith. Remember everything is as it should be.
Repeat your affirmations
Crush a corn-flake
Cyd is a Woman. She is pretty. She is my friend.
'Now' is all there is.
Breathe.
Remember Granpa and everyone loves me. Visit them often.
I forgive myself for the mistakes I've made.
Love is all around.
Be kind to myself.
Planet – thank you.
I am me, and proud to be.
Sit, breathe and visit your memory pods.
Clouds
Take time to just sit, and 'be'
It is safe to trust.
Visit my love yurt.
Remember the Sufi saying, and collect some 'bruises'.
I am committed to change.
Thank-you.
All there is is here and now.
Be Brave. Ribcage, and breathe.
Question the anxiety. Ask for evidence.
I am welcoming miracles into my life.
Practice. Believe change is possible, and then practice.
I am never alone.
Never be scared of your greatness. Be proud to shine.
I have my best friend, right here inside me. Together we can conquer the World!
Never forget I love you.
All is as it should be.

I turned to Ty's writing on the back page: 'Nell Greene, you are the woman I've always wanted to meet. You are the light of my life, and the love of my life – never forget that'.

"All is as it should be, Alice. I am pregnant, and Ty will be released."

"Ty and Shilly, will be released, you mean. Let's say it twenty times every day."

ACCUSATIONS

Affirmation for today: Thank-you, Thank-you, Thank-you, Thank-you.

To the Population Committee
I am writing to inform you I am six weeks pregnant and will therefore be honoured to receive the Award.

I look forward to attending the ceremony.

Nell Greene

To the Livelihood Committee
I would like to inform you of the fantastic news that I am pregnant. I will therefore not be taking up my reallocation assignment as Livingspace Monitor because I have accepted the Award.

My pregnancy can be verified by Docbot Peters at the emergency health clinic in Zone Cassava, West Africa.

The father of my child is Ty Martins. He has, therefore, been wrongly reallocated due to a mistake by the Health Committee, who claim he is sterile. I can personally promise you he is not!

I am hoping Ty will now be released, and he and I will be able to live on his farm with his two boys and our soon-to-be new addition to the family.

Nell Greene

No reply.

Granma ordered some bamboo sticks the minute I told her.

"I'm going to have a wagon made to pull the baby around in!" Alice said, spinning with excitement. "Shilly and I will take turns."

"My affirmation about welcoming a miracle worked, Alice," I said, "twice."

"Twice?"

"Granma turning up in Berlin was a miracle, and now this," I said. "It works, Alice. I've stuck with my toolkit, and it's worked!"

Not my place to remind you of the minor meltdown in Berlin then, is it?

To Nell Greene
Many congratulations on your exciting news. We are somewhat concerned, however, as we understand you are claiming the father is Ty Martins. As you are aware, Ty was proven to be sterile by ourselves, so we are wondering if you may have made a mistake?
The Health Committee

"Made a mistake!" I shouted. "How the hell does anyone do that?"

To the Health Committee
Are you calling me a liar?
Nell Greene

No point in beating around the bush.
I showed the messages to G.
"Not sure they'll like that too much," she said.
"I have to get Ty out, G, they need to take this seriously."

To Nell Greene
I am writing to confirm the farm of Ty Martins is scheduled to be redeveloped as an environmental ed facility. Ty's original reallocation assignment was designed specifically in recognition of the contribution Ty has made over the years to self-sufficiency. He was going to be developing materials for the ed facility, based on his farm. The rest of his family, however, would no longer live on the farm. Unfortunately, due to his anti-System behaviour, his reallocation assignment was downgraded to geological stability monitor.
The Livelihood Committee

"BASTARDS!" I screamed at my roamer.

"I know it's depressing, darling," Mum said, "but shouting isn't going to help. You need to calm down and concentrate on being well."

"Calm down! Mum, have you any idea what all of this means?" I read her the messages. "Not only has Ty been wrongly reallocated, but his original reallocation would have kept him on his own farm, and not once was he told that. Not once was he given any hope his life might be slightly normal. Maybe he wouldn't have protested if he'd known that. Maybe he wouldn't have had his assignment downgraded. Maybe I'd have been able to go and join him once I found out I was pregnant."

That's a lot of 'maybes'. Remember, Nell, 'all is as it should be'.

"Nell, you need to know when to drop this. You'll make yourself unwell," she said, her eyes full of concern.

"What's gotten into you, Jenny?" Granma shouted, "I can't believe I'm hearing this – where's your fight gone? What happened to Jenny and Rufus, the planet's most passionate activists? Keep fighting it, Nelly, that's what I say."

"That was a long time ago," Mum said, looking at G, "times have changed, and Nell isn't just thinking about herself now, is she?"

"It all seems so ridiculous, Mum. I can't believe any of this is real. I've always believed in the System, but I just don't understand any of this. Before the Award I wasn't fussed whether I had children or not. But now I've met Ty, and I'm pregnant, I can't imagine anything I'd rather do. But it's like now I've finally straightened my head out…"

Thank you, Cyd

Pleasure

"…and got everything in place, it's all being pulled out from under me."

I sat down next to Granma. She squeezed my thigh.

"How about the Original Human Foundation?" I asked Mum. "They helped Ty before, maybe they'll help me."

"Maybe. I'll see if your Dad can talk to someone."

"Docbot Peters told me to take time to choose which path to follow. What do you think he meant?"

"I have no idea, Nell."

THE FATHER

We understand from the Livelihood Committee you are six weeks pregnant. Congratulations! We have spoken to Derek, and he confirms you did have intimate encounters while you were at GreenWaters. We are happy to have been successful in providing a match for you, and wish yourself and Derek all happiness for the future
The Dating Committee

I read the message out loud.

"Absurd!" Alice said.

I burst out laughing.

"Is this for real?" Granma asked.

"They have to be kidding."

"It's so much more exciting than Australia. They're all ganging up against you, Nell."

To the Dating Committee
I'm afraid you have been wrongly informed by Derek, unless of course he considers a kiss on the left cheek an intimate encounter. I am unaware of any woman ever becoming pregnant by such a method. If, however, you have information to the contrary I would be keen to read it.
Nell Greene

"Excellent! Send it," Granma said, "they never detect sarcasm."

The Dating Committee's message made me feel uneasy. Maybe Derek had come round to mine after Ty had left purely so he could claim we had become more intimate than we had.

Derek, What the hell are you playing at? Did you tell the Dating Committee we'd slept together? Nell

No reply.

What a bloody nightmare.

"Oh, by the way, it's time for a PTP alert," Alice said, barely looking at me.

"It hardly seems worth it, Alice."

"I agree," she said, sloping off into a corner.

Not worth it! There are a hundred and one things to say 'thank you' for! You're alive: you're pregnant: Ty is alive: the world is still a beautiful place: G is here: you and I are friends: Ruby hasn't called since you've been back. I could go on. For goodness sake, lighten up a bit.

A MINOR BREAK-THROUGH?

The reply was almost instant.

"They expect us to believe they can't contact someone once they've been reallocated?" Granma said. "Who looks after the reallocated when they're poorly, then? I only know of one Health Committee, Nell, don't you?"

"There's only one I know of, G."

Try Derek then.

The reply came the day after my foetal DNA test with Peters.

To Nell Greene
We can now confirm Derek is not the father of your
child. That does *not*, however, prove Ty Martins is.
The Health Committee

"Bloody cheek! So they're insinuating I've been sleeping with
who, exactly?" I said, to Alice, and Granma.

To the Health Committee
May I suggest you test every man who was in
Scandinavia at the same time as I was there. That way
there will be no room for doubt.
Nell Greene

"Derek's not the father!" I shouted outside, to Mum.

Mum rushed in from the veranda. "I thought you already knew
that?"

"Yes, Mum. I did. But it feels like I was the only one."

"Don't be ridiculous."

"Now we just have to find a way of proving Ty is. It can't be
true the Health Committee has no contact with people after
reallocation, can it?"

"If that's what they say," Mum said.

"What about, TOHF?"

"No chance at all. They wouldn't have contacts able to do that
sort of thing."

"I'll have to contact the Director, then," I said, looking at
Mum's puffy eyes. "God, I'm being so selfish. I'm sorry, Mum –
I should be helping you with your party, or with the cassava.
Give me some jobs to do."

"Don't worry about me. You keep focussed on Ty," she said,
kissing my forehead.

"How about Ty's brother?" G said. "They could test him – it
would probably show a close enough match."

"G, you're a genius!" I said, rushing over and kissing her
cheek.

To the Livelihood Committee
I'm afraid I am having trouble getting the Health
Committee to believe Ty is the father of my child.
They have told me they cannot take a DNA sample from

him because he has already moved to his reallocation assignment, and they cannot contact him. I must say I find that hard to believe. As you are responsible for his assignment, please would you be kind enough to arrange for a DNA sample to be taken, so we can prove he is the father.

If that is not possible, could I suggest you ask the Health Committee to test, Mateo, Ty's brother? I believe a family-reconstruction DNA test should provide us with the proof we need.

Nell Greene

To Nell Greene

We note with interest your request. There are many implications arising from Ty testing positive as the father of your child.

We would, therefore, ask you to come in to have a meeting with the Committee, the day after tomorrow, at three in the afternoon.

The Livelihood Committee

"MAJOR RESULT!" I shouted, banging my fist on the kitchen table.

"What are you shouting about now?" Mum said, racing back in from potting up cassava saplings.

"I've got an appointment with the Livelihood Committee to discuss Ty being tested for DNA."

"When?"

"Day after tomorrow."

"What? That soon?" she said, rushing off to her office.

"Soon! What are you talking about?" Alice said. "That's still forever away."

THE LIVELIHOOD COMMITTEE

Affirmation for today: Have faith. All is as it should be.

Finally: time for my meeting with the Livelihood Committee. I wore my smartest green sweatshirt and even polished my shoes, which Alice thought was ridiculous. I tied my hair back into a pom-pom affair and put on some mascara. Why I have no idea.

The Committee Meetings building was a short sunbus ride. A trouser-suited Silver greeted me at the single-storey building's entrance, and she led me to a spacious, light room. There was a pony-shoe shaped rattan sofa, matching drinks table, and a wall to floor screen.

"Please," she said, beckoning towards the sofa. "Would you like refreshments?"

"Am I likely to be here long?"

"Your conference is scheduled to start in ten minutes."

"A nettle tea would be lovely, then, please."

I settled on the sofa. Trouser-Silver carried the tea in, and just as I took my first sip, the lights in the room dimmed. I put the cup on the drinks table, and the screen lit up. In front of me were four Silvers, neatly dressed in v-necked short-sleeve tops, each with different coloured hair. They were sitting behind a long, thin wooden desk which was completely empty. The light blue wall behind them was completely void of any form of decoration.

"Hello, Nell. Thank you for coming to the meeting."

"Thank you for inviting me."

"We wanted to explain things to you face to face, rather than through written messages," the woman on the right said.

Don't like the sound of that. Stay relaxed and breathe.

"In a nutshell, we cannot honour your request to test Ty Martins for paternity."

Why had I even thought this might work?

It's okay. Maybe they'll offer an alternative.

"Once we reallocate someone, their details are passed on to a subsystem, and then erased from the Livelihood database. The subsystem manages them until the age of eighty-five, at which point, their details are transferred to the Australia System. So we no longer hold information about Ty Martins. We're sorry."

"I don't believe you. I can't believe there are subsystems you have no access to. How can that possibly work? You're one of the main governing Committees!"

"I know it sounds unlikely, Nell, but it is the way we have been set up for the past five years."

"I don't believe it." I said, looking from one to the other.

Neither do I! Ridiculous idea.

"Can I contact the subsystem?"

"Not through us. It all became very complicated some years ago, when we had to work out how to manage people who weren't willing to contribute to the development of society to its highest potential. Reallocation was the healthiest option available, but it proved too complicated for the current Committees to manage, so a subsystem was established."

"How is it the healthiest option available? I don't understand – you take away the freedom of people for something as small as being sterile, which, by the way, in Ty's case, isn't even true!"

"You have to look at the bigger picture, Nell. Reallocation is so much better than locking people up in horrible buildings for years on end, like it was pre-disaster."

"At least when people were locked up they knew one day they'd be free again – depending on the offence, of course. Free to go back to their families."

"And back to non-conformity? It's just too expensive to manage. Our limited population can't afford it, financially or emotionally. Reallocation gives people a worthwhile job they can feel proud of, and we believe it's better for all concerned."

"Cheaper, you mean."

"That's the way it is, Nell. That's all we can say. It's not necessary for us to communicate with people once they have passed through reallocation. That's how it works."

"Don't you think that's a bit of a weak area for the System? Someone could go for re-allocation, escape, and not be recorded anywhere. What would happen then?"

"We are not here to enter into such discussions, Nell. We're sorry, but there is nothing more we can do for you."

"Why did you bother asking me to a meeting to tell me that?"

"It is the best way to tell you."

"What about, Mateo – Ty's brother? You could test him."

"We have asked the Health Committee if that will be possible, and they have informed us that they no longer consider family-reconstruction methods to be reliable."

"So they're not going to test him?"

"No."

"That's absurd!"

"They have recorded incorrect results in the past, and no longer use that method of testing."

"Can you change their minds?"

"It is not in our interest to do so."

"But it is in mine! Why won't you help me? I've trusted you – the System – all my life. What's happened to you?"

"We're sorry, Nell."

"Are there any other options open for me? There must be something – I could find the park where Ty has been sent. I could wait for him to leave on one of his family visits."

They looked to one another.

"Oh my God! That's a lie, isn't it? Once we're reallocated there are no family visits! It's all total lies," I said, panicking.

Silence.

"Everything I've believed in is a lie. You, the System, you're a lie."

"We hope you do not really believe what you are saying, Nell. We are really, very sorry."

"Sorry? I have to do something, please, can't you help me? What can I do? There must be something I can do!"

"Nothing we can think of," they said in unison, "we're very sorry."

"I have to go onto the Human Voices channel with this story. You must understand that I can't just accept your answers?"

"Reporting this to the general population will not help your case, Nell. We would advise against it."

"But if you are refusing to help me, I have no other choice."

"There is always a choice, Nell."

Hey – that's what I always say!

Their lips carried on moving, but I didn't hear them.

Don't give up now! There's always The Foundation, remember?

I think they wished me luck with the pregnancy before the screen cleared and I left the room.

I walked back to the elevator, my ears ringing in the silence.

"Doors closing," a high pitched automated voice said.

I stood to the back of the elevator, and once again my world turned black.

WAKING UP

My right hand was being squeezed, and the hair across my forehead stroked out of the way. I opened my eyes.

Ty smiled, "Hi, Spaghetti Head."

I stared.

He continued stroking my hair.

I looked up at Ty's unshaven face, into his big, dark, smiling eyes. I smelt the comfort of his sweater. I reached up and touched his hair. Tears rolled down the side of my face.

He kissed my forehead.

"Ty?" I whispered.

"It's me," I heard him say.

Then there was another voice to my left. "Nell, darling, everything's fine." I turned my head and saw Mum.

"I didn't mean to die," I said.

I heard distant laughing.

"You're just drugged," Ty said.

"Just drugged," I heard myself say.

"Get some sleep," he said, kissing my forehead.

"Drugged. How long?"

"Six hours."

"Water, please."

Mum and Ty helped me to sit up. "Ty's here," I said.

"I am, and I'm staying."

He stroked the back of my hand and forearm. Mum held my hand the other side of the bed.

"Where are we?"

"We're in Zone Cassava, not far from home. We're in one of those massive derelict groundnut warehouses – it's the headquarters for The Original Human Foundation."

I burst out crying. "We're prisoners!"

"We're totally safe, Nell – it's all going to be okay, I promise," Ty said, passing me some tissues.

Mum kissed me on the forehead, "I'll leave the explanations to Ty, my darling," she said. "I'll come back later. Please just remember I had no choice. I only hope you can forgive me."

There's always a choice.

"Forgive you?"

She left the room.

"Why would she say that?" I looked at Ty.

"She had a plan, Nell, all along."

"A plan for what?"

"Getting us here."

"Why are we in the headquarters of TOHF?"

"We're going to be alright, Nell. We're free," he said, helping me move over on the bed so he could sit facing me. He held my hands. "Are you ready to hear what's been going on?"

"I don't know," I said, feeling sick.

What? I can't bear the suspense. Get on with it!

REVELATIONS I

"Your Mum and Dad are the founders of the Original Human Foundation, Nell."

"WHAT?" I said – the drugs suddenly wearing off.

"I know! Crazy, isn't it?"

"Crazy! It's impossible!"

"They started it in 2072, the year they got married. They'd met at a public meeting, unhappy with how women were being selected to have children. That meeting generated so much interest they suggested setting up a Foundation to ensure humans would always have a voice. Everyone loved the idea, and shortly after that, the Original Human Foundation was born. And then they were elected as the leaders...."

"No."

"Your Mum and Dad, Nell, are the founders, *and* current leaders, of TOHF!"

"Current leaders! Don't be nul. I'd have known...they would have told me..."

"It's true, Nell," Ty said, holding my stare.

"No. It's the drugs you've given me. Or someone's given me. This isn't real."

Ty gave me a long, soft kiss. "Does that feel real?" he asked.

"Better than real – but all the other stuff – that just can't be true."

"It is, Nell."

"But...hang on...that means they were the ones who sent the letter to you at GreenWaters? That doesn't make sense. They would have helped you. They would have helped us. Why didn't they?"

"They did. That's why we're here now."

"But why didn't they tell us what was going on?"

"They couldn't. If they had sent us messages, and they had been traced, it would have blown the entire plan – and wrecked their relations with the new Director."

"What relations with the new Director? My Mum hates the System. Why would she care about the new Director?"

"I know it sounds bad, Nell…"

"Sounds bad! So what if their daughter has a nervous breakdown – as long as their relationship with the Director is okay?"

"No, Nell, you've got it wrong – you just have to believe they knew what they were doing."

"What were they doing?"

"Saving you. Originally, their focus was removing just you from the System – but when we fell in love it made things complicated for your parents…"

"…Oh well, pardon me for making their life difficult…"

"…because they quickly realised they needed to add me to their 'removal' plan as well."

Priceless!

"It still doesn't answer why Mum would prioritize the Director over me. There is nothing she despises more than the System."

"It's not a question of prioritizing, Nell – she was doing what she had to. The Director had contacted Jenny and Rufus to ask their opinion about the idea of an election including human candidates. They couldn't believe it!"

"I bet they couldn't."

"Don't mind if I call them Jenny and Rufus do you?" he said, handing me a glass of water.

"Course not."

"Well, about a year ago, eighteen out of the twenty-four governing-board Silvers started to raise concerns about various issues: one of them being the increasing number of human complaints about the introduction of more strict re-allocation rules. The Silvers computed, through the amount of complaints, that something was wrong. As the Silvers logged those complaints, they noticed some changes had been made to the System's method of operation. They computed that too, to be wrong, and flagged their findings to the Director. In their conclusion, they suggested that introducing even more rules to keep control would make humans protest in more aggressive ways – and if peace was to be maintained, protests must be avoided. As a solution, they suggested announcing a global election, one that included human candidates."

"And what did the Director say to that?"

"She, along with the six-remaining governing-board Silvers, thought the eighteen had misread the information, so they reviewed all of the statistics, and found them to be correct. The Director scanned operating systems and discovered significant logging changes – changes which, she concluded, had been made by the Programming Team without her knowledge. The governing-board decided an election, including humans was correct. They informed the Programming Team of their decision. Shortly after, the Director got in touch with your Mum."

"But why did the Programming Team agree?"

"The System threatened to go public."

"I can't believe Mum and Dad took the Director seriously – they don't trust the Silvers with anything they do."

"They trust certain ones, Nell."

I raised my eyebrows.

"The Director asked Jenny and Rufus to run in the election."

"And?"

"They're thinking about it."

"My God!"

"So that's why she couldn't have been directly involved with my protest at GreenWaters: because it would have drawn unwanted attention to the Foundation at a time when they're on good terms with the Director."

"But Sally helped, and she's a member of TOHF, so that's not even true."

He leant over and kissed me. God that felt good.

"But do you remember asking me why Sally had even bothered helping me protest, when you reckoned I could have written the message to the Committees myself?"

"Of course."

"Sally only helped to waste time, so Jenny and Rufus could get their plan together for saving us! It's pretty amazing, you must admit."

"Hang on! 'Jenny and Rufus', 'it's pretty amazing' – It sounds like you're one of them."

He stroked my arm.

"I have become a member, Nell."

"I've just had the worst few weeks of my life!" I said. "And you're telling me it was all organised by my Mum and Dad?"

"I think that's possibly why your Mum mentioned you forgiving her? For both of us to play our parts convincingly for the System, we couldn't have known about it."

"But all the lies."

"More untolds, than lies, Nell."

"Oh, fuck it. Where's Alice?"

"Under here!" Alice shouted.

"ALICE!" I said, bursting into tears again. She rolled out from under the bed, and Ty picked her up and put her in my lap.

"Easy! I'm going to buckle if you squeeze me any tighter!" she squeaked.

"And Shilly?"

She rolled out from under the bed too, and Ty put her up close to Alice, then climbed back on the bed himself.

"One of us is going to fall off in a minute," Alice said.

"No chance," I replied, hugging everyone into a big bundle.

Ty eventually surfaced for air. "When your Mum and Dad were elected as leaders of the Foundation all those years ago, there were two hundred members, Nell. Currently membership stands at one hundred and eighty-five thousand, and rising," Ty said, proudly. "That's pretty impressive, don't you think?"

Impressive? It's mind-boggling!

"Why didn't they ever tell me? Or Shoo? How could they have kept it a secret?"

Amazing. All this time!

"I don't think anyone outside the Foundation knew who the founders or leaders were for many years. They kept it a secret to protect you, Nell."

"But they signed me and Shoo up when we were about ten minutes old – so how was that protecting us? I don't get it. How could we not have known?" I said, tapping my chin on Alice's head. "Bloody hell, Alice, I just can't believe this."

"And that's just for starters," she said, tickling my cheek with her ear.

REVELATIONS II

"This may freak you," he said, waiting for me to drink. "You ready?"

Brilliant! I'm enjoying this.

"No, but you're going to tell me anyway."

"Your Mum had the livingspace surveillance devices activated," he said, studying my face. "With the help of Sally, of course."

Cringe.

I felt my face heating up.

"Remember the day we watched Sally communicating with, P?"

"Yes."

"Well, your Mum asked Sally to set that up. When Sally wrote 'I know it will be alright, but Nell and Ty don't, do they', she was hoping we'd realise we were being passed a message."

"I don't even remember that sentence."

"Me neither. All I remember is you shouting about S and P."

"God, all that seems like another life-time."

"And she had Sally activate the device in my livingspace at the centre, as another example? And I believe in Mara's space," he added, raising his eyebrows.

"Alice made me watch," I said, pathetically.

"That is NOT true," said Alice, butting me with her head.

"Apparently you were watching when Mara told me about the boys?"

I pulled a face.

"Sally told your Mum how you and I had bonded during the corn-flakes, and she thought there may be hope of a relationship. So she wanted you to see Mara and I verbally ending our marriage. Mara had told Sally when and where she was going to tell me about the boys, so all Sally had to do was activate the device. Easy. Of course your Mum had no idea I would also tell Mara I wanted to start my life again, with you. I don't think she could believe her luck!"

"Mum was watching too?"

"No. I've explained it all to her."

This is slightly awkward, but don't worry.

"Okay, so, Sally and Mum are obviously good friends, and they're both with the Foundation. So, does that mean Mum knew I would end up at GreenWaters where Sally's the therapist? She can't possibly have known that."

This is bloody good, I must say!

"Ah," Ty said. "I think Youssan might have something to do with that – he's a member of the Foundation too."

"Youssan." I stared at Ty. "Youssan....was set up....BY MY MUM?"

"That's the way I understand it, yes."

"My Mother set me up to become demented and paranoid?" I said, sitting upright.

Bit radical.

"What sort of Mum would do that?"

A desperate one, by the sounds of it!

"My entire life has been fucked up by my mother!" I said, slamming my glass of water down on the bedside table.

"Wait, Nell. Calm down, please."

"Calm fucking down? Are you joking? No wonder I've had trust issues!"

"Can I get down please," Alice said. I cuddled her tightly.

"Hear me out. Please Nell. Let me tell you everything she's told me, then you can get as angry as you like."

I picked my water back up and rested it on Alice's back.

"Your Mum knew you'd like Youssan, and she also knew SID – S.I.D. – would step in and try to wreck your relationship with him."

SID! I can't believe I ever was that nasty, bitter person.

I can.

"Once SID convinced you you couldn't trust Youssan, it made your Mum's plan easy," Ty continued. "With a little encouragement from her, Alice and your Granma, you finally accepted it was time to destroy SID once and for all. They all planted the idea of you using your therapy credits. Your Mum mentioned GreenWaters to your Granma, without your Granma knowing anything about Sally working there, and once G mentioned GreenWaters to you, it all worked out perfectly."

"Worked out perfectly for what? God, I feel sick. FOR WHAT? You still haven't answered that!"

"Please don't get angry with me, Nell, I'm only the messenger," Ty said, twiddling Shilly's ear.

No wonder you've had issues! Your mother was lying to you all your life! You thought I was bad! Okay. Never mind. Rise above it.

Bugger off.

Harsh!

"Your Mum will need to explain that part, Nell."

"Was Granma in on Mum's scheming too?" I asked him. "Please tell me she wasn't, I couldn't bear it."

"No, Nell, she wasn't – apart from mentioning GreenWaters to you."

"And she didn't know about Mum's plan?"

"She had no idea."

REVELATIONS III

"There's more? Oh for god's sake," I said, letting out a massive sigh. "This is too much to take after being drugged in an elevator!"

"I'm afraid so," Ty said. "Now we move onto Alice."

I looked down at her, and no surprises her ears were flat back against her head.

"No. Not my faithful Alice. Please, no."

"Alice fed all the information about how you were doing on the therapy course back to your Mum, with the help of, you guessed it, Sally."

"Alice!"

She didn't move.

"After you'd told your Mum about having been honoured with the Award, she knew you'd probably refuse it, so she altered Alice's chip giving her the ability to transmit."

"It makes my ears twitch," Alice said.

"That way, your Mum would know what you were planning, and how it was going with Youssan. Then, once you'd started at GreenWaters, Alice transmitted information about the therapy techniques at the centre – The Foundation were worried the Programming Team may be testing unauthorized thought pads."

"So Mum's no better than the System. No wonder she kept delaying Alice being sent for a scan. I believed her when she'd said it was too complicated to send her from Scandinavia. And you know – I've just spent nine effing weeks in therapy to sort out my problems with trust and love, and two of the people I trust and love the most have been lying to me all along!"

Glad I'm not included in that.

"We haven't been lying to you, Nell," Alice said, looking down at the sheets, "we didn't tell you any lies. We just didn't tell you what was..."

"What's the difference?"

"We couldn't have told you, it would never have worked if we had. You've got to believe it. Plus, I didn't have any choice – I didn't alter my own chip, did I. I've only ever been here to help you, Nell, you know that. And why? Because I love you," Alice said with her head down.

"But you could have told me what was going on, Alice. If you'd said I must keep it a secret, you know I would have."

"I couldn't. Telling you was forbidden."

"Well, Alice – thank goodness I love you too," I said, tickling behind her ear. "I don't blame you, there's nothing you could have done to stop someone interfering with your programming. It's Mum I don't understand."

Alice hid her head under my arm, "I feel silly now I've said the 'love' word," she said. "Life was so much easier before your Mum altered me. I don't really want emotions."

I ruffled her fur.

Only one more person to ask then, Nell. Deep breath. I know he had nothing to do with it. Be brave.

"And you, Ty?" I said, looking into his eyes, "were you part of the plan too?"

"No – I'm your added bonus, Nell," he said, kissing my hands. *Thank God for that.*

REVELATIONS IV

"Your Mum and Dad couldn't believe their luck when they found out I was on the course with you, and once you and I had got together all they had to do was figure out a way to get us both into this old groundnut warehouse!"

"This is too much! All this plotting, and planning and running around without me knowing about it. My head's hurting."

"Drink some more water."

"Did Mum and Dad set Derek up too?"

"He wasn't a plant by TOHF, Nell. He was working for the Programming Team."

I knew it. You couldn't make him answer your questions about it. I knew it!

"The liar! He said he was working for the Dating and Windfall Committees – on the love-test project."

"You didn't tell me that."

"He asked me not to."

"I see."

"God, Ty, there was so much going on at the time I didn't want to throw another reason for suspicion into the mix."

"No. Well, according to your Mum and Dad, Derek was there to see if you were secretly working with Sally. The Programming Team thought your need to be on therapy could be a cover for you and Sally planning the Foundation's election campaign. Also, they hoped you and Derek would get together and he could waste your time, so you wouldn't get pregnant before your 37th birthday, meaning you wouldn't need the windfall payment."

"OH MY GOD! But I *am* pregnant, Ty. We haven't even mentioned that! Can you believe it?"

"What. That we haven't mentioned it?"

I punched his arm.

"Not for a while, I couldn't believe it," he said, moving closer beside me.

"When did you find out?"

"Two days ago."

"Wow! You had no idea up until then?"

"None."

"Were you shocked?"

"I was speechless, Nell – I'd just been reallocated for being sterile. But then, when I saw the scan, I don't think I've ever felt happier," he said, moving over and kissing my forehead and cheeks.

"Can I get down please," Alice asked.

"And me," Shilly added.

Ty put them on the floor. He got back on the bed next to me, and we laid down, smiling at one another. I stroked his ear, and he ran his hand through my hair.

Nelly and I are skipping round and round in circles. Everyone's in love, for ever and ever.

"Can you believe it's all worked out?" I said.

"Now I'm with you, I can."

Oh happy days. Oh glorious, sunny, happy days. Oh beautiful frangipani trees and herds of zebu cows.

"You know, Derek was on for a good service-promotion if he could have proved you and Sally had been plotting for TOHF."

"I'll have to congratulate him some day on how miserably his mission failed. He kept asking me what Sally and I talked about all the time, but I didn't think any more of it – I thought maybe he was simply interested in the therapy techniques!"

We laughed.

"Honestly, Ty, you couldn't make all this up if you tried!"

Ty leant up on his elbow. "And as far as your Mum goes, the Health Committee reallocating me for being sterile was pure good luck."

"Why did the Committee even come up with that lie, do you know?"

"We think the Programming Team knew about the letter I received from TOHF, and they didn't want me to join. I have quite a few followers on the Self-Sufficiency stream, and the last thing they want is lots of 'relatively unknowns' like me, enlisting support for the Foundation in time for the elections. Same with you. I mean, I have what, a couple thousand regular followers? You have the same. If lots of people like us rally support, numbers quickly add up. They wanted me out of the way."

"You definitely have more than a couple thousand followers."

"Well anyway, my protest and reallocation worked brilliantly for your Mum."

"Really?"

"When your Granpa was in the survival park he became great friends with a couple of geologists. Do you ever remember him talking about Bo?"

"I met Bo once."

"Did you ever meet his children?"

"I don't remember ever meeting them – but I think he had two, didn't he – and one was the same age as mum and dad."

"He did have two, and they're both members of TOHF. The one you mention, Chan, currently works at the geology reallocation centre, where I was going. So your Dad got in touch with him, and they developed the plan for me to 'disappear'. The day after I arrived at the reallocation centre, Chan explained the plan to me and asked if I was willing to risk defying the System. Stupid question – I arrived here yesterday morning."

"So you were already here when I went for the meeting with the Livelihood Committee?"

"The minute you stepped onto the sunbus to travel to the meeting, your Dad came to collect me from Docbot Peters' residence."

"They could have fucking told me."

"Would you have reacted the same way in the meeting if you'd known? No."

"And what happens when the System find out you're not at the reallocation centre, but you and I are now living with TOHF? There's no way they're going to take that!"

"Your Mum's theory is nothing will happen: in the election build-up, they won't want any negative publicity. Your Dad has another idea – which he'll explain to you."

"There's no way they'll accept it – elections or no elections. What about everyone else in their reallocation assignments? They could just leave. It would be total chaos."

"We'll see."

"Ask what happened to Derek!" Alice shouted from under the bed.

"He was reallocated the day the Health Committee proved he wasn't the father of our baby."

"Brilliant," Alice said.

"It's all mad," I said.

Ashing clever though!

MUM'S EXPLANATION

Ty and I dozed and cuddled and I tried to digest all he'd told me. Then there was a tentative knock at the door, and Mum and Dad walked into the room.

Mum grimaced and raised her eyebrows, whilst Dad just threw his arms open and rushed over to our love-island of a bed.

"I'm so sorry, Nell," Mum said, "if there'd been any other way I could have done this, I would have. You understand that, don't you?"

Dad let go of me, and Ty and I sat up.

"No, I don't understand, Mum."

She came over and hugged me. I kept my arms down by my side.

"Thanks for saving Ty," I said, "I'm grateful for that. It's hard to believe we're all together."

"Together, and staying that way, we hope!" Mum said, looking across at Dad.

"I'm not going through this effing nightmare again," he said. "Your mum hasn't slept for weeks, Nell, and I've run myself ragged between the Silvers we can trust and those we can't."

"I can't believe the two of you are the founders, and leaders, of TOHF!"

"We decided many years ago, Nell, that it was something we shouldn't broadcast," Dad said.

"Not even to your own children? No wonder Shoo and I have got issues."

You haven't anymore.

"When we formed TOHF, you wouldn't believe how unpopular it was with the System – we didn't really have much choice," Dad said.

There's always a choice.

"Listen," Mum said, "can we not focus on all of that? The important thing is we're all together. Ty is free, you're free, and you're pregnant!"

"Are we free, Mum? Will we ever be free now we've really pissed the System off?"

"We hope so," Dad said, hugging me again.

"Boy, or girl?" Mum asked.

"I'll put units on it being a boy, who we'll call, Jed," Ty said, squeezing my hand.

"And if it's a girl?" Dad asked.

"Jedina?" Alice said.

We all laughed, and I told them about Ty's thought-projection involving Jed.

"What I don't get though, Mum, is why this massively elaborate plan to get us here?"

"Well, there was no other way, Nell. The System had given you a choice between the Award or reallocation. Either scenario meant you would never know freedom again. The Ambassador scheme that comes with the Award, which Granma told you about, takes away your freedom. Yes, you'd have your family, and we'd be able to see you now and again – but you'd be controlled by the System."

"I'm already controlled by the System – we all are."

"Some more than others," Dad said.

"Well anyway, there was no way your father and I were going to let you be either reallocated or become an Ambassador. You, Nell Greene, were going to become a livingspace monitor! Not whilst your Dad and I could still breathe. So what other choice did we have?"

"And now you're controlling my life just as much as the System does – how does that make you any better than them?"

"I'm sorry you think of it that way," Dad said. "We don't see it like that."

"Obviously."

"Things are changing, Nell, and not for the better."

"But surely the last thing Ty and I can be now, is free!" I said. "I mean, the System aren't going to just overlook Ty Martins and Nell Greene defecting to the Foundation, are they? And anyway, what role can we play? The Foundation don't have specific roles that earn units, do they? So what will our lives become now? Hiding in disused peanut sheds for ever more?"

"Not exactly," Dad said. "There is..."

"I think you'll be surprised, Nell," Mum said. "You can earn units from any service provided, no matter how small. I could even transfer you some units for helping me decorate the warehouse for our party!"

"I don't really see that as holding great future prospects, do you Ty?"

"When is the party?" Ty asked.

"The day after tomorrow," Dad said.

"Where?"

"Here. Well not here, in the bedroom. Out there, in the warehouse."

THE SYSTEM'S MANIFESTO

"About two weeks ago, your Dad and I received a communication from the Director, saying a statement was being developed for the System's future governance of the planet. A statement they would use leading up to the elections. She asked if we would give our opinion on it. Why were they asking our opinion? It was very weird, and very suspicious."

"Was it? Ty said that she'd already been in touch with you before announcing the global election."

"They had – but since that first contact, we'd had very sporadic communication. Docbot Peters – one of our foundation-friendly Silvers – told us the governing-board were putting pressure on the Director to work more closely with the Foundation, because they were worried about a human uprising before the elections."

"Sounds a bit paranoid," Alice said.

"Docbot Peters said the Director hadn't known anything about Ty's reallocation until the Livelihood Committee reported receiving the sheep sperm," Dad said.

"Well she can't know about everybody's reallocation, can she."

"No, she can't. But because of Ty's protest, and other peoples' previously logged complaints, it re-highlighted the discontent regarding new reallocation rules. More drastic protests, like Ty's, that the eighteen Governing-Board Silvers had predicted, were becoming reality. The Director agreed that Ty's reallocation was wrong, but she couldn't intervene in just one case. And then, when she read your communications, Nell, saying Ty is the father of your baby, and saw the Health Committee's replies refusing to help, she started to investigate records to see if the Silvers themselves could be corrupt."

"Bizarre," I said. "How can that even be true? I mean the corruption can only come from the women programming the Silvers, can't it, not from the Silvers themselves?"

"Exactly what we thought – but artificial intelligence is developing at such rapid rates we're not so sure anymore. We have a contact in the programming team based at the intelligence facility. She says that security there has been very relaxed for many years, and her theory is someone has tampered with certain committee programming codes. She has no proof, but she has pushed the facility into starting an investigation."

"So, someone in the programming team is getting scared about the election results – is that what you think?"

"Maybe," Mum said. "Anyway, it'll be a while before the results of that investigation are released, but have a look at this – what do you think of their statement?" Mum pulled up a file on her roamer.

I read it out loud.

'A peaceful Planet. A clean Planet. A healthy Planet. A Planet where everyone's voice is heard, and Leadership is fairly elected. A Planet where everyone feels valued, and equal, and lives in harmony with nature. This is what we, the System, have achieved, and it is what we wish for our Planet's future.'

"That's pretty boring," I said.

"How do people who have been reallocated feel valued and equal!" Ty said.

"Exactly!" Dad said. "We couldn't believe it when we read it. But anyway, back to how we think all of this can work. Jenny, I'll let you explain."

MUM AND DAD'S PLAN

"Well," Mum said. "Our plan is, to prove, with DNA testing – purely for the sake of the System you understand – that Ty is the father of your baby. And the father of his two boys. Then your Dad is going to contact the Director and tell her you are both here in Zone Cassava. He's going to suggest Ty makes a public apology – which he's agreed to do, thank-you, Ty – saying he understands the need for rules, but suggests that in the case of health-related reallocations, there should be verification of the facts to prevent any future mistakes. He's going to suggest the Foundation could have a role to play in the development of the reallocation programme, and that it would be beneficial for the Foundation and the System to work more closely together in an official capacity. The Foundation believes this will help rebuild people's trust in the Committees if they know there is human representation. Ty will say he hopes the System will agree to create a kind of coalition."

"And you'd want to work that closely with them? You hate the System."

"It's time for TOHF to move out of the shadows, Nell," Dad said.

"But if the Silvers only function through their programming, then we don't need to ask them for their agreement, do we? We just have to programme it in!"

"And if it was the Programming Team who wanted Ty out of the way, how do we do that! It is safer if Ty follows the protocol of the Silvers being the first point of contact, then they are aware of the situation before the Programming Team realise what has happened. Plus, as your Mum alluded to before, the Silvers' artificial intelligence is improving, actually to the point of becoming self-improving. It is, therefore, in our interests to work more closely with the System – so that we can keep an eye on how they are developing."

"Makes sense," Alice said.

"Then," Dad continued, "we remind the Director you are a couple and that you, Nell, are pregnant – therefore, you satisfy the criteria for the Award. However, you would like to suggest the Director looks at both of your life-time's service in helping the planet, and ask if she will agree to allowing you to go and live on Ty's farm and develop it into a global ed facility, rather than a reallocation ed facility."

"You've agreed to that, Ty?"

He nodded.

"And you think the Director will go for it, Dad? I doubt it. And even if she agrees, what about the other Committees – and the Programming Team?"

"We can only try. They'll know if they don't agree you will appear on the Human Voices sites, and that will probably start a movement of human unrest."

"They'll just close down the sites."

"No they won't – that would create even more trouble – you have to remember the Programming Team think their roles are threatened by the elections as it is. They want the System to win, don't forget!"

"I think two boys being reunited with their father on a few of the streaming sites will work in your favour," Mum said, smiling.

"Shit!" I said, "I haven't even met your boys yet!"

"Your Granma's looking after them, Nell. She'll bring them in tomorrow, when you've recovered from the shock of all this!" Ty said.

"And the drugs!" Alice added.

"We believe the System will accept it," Mum said.

Ty and I raised our eyebrows at one another.

"And what about Youssan, and the surveillance device at the centre, and Alice's chip, and all that other stuff, Mum?"

"I know it all seems rather overwhelming at the moment, Nell, and I promise to explain it all to you one day, but for now you need to rest and recover. Tomorrow you'll meet the boys, and have time to get your head round everything," she said. "We're hoping you're going to be on good form for our birthday party."

PARTY

The peanut warehouse was transformed for Mum and Dad's joint 70th party. I had never seen so many brightly painted bottle gourds hanging from a ceiling.

Granma had her favourite dancing shoes on, and even when they played all the bot generated stuff – she was out there, body popping with the best of them.

"Isn't all of this exciting!" she shouted to me across the floor. I held her hands and we danced together to some robo-pop.

"Look. Over there!" she shouted, pointing towards Sally.

Love is all around. Oh this is such fun! Nelly and I are having a great time – we've cleared a dance floor in the cabin.

I walked over to Sally, who introduced me to 'P' – Patsy Shen – Sally's girlfriend, and the woman who had driven me from the port in Rostock to Berlin.

"Have you forgiven me yet?" Sally asked, as we hugged.

"Forgiving you is the easy part, Sally, it's Mum that could be a little trickier! How the heck did she ever dream all of it up. Just to save me from the Award!"

"Your Mum and Dad aren't leaders of the Foundation for no reason, Nell – they're clever, and they've got contacts in all the right places."

A bot presented us with a glass of cassava beer each.

"I start with another group back at GreenWaters in ten days," she replied. "I'm hoping they'll be as interesting! I'll be more relaxed this time, though, knowing you and Ty are okay, and the Foundation is in safe hands."

"Sounds like it's always been in safe hands, but Mum and Dad can't go on forever – maybe you should go for leadership, Sally?"

"Not really my thing."

Ty, dancing wildly with his two boys, caught my eye, just as someone tapped me on the shoulder.

Great mover, is old Ty.

I looked round, and Youssan was standing there. My heart changed gear. God he looked great.

Breathe. Relax.

"Hi Nell," he said. "Sally. Patsy. Great to see you." He kissed their cheeks.

Sally whispered into my ear, "This is a good time to practice forgiveness, Nell," and wandered off towards the dance floor with Patsy.

"I'm so sorry, Nell," he said.

If it wasn't for Youssan, you would never have met Ty. Think of it that way!

I looked over towards Ty, attempting a jive with Granma.

"Thanks, Youss, for the apology. Even though it is rather late!"

"I know, I'm sorry," he said. "You do know us meeting on New Year's Eve, and me inviting you to the restaurant the next day, wasn't set up though, don't you?"

"I didn't, no."

"Us dancing all night together, and the next evening, eating with Yolandé – she sends her love, by the way – that was all genuine, Nell. It was only after you'd received the Award communication that your Mum came and talked to me. I was pissed off to begin with, but I honestly thought there'd be a chance for us once you'd finished therapy."

"Really? Maybe if you'd have stayed in contact…"

"I didn't know how to – without having to lie."

"And it was all worth it, 'for the foundation's cause'?"

"I certainly hope so. But none of it matters anyway, now, Nell – congratulations on being pregnant."

"Thanks. Have you met Ty?"

"Yes. I was a bit nervous. I follow the self-sufficiency streams, obviously, working with compost. I couldn't believe I was actually shaking Ty Martin's hand. He seems like an amazing guy,"

"He is."

"Friends?" he said.

Ruby bounded up behind him and kissed him on the cheek.

"Youss! And, Nell!" she said. "I've missed you."

Liar.

"Hi, Ruby."

"Well done netting, Ty. He's effing gorgeous."

He is.

"Thanks," I said. I felt an arm around my shoulder. "Your Granma's worn me out!" Ty said.

"Ty, meet, Ruby. Ruby, meet, Ty," I said.

I feel totally okay with this. Ruby is no threat at all.

"Ruby. Nice to meet you. Youssan," Ty said, shaking their hands. "Great party."

Calm. Secure.

In love.

"It's banging. I'm off to find a single to dance with," Ruby said, looking through the crowd, "unless you fancy it, Ty?"

"No thanks, Ruby," Ty said, kissing my forehead.

"How about Youssan?" I said.

"God no," Youssan said. "She nearly killed me the last time we tried a robo-rock."

We all laughed.

"Why not come over for a drink one evening, the two of you?" I said.

Hang on. That could be pushing it a bit.

It's fine. Ruby's just Ruby.

"Great idea," Youssan said. "So, Nell. Friends?"

I felt calm.

"Why not." I shook his hand. Ty shook his hand. Ruby walked off into the crowd and Youssan grabbed another beer.

"Well done, Nell, that can't have been easy," Ty said, kissing me.

"It was easier than I'd imagined, Ty. The corn-flakes worked," I said, laughing.

The atmosphere was electric.

Well done! Ruby is just Ruby – no one to fear. I'm so happy we became friends – or I'd have missed out on all of this. Thank you.

Thank you, Cyd, for being open to change.

Are you mad? You're the one who chose change.

ONE LAST SURPRISE

At midnight, the warehouse fell silent. Granma and Ty looked upwards, I followed their gaze, and saw Mum and Dad standing on a platform, way above us all.

"Could we ask Nell and Ty to join us, please?" Dad's voice came through the sound system.

I looked at Ty. He smiled. I looked at Granma. She raised her eyebrows.

Can't be anything worse than reallocation, can it?

I grabbed Ty's hand, "I don't like the sound of this."

"Nell, it's their seventieth birthday! Let's go up and celebrate with them."

I walked, reluctantly, over to the bottom of the metal stairs, and Ty and I slowly climbed together.

"Have you any idea what this is about?" I asked. My legs were like jelly.

He shook his head.

"No more surprises, please, Mum. I'm not sure I could take anymore," I said, when we joined them on the platform.

Mum and Dad laughed. "Oh go on, just one," she said, and with that she turned to address the warehouse.

I practically squeezed the blood out of Ty's hand.

"As you know, Rufus and I are both seventy this year," she shouted.

A cheer erupted from below.

Mum blushed, Dad tipped his head.

"When we started the Original Human Foundation, it was agreed there would be an annual vote by all members with regards to leadership. Every year, Foundation members have voted that if Rufus and I are fit and able, we should remain as leaders. Fortunately, we have been able to do so."

An even more enormous cheer erupted upwards.

"More recently members have voted for our election candidate. With an eighty-four percent majority vote, you have chosen Rufus and I. Thank you."

I cheered along with everyone else.

"During the voting process, you also suggested the Foundation would benefit from having a younger 'face' to promote their campaign," she continued, smiling over towards me.

Younger 'face'? I looked at Ty.

Shit! Does she mean ME?

Us! Shit! Breathe!

As the crowd roared, I finally understood her plan: myself and Ty to become Ambassadors for the Foundation. Fuck that.

SHIT! Breathe!

Okay, Breathe, Nell. All is as it should be.

"Did you know?" I mouthed to Ty.

He shook his head.

Not sure that's the truth.

I could feel my forehead getting hot. Fucking nerve! She is no better than the System.

Ty put his arm around my waist and kissed my cheek.

"Well, faithful members, may I present to you the new Ambassadors for the Foundation: Ty Martins…"

The roar from below eventually quietened.

"And our very own Nell Greene, lovingly known to us, as Spaghetti Head. Hopefully, once they've recovered from the shock, they will be happy to accept their new role."

Laughter wafted upwards.

I am SO HAPPY. We're safe. We're going to work with the Foundation!

I smiled, walked over to Mum, and whispered in her ear. "You can't do this without asking me!"

"Well I have. We'll make a fantastic team."

"You didn't want me to be an Ambassador for the System – how is being one for the Foundation any different?"

"It's totally different, Nell, you know that."

"I've never had anything to do with the Foundation!"

"Doesn't matter."

She's right – it doesn't matter – you'll be FANTASTIC.

You're wrong, Cyd – of course it matters.

Ty pulled me towards him, held my hand in the air and kissed me on the cheek. Mum and Dad kissed us both. Ty's two boys started to climb the stairs towards us, through the fog of cheers.

I looked down at the smiling faces and saw Granma waving like a meltdown patient. Over in one corner I saw Alice and Shilly, spinning round and around in circles as fast as they could go, ears forward.

MANIPULATION

"We need to talk," I said to Ty, once we were back at ground level and had survived the congratulatory hand slaps. "I'm fed up with this old warehouse. I'd like to go home."

"Is that a good idea? We haven't been given clearance to leave Foundation headquarters yet."

"I don't care."

"Well, let's at least tell someone we're going."

"Granma, if Alice or Ty's boys look for us, we're going back to mine. I've been shut up in here for way too long."

"Don't be angry with your Mum, Nell. She only wants the best for you both."

"Does she? The way I see it she wants what's best for her."

I took my shoes off to walk along the sandy tracks with Ty. He stopped inside the first sparkling circle-junction. "What's going on?" he asked, holding my hands.

"Can we just enjoy the walk?" I kissed him. "We can get on to the serious stuff when we're home."

"Is it far?"

"Fifteen minutes."

"This solar-circle is pretty special, Nell. We could talk about it here."

"I'd rather go home – I feel it's where I need to be right now."

I opened the door to my livingspace and showed Ty around – which took all of thirty seconds. I flipped open a drawer in my office zone and took out a piece of paper and a highlighting pen. From there, to the kitchen to pick up a lighter. I sat at one end of my dining table, Ty came and sat next to me, and I placed the paper, pen and lighter in front of us. He raised his eyebrows.

"Right." I picked up the pen, and wrote on the paper, in capitals, MANIPULATION.

"Am I likely to need a corn-flake?" Ty asked. We laughed. He kissed my forehead.

"I cannot believe Mum and Dad think I'll go along with this! I'm not interested in being an Ambassador for the Foundation.

They're such complete hypocrites – they did all of this to stop me being an Ambassador for the System – how is this any better? I've never had anything to do with their fucking Foundation – so why she thinks I'm going to want to represent it in the elections I've no idea."

She knows you'll be good at it.

"Maybe she thinks you'll be so proud of them as leaders that you'll want to get involved – as a matter of family bonds?"

"If she hadn't lied to me my entire life, maybe I'd think more positively about it – but right now, I'm having stronger feelings about killing her than I am working with her."

Harsh.

"And don't forget – they've saved you from reallocation."

"No they haven't – I was never going to be reallocated once I was pregnant, was I. How effing dare they announce, in front of Foundation members, that you and I are the new Ambassadors without having effing asked us!"

"Would it be so bad?"

"Being Ambassadors? Yes."

"Why?"

"Because it isn't my choice. You and I can carry on the human cause in our own way, Ty. I don't want to turn my back on promoting peace and transparency, and all that – I just want to do it on my own terms. I have been totally manipulated. No wonder I've got effing trust issues."

Had, effing trust issues!

"And what about the System? Do Mum and Dad really think they will just accept you and I working for the Foundation? They're nul if they think they will. I'm not going with it, Ty. I'm sorry. I can't believe you think it's a good thing."

"I don't think it's a bad thing – and I want us to be involved with the election build-up in any way we can, but I see why you're feeling jipped. I do think your Dad's plan of us going to my farm and developing it into an ed facility could work. But to be honest, I was so happy to be out of reallocation and reunited with you, I'd have gone along with anything."

Beautiful.

"I can't accept their proposal. If you feel that staying with the Foundation is something you really want to do, then I understand that. But please understand that I cannot."

"I'm going wherever you go, Nell."

"Really?"

Well yes, otherwise he wouldn't have said it!

"Really."

"Thank-you." We kissed and smiled and kissed.

"We could try and make it back to the farm. Or we just disappear? We're not on any system anymore I assume, we might get away with it," he said.

"Until we use our units to pay for anything, or to travel anywhere."

"Yes, good point. So, what's your plan?"

"Long term: tell Mum and Dad: tell G: tell the System: figure it out. Right now? My plan is to go outside and set fire to this piece of paper."

"Sally would be proud."

We walked outside and sat at the edge of the terrace. I scrunched the paper into a ball and held it in my hands. "Manipulation: I realise now how passive I have been all my life. I allowed SID – S.I.D – to manipulate my behaviour for many years. I have – although I didn't realise it – allowed Mum and Dad to manipulate my life. But recently I have changed: Cyd and I are now friends: I have fallen in love, and I am now choosing to live my life the way I want to live it. I choose to live my life with Ty and to make a family with his boys and our child – wherever that may be. We will work it out with the System somehow. I will not live under the control of my parents. If Mum and Dad don't like it, then I will live without them. I am burning you, manipulation, because I am no longer the person I was six months ago, and I no longer need your energy in my life."

Fair enough.

"Why do I have to arrive at the exact moment you are chatting to a ball of paper!" Alice said, rolling up with Shilly.

"It's the perfect moment to arrive, Alice," I said, tickling behind her ear.

"We should have stayed with the boys, Shilly."

"Where are they?" Ty said.

"On their way. They kept stopping to look for tortoises, and we got bored," Shilly said.

"Please don't let them arrive and see you talking to a piece of paper, Nell," Alice said.

"She has got a point," Ty said, laughing.

"Listen, you two – we're not going to be Ambassadors for the Foundation."

"Shit," Alice said. "Well I'm not going back to GreenWaters."

"Neither am I, Alice – don't worry. No – the six of us – seven including to-be," I said, patting my tummy, "are going to go and live somewhere else."

Nine of us! Don't forget Nelly and me.

"Nine of us, sorry – thank-you Cyd for reminding me."

"Where are we going?" Alice said.

"Not sure yet."

"We could go and stay with G for a few months in Australia."

"Maybe we could, Alice. That's not a bad idea."

"FAN-TAS-TIC! I'm excited now," she said, rolling back and forth, bumping shoulders with Shilly.

"Let's not pre-view," Ty said. "There are a lot of people we need to tell first. And who knows what is going to happen from there."

"Will we be reallocated again?" Shilly asked.

"No, Shills, I'm sure we won't be. But we'll have a lot of negotiating to do before we can be sure of our future."

"Hang on, let me just finish off manipulation, then we'll go inside and start to formulate a plan."

"Thank God it's dark," Alice said.

I lifted my paper-ball of manipulation up to my face and closed my eyes. I had an image of myself lying on my back in the sand, with Mum, Dad and Docbot Peters stamping on my stomach. I took a deep breath in and blew the image out into the ball.

"Goodbye, manipulation," I said, putting the ball down on the sand in front of me. Alice, Shilly, and Ty, looked down at it.

"Lighter, please," I said, holding my hand out to Ty.

I set fire to the paper and we watched the flames dance. Within 30 seconds, manipulation was nothing more than ash.

"Right then," I said, rubbing my palms together, "let's go and get started on a plan."

Excellent. Nelly and I will make one too.

Ty stood up, held out his hand and pulled me up to join him. He put his arm around my waist and we turned to look up at Sirius. We took deep breaths in and out.

"All is as it should be," Alice said.

"Indeed, it is, Alice."

Laughing, we turned to walk back into my livingspace.

"Come on, you two," I said, looking over my shoulder.

Shilly and Alice were side by side, whizzing backwards and forwards over the ash, brushing it into the sand: ears forward.

THE END

Thank you for reading! If you enjoyed this book please consider leaving a review.

A little bit about me

I grew up on a dairy farm in Somerset and had the most fantastic childhood, during which I developed an unwavering love for cows. I would have to be biased towards Friesians, but really, any cow will do. And the funny things is, that for 90% of my adult years, I have travelled, lived and worked overseas – and during that time I have found myself never very far from a herd of cows.

I have written a diary since I was twelve, and some years ago I thought to myself 'hey, that must mean I'm a writer' – and so I embarked on short stories. I never quite got the hang of those, but I did, one day, sit with a pen trying to come up with ideas – and I drew a picture of a jumbled pile of spaghetti, which I felt represented my thoughts and emotions at the time. I sat looking at the drawing – and the seed of Spaghetti Head was sown. In 2006, I took the month of November off work, dusted down my laptop and signed up for Nanowrimo. 30 days later I had written 90,000 words, and the first draft for what has become Spaghetti Head.

I currently live in France spending my time between my gardening business, writing and playing tennis. Roger Federer: if you, or Mirka ever read Spaghetti Head, I would like to invite you round for a cup of tea.

You can find me at:
https://www.facebook.com/SarahTyleyAuthor/
https://twitter.com/sarah_tyley
www.sarahtyley.co.uk

Printed in Great Britain
by Amazon